D1503409

SPIRIT OF THE MIST

The *Celtic Journeys* Series

*Romance and High Fantasy
in Ancient Ireland*

JANEEN O'KERRY

NOVELS BY JANEEN O'KERRY

The *CASTLES OF IRELAND* Series
Family Saga and High Fantasy
Seven Castles in Ireland

THE *CELTIC JOURNEYS* SERIES
Romance and High Fantasy in Ancient Ireland
Lady of Fire
Queen of the Sun
Mistress of the Waters
Sister of the Moon
Spirit of the Mist
Keeper of the Light
Maiden of the Winds
Daughter of Gold
Goddess of Eire

With Hazel Ann Williams
Sweet Contemporary Romance
April's Christmas

PRONUNCIATION GUIDE

Aed - ed

Curragh– KURR-ah

Darragh– DAHRR-ah
dun– doon
Dun Bochna– doon BOWKH-nah
Dun Camas– doon CAM-iss
Dun Farraige– doon ARR-ih-gah

Fidchell– fikh-YEL

Grania– GRAHN-yah

Killian– KIL-ee-an

Lughnasa– LOO-nah-sah

Moina– MOY-na
Murrough– MURR-oh

Odhran– OH-dran

TABLE OF CONTENTS

. . . for every lady who ever loved a king.

I. THE EXILE IN THE STORM

In the darkness, lightning flashed, and in its glare raged a storm-lashed sea. Rain drove hard against the waves and against the rocks of the nearby cliffs. And approaching those cliffs, tossed on the waves like a bit of bark, was a tiny curragh with a lone man inside.

He knelt in the center of the craft with his hands over the sides, trying with all his strength to steer his flimsy boat towards the beach and away from the rocks; but it was a losing battle against the wind that tore at his hair and tattered clothes. He had no oar and no sail. There was nothing between him and the howling storm except the bare wooden frame and leather skin of the curragh, and the strength of his own two arms.

He rubbed his face against his arm in an effort to push his wind-whipped hair out of his eyes. It was a young face, brave against the howling storm, with smooth skin and determined eyes. He kept on pushing the boat towards the shore but it was no use. With every heartbeat the roaring waves carried him closer to the jagged cliffside.

Even his strong young shoulders were no match for such a storm.

The image wavered. Muriel tensed, trying to focus her thoughts in an effort to bring it back... and then realized that she had caught hold of the sides of her water mirror, vibrating the sea water within and disturbing the vision it showed.

She tried with all the power she possessed to recall the image of the man lost in the storm, but the water in the polished bronze dish turned clear and dark even as she watched. It was no use. The storm clouds rolling in from the sea had swallowed up the moon, and without the moon shining down there would be no visions in her mirror.

Yet Muriel had seen all she needed. She pulled the window shutter closed, caught up her purple-blue woolen cloak from her bed, threw it around her shoulders, and ran out into the night.

The great fortress of Dun Farraige lay dark and silent before the approaching storm. Muriel crept through the shadowy grounds, between the scattered homes and around the King's Hall, until she reached the huge wooden gate in the dun's circular earthen walls. It was shut tight against the night and the wind. Two watchmen sat huddled on the covered walkway above.

Muriel pulled up her heavy rectangular cloak so that the top of it fell over head, stepped into the shadows, and waited.

Rain began to fall. It ran down the leaves and gathered in the hollows of the trees outside the walls, especially the tall willow near the gate. Muriel lifted her hand and made a small flinging motion, and the collected rainwater splashed down with a *thump* against the outside of the tall wooden gates of the dun.

The two watchmen got to their feet. "Who's there?" one of them called.

"Ah, it's just the wind rising. No one's there," the second complained.

Muriel made the small gesture again. There was another *thump* against the gate.

"Someone is there," said the first watchman, leaning out over the walkway. "Who is it?"

"Somebody lost in the storm. Or a farmer whose wife's birthing time has come," decided the second, climbing down the ladder. "You watch for them. I'll open the gate."

Grunting with effort, he pulled out the heavy wooden bar from its iron holders and dragged the gate partly open. "Who's there? Answer!"

Muriel breathed deeply, gathering the last of her reserves, and made the flinging motion one last time. Another *thump*, farther away on the earthen wall, made the watchman step out into the grass beyond the gate. "Answer, now! I'll not ask again. If you're there, show yourself, or the gate will be closed!"

While he peered out into the night, Muriel quickly slipped past him and crept into the darkness. Moving along the curving wall of the dun, she raced into the night and the storm.

* * *

Muriel fought headlong through the howling wind, struggling to fasten the heavy bronze brooch at the shoulder of her woolen cloak. She could see almost nothing in the heavy darkness and had to find the path to the sea from memory and from the sound of the crashing waves.

Never had the journey seemed so long.

At last, reaching the wet sand of the beach, she untied the strings of her folded leather boots, pulled them off, and threw them aside. Closing her eyes as the rain poured down, she waded ankle deep into the cold white surf.

Now in contact with the water of the sea and the life within it, Muriel raised her arms and spoke to two of those she treasured most: sleek grey swimmers, smooth and swift, who laughed at storms and considered the roughest waves to be their playground.

Come to me... come to me... there is one who needs your help...

9

Lightning flashed and the thunder rumbled. A short distance away a pair of dolphins arced up out of the ocean, one after the other.

Near the rocks... the storm has him but you are stronger... help him... bring him here... bring him to me...

The dolphins leaped again and then vanished beneath the waves. Muriel shielded her eyes against the cold driving rain and looked out towards the rocks, where she knew the man in the curragh struggled against the storm.

He was surely facing his death at this very moment.

Another flash. This time she saw it: the curragh riding high on the whitecapped waves, heading straight towards the boulders at the foot of the nearby cliff. Then there was only darkness and howling wind as before, with lashing rain and crashing surf.

She took another step into the rushing sea. The sand tugged hard at the soles of her feet each time the waves receded.

Help him, she called to the dolphins once more, closing her eyes and stretching her hands towards the cliffs. *You can do this thing... you can bring him ... you can save his life...*

She was almost afraid to open her eyes, fearing she would see nothing but roaring waves. But she did open them, blinking against the rain, and looked hard into the darkness.

A brilliant rippling flash showed her the little curragh bouncing and leaping towards her on the waves, pushed and guided by the two dolphins.

But there was no sign of the man. Had she been too late? Had her friends rescued only the curragh and not its passenger?

The two creatures slapped the waves with their tails as they forced the craft up onto the shore, near where Muriel stood; and then immediately turned away and swam back out to sea.

Thank you… thank you! The two dolphins leaped up out of the surf once more and then were gone.

Muriel grabbed hold of the boat's drenched leather sides and looked in. The man lay on the floor of the craft, exhausted from the struggle and from the cold. The last of his strength had been spent in his battle against the waves.

"Get out! You must get out!" She struggled to drag the heavy boat farther onto the beach before the waves could get hold of it again. "Get out!"

But the man lay unmoving on his side, his face half-covered by the cold water pooling in the bottom of the craft.

Muriel reached in and got him by the shoulder. With some effort she managed to roll him over onto his back. Was he dead? She placed her fingers at his neck. The skin was chilled by the rain but warm beneath, and the pulse was steady and strong.

He was alive. But she had to get him out of his boat before the sea dragged it away again. "Wake up! You must come with me! Wake up. Wake *up!*"

The man stirred a little but then fell back again. Muriel raised her hand and slapped him sharply on the face, enough to sting his cheek and make him open his eyes.

He sat up suddenly and caught her wrist. In an instant he had come fully awake. "Who are you?" he whispered, staring up at her.

The lightning flashed and she caught her breath, for his were the strangest eyes she had ever seen. She'd seen them for only an instant, in the brilliance of the storm; but they were unlike the eyes of any other man.

The sight of them was enough to make her wonder just what it was she had rescued.

But as she stared at him and the rain pelted her face, he began to lose his grip on her wrist. The sea had grabbed hold of the curragh and was dragging it out on the waves again. In a moment the man would be far beyond her reach.

"Get out! Get out!" she cried, as the boat moved further away. "I have not the power to help you again tonight. You must get out!"

In one move the man rolled over the side of the curragh and into the chest-high surf. He struggled against it, battling the water with the last of his strength– and then the waves took him down and he vanished beneath them.

Muriel started to cry out, started to go to him, but there was nothing she could do. The sea would only take her, too.

Come back! Come back... come back to me...

With a great gasp for air, the man flung himself up out of the waves and forced himself forward, one step, another, and then another, until at last he struggled out of the grip of the angry sea and dropped to his knees at the edge of the beach. Muriel reached for him but he only closed his eyes and collapsed to the wet sand at her feet.

At last Muriel felt that she could breathe once again. The stranger would be safe where he was, at least for a little while. He was finally out of reach of the storm and the tide would not come in again before dawn.

She unpinned her heavy purple-blue cloak and wrapped it around him as best she could. The good wool would help keep him warm even though it, too, was soaked from the storm. "I will come back for you," Muriel promised. Then she ran across the beach, grabbed her wet leather boots, and hurried back to the dun.

* * *

The storm clouds had gone and the night sky shone with stars by the time Muriel returned to the beach, followed closely by four armed men from the fortress. She maintained her outward calm but beneath it, her heart pounded and her breath came increasingly fast.

Hurry, hurry! she wanted to say to the four men. *Our visitor is cold. Exhausted. He lies awash in the surf at the edge of the sea. He cannot survive there for long. Hurry! Hurry!*

But the men only made their methodical way down the rocky hillside patch to the beach, moving quietly and carefully in the windy darkness. "You're sure he was alone?" Ronan questioned as they walked. "You're sure he was not the first of some invading force?"

"He was nothing of the kind. I told you, I found him alone in a leaky little curragh with nothing and no one to help him. No sail. No supplies. Not so much as an oar."

"An exile," said Flannan. "Set adrift with no way to steer, for the sea to take where it wanted."

13

"Well, it has taken him here," said Muriel. "And we will care for him as hospitality demands."

"If he lives," added Ronan, with a shrug.

They reached the bottom of the hill and walked out onto the beach. Muriel left the men behind as she raced across the wet sand to the dark bundle at the water's edge.

"Is he still alive?" called Flannan.

Muriel looked up from the fallen stranger and nodded. "He lives. But he grows colder. We must move him now, or it will be too late."

"Well, that we can do. Grab a corner, lads, and lift."

The four warriors each took hold of an arm or a leg and began hauling their half-drowned guest back towards the dun. The purple-blue cloak that Muriel had wrapped around him fell to the sand and she quickly gathered it up.

"Look at him," remarked Flannan as Muriel hurried to catch up. "Ragged clothes of worn linen. No sword. No dagger. No gold at his throat or at his wrists. Hair cut short. Not even a pair of boots on his cold, bare feet. And I suppose that's his boat out there."

Muriel followed the warrior's gaze. The battered remains of the stranger's curragh smashed against the rocks in the moonlight, breaking up into pieces.

She turned away from the sight. "You said he was an exile. Perhaps he was taken prisoner in a battle. Perhaps–"

"He's a criminal," interrupted Ronan, pulling up the unconscious man's wet arm to get a better grip on it. "Battle prisoners are not exiled. They are held for ransom, if noblemen, or simply kept as slaves or soldiers if they are not."

"He is no criminal," Muriel whispered.

"You are so sure? I don't think–" Suddenly Ronan's burden arched his back, twisted around, and wrenched himself out of the grasp of all four men, only to fall facedown on the beach.

He was quick, but he was also numb with cold and exhaustion. Dun Farraige's four warriors had him surrounded at swordpoint before he could stand. They shoved him down onto the sand, where he sat very still with his hands braced at his sides.

Muriel moved past the swords and stood over him. Though the man was pale and shivering with cold, he was nonetheless wide awake and surprisingly calm. He looked up at her and smiled, as if the two of them were alone together.

"I did see you," he said. "You were no dream. I feared you existed only in the delirium of a dying man. But you are real, and that makes me very happy."

She could only stare back at him, seeing nothing but those eyes. The moonlight revealed that one was blue and one was brown. Never had she seen anyone with eyes like that.

Still smiling up at her, he got slowly to his feet. Even in his weariness Muriel could see that he was tall and strong and broad-shouldered, and carried himself like a warrior. He seemed not to notice as his four captors glared at him and pushed their sword points closer.

"Please, can you not put those away?" Muriel pleaded. "He is unarmed. He is no threat."

"We don't know what he is," said Ronan.

"Oh, we know," growled Flannan. "He is an exile. A criminal. A slave."

The stranger glanced over at Flannan, looking him fearlessly in the eye. "I am no slave," the man said, with a laugh. "My name is Brendan. I am a prince. I am the tanist of Dun Bochna."

Now it was his captors' turn to laugh. "Oh, I am indeed sorry! We should have known. You certainly do look like a prince," said Flannan with a sneer. "Such fine clothes. Such fine weapons!"

"A broken-down boat for a steed, and a school of eels for an army!" added Ronan.

Muriel looked up at Brendan, but he simply waited patiently as the others laughed.

"You were found adrift without even food or water, as the law requires," said Ronan, after the others quieted. "Who would do such a thing to a prince?"

Again the man named Brendan looked straight at him. "Odhran."

This time the men of Dun Farraige were silent. They glanced at each other and back at Brendan. "We've had our own dealings with King Odhran," said Flannan.

"Something will have to be done about him soon," added Ronan.

"A more false and wrongful king I have never heard of, not even in the old tales." Flannan looked closely at Brendan again. "Tell me, tanist: Who is your tribe? Who is your king?"

"Surely you know of Dun Bochna. And of Galvin, king there for more years than I have been alive."

"We do," answered Flannan. "But Dun Bochna is at least five days' ride from here, on the other side of the bay. You must have drifted for a good long time."

"I was not set adrift from my home. As I said, I am no criminal." Brendan glanced away, out at the rocks

16

where the little pieces of his curragh clung to the dark waves. Muriel saw how much he still shivered.

"I will confess that I am not sure how long I was at sea," he said quietly. "I only know that there was no food. No water to drink. I fought the waves for a very long time."

"Please! We've been out here long enough!" she cried, and reached up to wrap her cloak around his shoulders. "What sort of hospitality does Dun Farraige offer to an unarmed stranger, leaving him hungry and cold on our shores? We are taking him back with us right now!"

The four men of her dun looked at each other. Finally Ronan and Flannan each pulled one of Brendan's arms across their shoulders and began helping him walk towards the cliff.

"Very well," said Ronan, as they moved along. "We'll take you back to the dun. In the morning King Murrough and the druids will decide what's to be done with you. if you are a prince, as you say, then you will be treated to the finest hospitality we can offer.

"But if you are a slave– or a criminal– then understand that your life will never again hold uncertainty."

* * *

The two men shoved open the door of Muriel's little round house. Inside, her servant, Alvy, nearly dropped the iron poker into the hearth fire. "Mistress!" the old woman cried, hurrying over as quickly as her bent back would allow. "I was so worried about you. Oh, but what is this?"

Muriel stepped into the deep clean rushes on the floor. "Put him there," she said to Ronan, and pointed across the room to the fine rope-and-wood frame bed against the white clay wall.

Ronan and Flannan pushed their way through the door, still supporting Brendan between them with his arms up on their shoulders. As they moved past her, she lifted her heavy, wet, purple-blue cloak off of Brendan just as they got him to the bed.

The men let him fall on his back to the straw-stuffed mattress. His long bare legs trailed off to one side. "Thank you," Muriel said, and hung the drenched cloak on a peg in the corner. "We will take care of him and bring him to the king in the morning."

The two warriors glanced at her and at each other, and then filed out of the house. Muriel closed the door tight behind them. Alvy stayed safely behind the central hearth and stared wide-eyed at their guest.

"Lady, what is this? I have never seen this man before. Who is he? And what's wrong with him?"

Muriel hurried over to the bed. "His name is Brendan," she answered, easing the man's long legs up onto the bed. "His curragh wrecked on the beach. He nearly drowned."

"He doesn't look like much," Alvy commented, standing up and moving closer. "So pale… dressed in rags… no gold…" She paused. "Is he a slave?"

"He's not a slave. I'm sure of it." Muriel got her arm beneath Brendan's broad shoulders and helped him to sit up. "Alvy, bring all the furs we have. Stir up the fire, too. He's cold to the bone. We've got to get him warm or he may not– he may not be with us for long."

"Thank you, Lady Muriel," whispered Brendan. "I am sorry to trouble you…"

Muriel took the dry, warm furs that Alvy held out to her and smiled briefly. "It is no trouble. We could

18

not leave you out in that storm. But if you don't get these wet clothes off and let us warm you, we may as well have left you there on the beach."

He gave a slight nod. Slowly he reached up for his ragged linen tunic as if to pull it off, but then his head fell forward and his arms dropped back to the bed.

Quickly Muriel eased him back down. His eyes were closed and his breathing shallow. His skin was paler than ever and his lips had turned a strange shade of blue-grey. Most frightening of all, his shivering had stopped.

Muriel pulled her small knife from the small leather scabbard at her belt and used it to rip away the man's wet tunic. She started to tear open the heavy linen pants, but an indignant voice stopped her.

"My lady! You cannot!" Alvy came bustling over and took the knife from Muriel's hand. "Let an old servant woman get the britches off him. You stir the fire, and see about getting him something hot to drink."

With some reluctance, Muriel got up from beside the unconscious Brendan. There would be no use trying to argue such a thing with Alvy, protective as she was. Muriel could only smile as she moved to the hearth and took care to keep her back turned to the bed.

There was the ripping and tearing of old clothe. Muriel started to glance back, peering out from beneath her long dark hair, but then quickly turned away at the sound of Alvy's voice. "Muriel! Is the fire stirred up yet? He is still cold, so very cold!"

Muriel busied herself by placing the last two bricks of peat on the fire. She stirred the blaze with the iron poker, feeling warmth spread out from those small crackling flames.

She set down the poker and held her own hands over the fire, realizing just how cold and tired she was herself. For a time she simply stood by the hearth and watch the wispy blue smoke rise up into the night through the narrow slot in the center of her dwelling's thatched roof.

Finally she heard the rustling of fabrics and furs as Alvy covered the man's unconscious form. "All done, lady! I've found dry cloaks and a few more sealskins for him."

Muriel turned around. The man called Brendan was tightly tucked in beneath a heavy stack of woolen cloaks and grey-brown furs flecked with black. Only his face showed in the soft light from the hearth, and she was relieved to see that he did look a little better. There was a bit of color coming back to him now and his breathing seemed to be deeper and more regular.

He would live. He would recover. She would see those strange eyes again.

With the relief of knowing he would survive came another wave of fatigue. The long time spent in the cold, wet night… the use of her powers to their greatest limit… the struggle to save a dying man… all of it seemed to catch up to her at once.

There was a gentle, familiar hand on her arm. "Come, dear one," said Alvy. "I've made you a warm bed in the rushes, near mine. We'll find him another place in the morning and you'll have your own good bed back."

"Thank you, Alvy. I'm just glad he will live."

"Oh, he will. And… Lady Muriel? I did catch a glimpse of him while getting his wet clothes off. I'd say he was worth the trouble."

Muriel smiled as she looked back at the old woman, but shook her head with some sadness. "Perhaps he is worth it for someone," she whispered," but I cannot dare to hope that he is what he says he is. And even if he were…"

"What does he say he is?"

"A prince. The tanist of his people."

"Tanist!" Alvy stared at her. "The next king?"

Muriel shrugged. "We have no way of knowing. He could say anything, sick with cold as he is, and it could mean nothing." She looked away. "He is only a stranger in need of help on a storm-wracked night. In the morning he will be gone. I cannot allow him to be any more to me than that."

"Well, he is a pretty one, though," Alvy said, glancing at Brendan again. "And there are so few men that you can safely look to. If it's true about who he is, then perhaps he will be worth it to you, too."

Muriel smiled gently. "Thank you again, Alvy. Good night, now. She turned away and lay down on the furs in the rushes for what remained of the night, still seeing Brendan's eyes as they had looked in that bright flash of lightning out in the storm.

* * *

Muriel awoke to find herself lying on the floor, nestled beneath warm sealskin furs in a thick pile of rushes. The grey light of dawn was just beginning to fill her house and for a moment she was puzzled. What was she doing sleeping in the rushes?

Then she remembered. In an instant she threw off the furs and got to her feet. Cautiously she moved towards the bed, almost afraid to look– and then she let out her breath.

21

He was still there, sleeping soundly, warm and safe in her own fine bed, snugly wrapped in her own good wool cloaks and softest sealskins. His fair skin looked normal now, warm and alive, with just a touch of redness at the cheek. His golden brown hair, cut short to the level of his chin, lay smooth and soft on the feather-stuffed linen pillow. And his breathing was light and steady, she noted, as she watched the slight rise and fall of the black-flecked furs that covered him.

It was an odd feeling to see a strange man lying in her bed. Muriel reminded herself that she should be glad he was alive and think no more about him; but now that she knew he would recover, her curiosity grew stronger as to exactly who and what he really was. She had told Alvy that this man was not a slave and she was more certain than ever of it now.

A servant was simply a man or woman of the land willing to trade labor for the good food and dry bed and measure of protection that living in the king's fortress would provide. A slave was far different.

Being a slave was not a matter of birth. Only hated enemies captured in battle, or those paying for the worst of crimes, were forced to become the property of others and serve without a choice. Servants were not property, but a slave was no better than any cow or dog and could be used or traded as his master saw fit. And everyone knew that the child of a slave could hope for nothing better in life than to be the lowest of servants.

Looking down at Brendan's strong and gentle face, and remembering his well-spoken words from the night before, Muriel was certain that this man was no criminal. She did not dare to hope that he might really be a prince, as he had said, but he surely seemed to be an educated man of the warrior class.

Perhaps he had indeed been captured in battle, and then stripped of his gold and weapons and fine clothes before managing to escape... and then the sea had brought him here and left him at her feet.

Her mouth tightened. She closed her eyes. Why had the sea brought this beautiful young man to *her* doorstep? Already she was drawn to his handsome form and kind manner. Already she felt care and concern for him after pulling him from death. And already she was forcing herself to pull away, knowing there was almost no chance that he could be one of the very few men with whom she might dare to fall in love.

Muriel started to reach out to him with one hand. She could almost feel the smooth fair skin of his neck and the gentle pulse beneath it, warm and strong and reassuring... and then she quickly clenched her fist and pulled her hand back.

Brendan must remain nothing more than a guest in need who had briefly stayed beneath her roof. If he should try to be anything more than that to her, she must immediately put him in his place and keep him far from her.

He could not know what she risked by allowing herself to love any man. He could not know what had happened to the other women of her family, of the curse they had endured for so many years, of the care they must take not to fall in love with any man except–

He began to stir, turning over onto his side. Muriel quickly went over to the hearth to build up the fire once again.

Brendan he had told her. His name was Brendan.

She found the fire already glowing nicely. On the stone ledge surrounding it were two wooden plates, well filled with hot, flat, buttered oatbread and chunks of

23

steamed eel with a little green-black carrageen stirred in. The seaweed was there partly for salty flavoring and partly because Alvy insisted it gave a person strength.

Beside the plates were two wooden cups filled with fresh water hauled in from the stream outside the gates.

In a third wooden cup was a streaming hot brew whose scent she recognized. Alvy had been quite busy this morning. Muriel picked up the hot drink and moved to the bed.

Her guest now lay sprawled on his side, facing the dwelling's white wall. His arms were stretched out in utter relaxation as though this were his house and his bed. Muriel sat down on the edge of the wooden frame. "Brendan," she said quietly.

There was no response. She heard only a faint snoring sound.

"Brendan," she said again, a little louder. "Wake up. It's dawn."

More snoring. Carefully she reached out and placed her fingers on the warm skin of his bare shoulder. "Brendan–"

He jerked awake. In one move he rolled onto his back and reached for her wrist– but stopped just short of touching her.

Muriel sat motionless, holding the hot drink away from the bed. "Good morning," she managed at last. "I'm glad to see you are still alive."

"More than alive," he answered, sitting up against the wall and smiling. "Once you've thought yourself facing certain death, every new breath is like a gift."

Muriel stared back at him, still unmoving save for lifting one eyebrow. Those eyes of his, one light blue and one dark brown, were like something she had only imagined. But now, in the cool grey light of day, she could see that they were very real.

"And to wake up with you at my bedside is more than a gift. It is a wonder."

"It is not something that has ever happened to anyone before, I assure you." Muriel looked away, studying the cup on her hand, the walls, the rushes on the floor... anything except the gaze from one blue eye and one brown one. That gaze was too distracting, too full of other things she had never before contemplated.

"Oh, but I did not mean–"

"Here. Drink this." She handed him the cup.

Brendan looked at it, but kept still. "What is it?"

Muriel shrugged. "My serving woman, Alvy, knows quite a lot about herbs and things. This will warm and strengthen you. She wanted you to have it last night, but you fell asleep."

"My apologies. The last thing I would do is miss your company, even for a moment."

She held out the cup again. "Please. Drink."

He took the offering carefully, eyed the dark and steaming liquid within, and then breathed in its aroma. He looked at Muriel across the rim of the cup but made no move to drink it.

Muriel found herself impatient and reached for the cup. "Let me have it. I will drink first, if you do not trust my hospitality."

He stopped her with the touch of his fingers on her wrist. "I trust you, lady. You have already done more than I can ever repay." Smiling good-naturedly, he took a small sip– and then tried not to frown at the sour taste. He took another draught, and then another, and in

25

a moment the cup was drained. "I feel better already. It was very kind of Alvy to prepare this for me."

Muriel shook her head. "She would do the same for anyone who turned up on our doorstep, cold and in need. She has been a part of my life, caring for me, as long as I can remember. I am lucky to have her."

"And I am lucky to have you." The man called Brendan set down the cup in the rushes beside the bed and reached for Muriel's hand before she could pull it away. Slowly, gently, he stroked the skin of her fingers, smiling as he looked at her with those strange eyes.

She stared at him. It seemed she had forgotten how to move. It was as if the warmth he had regained from sleeping in her bed, beneath her furs, beside her fire, was being returned to her now. Slow heat crept from his skin into her fingers, through her hand, up the length of her arm, and–

Muriel withdrew her hand and looked away.

"I am sorry. I did not mean to offend you."

"You have not offended me." Clasping her hands together, she rose from the bed and walked to the far side of the central hearth where the plates of food sat waiting.

"There must be a man in your life already," he said quietly. "I should have realized that a lady of your beauty and kindness would surely have many men vying for her attention."

She lifted the plates of food, smiling coolly at him. "There is no man in my life at all."

"I see," he answered, after a moment; but it was plain that he did not.

Muriel sat down at the edge of the bed once more– a little farther back this time– and handed him one of the plates.

"Perhaps you will tell me why you have no man in your life, Lady Muriel."

"Perhaps you will tell me why you were adrift in the storm, Brendan."

He laughed. "Fair enough! I told you part of the story last night, but I will tell you all you wish to hear of my life and my predicament. You see–"

The door of the house creaked open. Alvy came in with a stack of folded clothes and woolen cloaks, topped by a pair of leather boots. The stack was so tall that she could hardly see over it and had to peer around the side.

"Good morning to you both!" Alvy said, elbowing the door closed. "Ah, Brendan! I am glad to see you looking well. We feared for you last night."

"No need to worry over me, kind servant," he said, sitting up a little taller in the bed. "I am as indestructible as the wind, as unrelenting as the sea."

"And as loud and braying as the gulls," said Muriel under her breath, taking a bite of bread.

He looked over at her, seeming to have a terribly wounded expression on his face; but then she saw the amusement around his eyes. "Now, can the simple truth be termed 'loud and braying?' Would any ordinary man have survived an ordeal such as mine, or gained the attention of a woman such as you to save him?"

She looked back at him with all the calm and coolness that she could summon. "An ordinary man would not. But that could mean you are far more than ordinary– or far less."

Brendan stared at her for a moment, blinking in silence– and then burst out laughing. "I can see it will take more than words to impress you. So be it! I will show you what I am made of."

He set his plate aside and started to throw off his blankets, only to be quickly stopped as Alvy came around the hearth and shoved the stack of clothes into his arms.

"You will show her none of what you are made of until you're wearing these," she said firmly, as he fell back against the cushions. "And after that, the king wants to see you."

"The king? Ah, good! Then you will all hear my story together. Now, Lady Muriel, and Alvy, if you would be so kind as to turn your backs, I will be ready in a moment. It's never a good idea to keep a king waiting."

* * *

Muriel stood outside in the warmth of the early summer sunshine, the sky clear blue after last night's storm. She had combed out her long black hair and put on another cloak. Like the one she'd worn last night, it, too, was dyed in her favorite shade of deep purple and she wore it over her dark blue gown. A bronze pin gleamed at her shoulder where it fastened the cloak, and bracelets made of polished bronze beads adorned each wrist.

She was ready.

The door of the house opened. Muriel looked up to see Brendan step outside. He looked nothing like the cold, pale, half-drowned victim she had rescued the night before. Now his fair skin glowed with life and warmth, and his short golden brown hair gleamed brightly in the sun.

The clothes suited him. Though simple, the garments were well made. Alvy must have gone straight to the king's household and asked for whatever extra pieces they could spare for their unexpected guest. The pants and folded boots were of fine black leather. The linen tunic had been dyed a soft grey. The light wool cloak thrown over his shoulder was also grey, and it was pinned at his shoulder with a plain bronze disk.

He stood so tall that the top of Muriel's head would scarcely reach his shoulder. As he walked to her over the green grass, she could feel the great physical strength that had allowed him to survive for a day and most of a night in his terrible battle against the storm-driven sea.

"Ah, I cannot tell you how much better I feel!" he said, breathing deeply of the sweet morning air.

"I cannot tell you how much better you look," she murmured, with as much detachment in her voice as she could manage.

"I am glad my appearance is pleasing to you, Lady Muriel. That alone makes my journey here worthwhile."

When she did not respond, he bent down a little as they walked and tried to catch her eye. "Most women would be pleased at hearing such a sentiment. Yet you seem entirely unmoved."

She could hear the genuine puzzlement in his voice as he finally added, "You did say you found my appearance pleasing."

Muriel stopped then, her dark purple-blue cloak swinging around her. "I said your appearance was *better*. Not *pleasing*." She looked up into his shining eyes. Somewhat to her relief, that strange coloring was not quite so noticeable in the sunlight as it had been in the fire's glow... or in the lightning.

"You must understand something, Brendan," she explained. "I am not 'most women.' I care nothing for how you may have dealt with other females, for I can tell you that I am not like them."

His eyes softened, though he continued to hold her gaze. "I will not ever make that mistake, Lady Muriel," he said, and then smiled. "But I hope you will allow me to tell you how lovely you look, with your shining black hair and deep blue gown all set off by gleaming bronze. I am happy to see that you chose to wear your best for me."

She could hardly believe what she was hearing. Was he serious? Or mocking her? Maybe it was a little of both.

All she could do was draw herself up as tall as possible and fix him with a cool stare. "I am on my way to see the king. Of course I would wish to look my best. It has nothing to do with you." Muriel turned before he could say any more and started off across the dun.

"Will you be so kind as to escort me to the house of your king?" he called after her. "I am told he waits to see me."

"You may follow if you wish, Brendan," she called over her shoulder. Right away came the sound of his footsteps in the grass as he caught up. She could not quite see him, but she could hear him following a few paces back.

And she could hear him laughing.

Her temper rising with every step, Muriel strode across the grassy, sun-warmed grounds of Dun Farraige with Brendan following behind her like a servant.

She was very glad that she had not allowed sympathy for his plight to affect her feelings towards him. He might be attractive to the eye, but he had proved to have a common, mocking manner with women. For all his courage in surviving the storm, he was just another ill-mannered, handsome young male who

30

assumed every woman he met would instantly fall in love with him.

It was almost a relief to find that he was no different from any other man. She told herself that when word came back to them– as it surely would– that he was not a prince at all but just a wily captive lying about his rank, she would be free to go on with her life without giving him another thought.

He was certainly no prince… and even if he was, he was still nothing of what she wanted in a husband.

They walked through the scattering of the dun's round white houses until they reached the long rectangular building of the King's Hall sitting at the center of the fortress. Muriel raised her chin and turned to Brendan as she stopped before the wide central door of the Hall.

"King Murrough is waiting for you." She stepped back to allow Brendan to pass.

He hesitated, but then smiled and made her a little bow. "Thank you." Then he went striding through the doors and into the unfamiliar hall as though it were his very own.

* * *

Muriel followed Brendan into the vast, high-ceilinged room. Sunlight filtered down through the thatched roof and streamed in through the hole above the huge round firepit at its center. But her attention was drawn to the far end of the building, where the king and a group of his warriors and druids stood waiting. Brendan moved towards them in perfect relaxation.

She found herself staring at his tall form as he strode across the rushes. His plain grey cloak billowed out from his broad shoulders, ending midway down his long legs in a striking contrast against the sleek black leather of his new pants and boots.

Even in his plain borrowed clothes Brendan stood tall before King Murrough. The man seemed to think he was just as regal and noble as the king, who wore bright blue and red and purple wool and who fairly glittered with heavy gold brooches and armbands.

"Good morning to you, King Murrough," said Brendan, in his clear and pleasant voice. Muriel moved to stand with him, careful to look only at the king and not at the tall, grey-clad figure beside her.

"Brendan," said the king. "You are welcome here at Dun Farraige. I hope that the hospitality you have received has been satisfactory."

"It has been more than I could ask for and more than I deserve. I am grateful to you, and to your people, and especially to this lady who stands near me now. Lady Muriel."

He turned to her and smiled, and in that moment she saw only his blue and brown eyes and the smooth skin of his face. She made herself look away and did not answer; instead, she simply inclined her head in recognition. Her voice might quaver if she spoke… if those shining eyes gazed at her again… if that dazzling smile was fixed on her once more…

Brendan turned back to the king. Muriel drew a deep breath and willed herself to remain clam and unruffled. He was just a man, no different from any other. It was simply his eyes that were different. That was all.

"You are welcome to what we have," the king said. "If you are now comfortable, we invite you to tell us your story." He sat down on a bench, and the nine warriors and five druids around him all looked

32

expectantly at their guest. News and stories brought by an outsider, a visitor, were always most welcome and would be quite enjoyed by all at Dun Farraige.

"I will be happy to do so." Brendan's smile included everyone in the room. "My name is Brendan. I am from Dun Bochna, the home of King Galvin, my father. It is a long way from here, far across the bay."

"It is," agreed the king. "It is five days' ride form here, if one has five good days. I have been there twice. And on neither of those visits do I recall seeing you."

Brendan regarded him. "No doubt I was out riding with the other men patrolling our borders, or checking on the herd boys out with the cattle in the hills. Or I was hunting deer or boar. When summer comes, I am not often to be found within the walls of the dun."

"That is possible," conceded the king. "But do you also set out alone in a little curragh when the summer comes?"

Brendan laughed. "I do not. That is another story."

"I do not doubt that it is." Murrough's eyes narrowed. "You were found alone in such a craft without weapon, sail, or oar. You were dressed in rags. Your hair was cut short in the manner of a slave."

"Criminals are cast out on the sea just as you describe," murmured the druid nearest the king.

Brendan drew himself up even taller. "I am no criminal."

"You had neither food nor water, as the law requires," the druid continued. "Were your supplies lost in the storm? Or do you mean to tell us that someone deliberately set you adrift in this way?"

"Someone did exactly that. It was King Odhran."

There was a murmuring among the druids and warriors. King Murrough glanced up at them and they immediately fell silent.

"I was told you had spoken of Odhran," the king said to Brendan. "We know him far too well. He has tried to establish a hold on the rugged lands at the eastern end of the bay."

"He has done more than try," Brendan proclaimed. "He has defeated the old king there and taken over his fortress. Odhran now holds Dun Camas."

"We got word of a battle held some nine, ten nights ago," Murrough said. "The farmers there believe that both King Fallon and Queen Grania were killed in the takeover. We could find no one who saw such a thing, however."

"That is because they were not killed. They were taken captive for a time. Then King Fallon was blinded with the same pin that King Odhran uses to fasten his cloak. Odhran rules there now."

Again the men of Dun Farraige talked in low voices among themselves. Their king's face grew even more serious and he looked hard at Brendan. "They may as well have killed Fallon outright. No man can be king with such a disfigurement."

"That is why they had it done: to shame him," said Brendan. "Fallon tried to walk off of the cliffs, but his queen begged him not to. I know this because he and Grania and one of their men were allowed to walk out through the gates while Odhran laughed.

"After many days, they found their way to Dun Bochna. The former king now lives quietly there in the shadows with his queen. He remains alive only for her sake, and I can tell you that on the day she dies he, too, will be gone before the sun sets."

34

King Murrough gazed into the distance, nodding slowly and thoughtfully. "Something will have to be done about Odhran very soon." He looked back at Brendan. "You still have not told us how you came to be set adrift."

Brendan smiled. "I am the second son of King Galvin. I wished to be named tanist, for I want nothing more in life than to be king after my father moves on to the next life. So, not long after King Odhran took over, I led sixteen men in a cattle raid against him."

The king raised his eyebrows, a slow smile spreading across his face. He nodded at Brendan. "A bold move," he said. "Did you get the cattle?"

Brendan grinned. "We got half of his herd. And all my men got away safely."

"All except you."

"All except me. I stayed behind to draw off the pursuit when it finally came. My men got away. I did not."

"Another bold move. But you cannot be a king if you are held captive, or if you are dead."

"That is true, King Murrough," agreed Brendan coolly. He paced a couple of steps, then cocked his head and grinned. "But as you can see, I am neither."

Muriel let out her breath. She wondered how this man's bravado would strike the king and his men. Never had she seen anyone with such confidence, anyone who was so sure of himself.

The king seemed to be enjoying his guest's story. "So you were the only captive," he noted. "I am sure King Odhran was not pleased to know that you led the raid that took half his cattle."

For the first time, Brendan's smile faded completely. He stood very still and faced the king. "You are right. He was not. He meant to kill me."

"Kill you?" Now Murrough was frowning. "If you are the tanist, as you say, why would they not hold you for the generous ransom your own king– your own father– would surely pay to have you back?"

"Because when the attackers came, I fought with them so that my own men could ride away. I killed one of King Odhran's men... and he turned out to be Oscar, the king's own son and the tanist of his tribe."

The king raised his head. "Oscar?" he repeated. "Oscar is dead? At your hands?"

"I did not wish to kill him, or anyone else. But he was determined to kill me. I had no choice if I wished to live."

"Oscar was as mad as his father. He was vicious. Cruel. No regard for the law." Murrough nodded. "You have done us all a favor."

But before Brendan could respond, the king fixed him with a cool stare. "Tell us, then. If you killed the mad son of an equally mad king, how is it that you stand before us here today?"

Brendan smiled again, but this time there was no humor in it. He glanced away and seemed to look inward, clearly reliving a terrible moment.

"Odhran meant to kill me with his own hands. He drew his sword and ran at me. I would be dead were it not for his druids."

Muriel saw Brendan falling to the grass with shock and pain in his strange blue and brown eyes... his fair skin suddenly white as death and splashed with bright red... his golden brown hair moving in the breeze against the green grass...

36

She took a sudden breath and looked away. The image faded and she was greatly relieved to see that he still stood before her, draped in his soft grey borrowed clothes and calmly speaking to the king.

"They said that one dead tanist was enough. Two would be a disaster," Brendan continued. "Though I believe they simply did not want Dun Bochna to attack them while they were still trying to establish themselves at their new home."

"The druids were much wiser than their king," acknowledged King Murrough.

Brendan nodded. "They persuaded Odhran to exile me instead, and once he got that idea in his head he came to prefer it. He went on at some length about how much longer it would take me to die, and how much more painful it would be, if I were cast out onto the ocean with no food and no water.

"When the druids protested this, he asked if they would prefer that he killed me on the spot with his sword. They had little choice but to relent.

"That evening, Odhran and a few of his warriors stripped me of everything I had, gave me rags to wear, and cut my hair in the manner of a slave. Then they threw me into a boat and pushed me out with the tide. All of them laughed as I drifted away, certain they had seen the last of me."

He turned to Muriel. "But thanks to this lady, they have not."

The king studied him, and then whispered to his druids before turning back to Brendan. "All this would explain why you had the appearance of a slave when we found you."

A look of relief crossed his face. "It would. It does."

"We have enjoyed your story, Brendan. But there is not a word of it that you can prove. You could just as well be a criminal who tells a fine tale– a criminal stripped of all you own and set adrift for your transgressions, to become the property of anyone who might find you."

"If you survived the waves," added the druid.

Brendan took a step back. "King Murrough, I assure you my story is true. I am Brendan, the second son of King Galvin, the tanist of–"

The king abruptly stood up, cutting off his guest's protests. "Tomorrow I will send five men to Dun Bochna to ask about your story. They will be gone at least a fortnight, since they will be forced to ride far inland to get around King Odhran's fortress.

"In the meantime, you will remain here. But you shall be neither noble nor slave, with neither weapon nor gold, until we know for certain who you are.

"If your story is true, your king and father will no doubt send men with a ransom to bring you home. If it is not, you will go back to the rags we found you in and live out your life as a servant of my people– the ones who rescued you. Which will be more than you deserve should we find you have lied to us."

Brendan bowed to the king. "I thank you, King Murrough."

"Do not thank me yet." With that, the king walked down past the firepit and out through the door, followed closely by his druids and his warriors. Brendan and Muriel were left standing alone in the filtered light of the hall.

She looked at him, and he stared back, and for the first time Muriel saw doubt and worry on his face. Not even when he had been facing death out on the waves had she seen anything but boldness in his eyes. Now, though, the supremely confident Brendan was beginning to realize just how precarious his position really was.

"Perhaps you would like to see the ocean from the hills up above the dun," she said.

His expression remained serious for a moment; but then his eyes sparkled and he grinned like a boy flirting with a pretty girl he was quite certain of. "Thank you. I would like that very much. I am sure the view is quite lovely from up there," he said, as his eyes flicked over her.

Muriel smiled, too, as sweetly as she could. "Now that you are not so tall, I thought it would be necessary for you to stand on the highest hill to get a view of that same ocean."

Oh, it was enjoyable, the way the stunned expression spread across his fine features. It was clear now that she would be able to keep him at arm's length quite easily, and simply enjoy his company for a little while before he returned to his own people. There would be no danger of her head being turned by his tall fair form, by his strange and beautiful eyes...

"I am fortunate that it was you who saved my life," he said wryly. "That must mean you like me a little. If you did not, think of how cruel you could be with a wit as quick as yours."

Then, to her surprise, he sank gracefully to one knee before her in the rushes. "My lady, before you I am never any taller than this. Will you still show me the way to the highest hill?"

She blushed. "Only if you get up off of your knees."

"That is kind of you. I am glad you would not have me travel on my knees. The rocks–"

"Would ruin a good pair of leathers," she retorted, cutting him off. But he got to his feet and stood back a bit, extending his arm towards the door with a little bow.

Muriel brushed past him and he followed closely as she walked outside. She was fairly certain she heard him chuckling.

* * *

Muriel looked neither left nor right but simply walked straight across the grass towards the heavy wooden gates in the outer wall of the dun. It helped to keep her mind from dwelling on the tall stranger who followed her.

And he is a stranger, she reminded herself. As the king had wisely pointed out, his story was still very much in question. She could not allow herself to forget that.

The gates stood open to the day, allowing workers and servants to come and go as they hauled water in and refuse out. Muriel and Brendan walked outside and began the climb up the grassy hillside above Dun Farraige, until the reached the wide rolling hilltops scattered with oak and willow trees.

The great size of the dun could only be properly appreciated from up here. Its two solid, grass-covered earthen walls– one inside the other, with a rain-filled ditch in between– formed vast circles around the twenty round houses and the long rectangle that was the King's Hall. The buildings had all had their straw thatching repaired, and the rooftops shone golden in the sun above white walls newly finished with clay to keep out the cold winds from the sea.

Along the inner wall were an armory, a smokehouse, and a huge stack of peat bricks for fuel. A few large pens held horses with glossy springtime coats as well as a few sleek calves and fat lambs. The whole place held an air of prosperity and plenty, as well as safety against the elements and against invaders.

Beyond the two circles of the dun was the edge of the cliff and the steep pathways that led down to the sea far below.

But Brendan only glanced at the spectacular view before turning back to Muriel. "I do think you must like me, Lady Muriel. Why else would you invite me to come up here with you?"

She started to give him a cold reply, but then saw how his eyes sparkled in the sunlight and how he was all but grinning. He was baiting her, hoping to make her lose her temper and quite possibly make a fool of herself.

That was not going to happen on this day!

Muriel merely smiled politely at him. "I thought only to show a small kindness to a lost stranger. If you would rather go back to the dun, please feel free to do so. The path is easily found."

"I appreciate your kindness very much, as I have told you. But are you saying you would have brought any stranger up here? Was there nothing about me at all that you found interesting?"

She shrugged. "I simply asked you to walk with me. Nothing more. I am sorry, Brendan, but you have no effect on me at all... not for good or for ill." Muriel turned to gaze out at the bay.

"You are saying I do not touch your feelings at all?" His voice was filled with disbelief.

"I am saying that I have never let myself be swept away by a handsome face or a set of broad shoulders– much less a sweet voice. I have learned to control my emotions very well."

"Ah, I think I understand now."

"Oh?"

"Of course. You sound like any woman who has never known love. That can only be what your trouble is."

She turned to face him. "I have never *allowed* myself to know love. I have been determined that I would never love any man unless I was certain he was the right one. So far, I have succeeded quite well."

"So far." He sounded very amused.

Muriel raised her chin. "Do your best, Brendan. Talk sweetly to me, gaze into my eyes, bring me little gifts. None of it will make any difference. I will be the one to control my feelings. Not you. That is one thing I can promise."

He merely nodded, his eyes shining.

They continued their walk. The hills around the dun were sprinkled with color, as though last night's storm had dropped flowers instead of rain.

Scattered in the sunniest open grass were bright yellow dandelions and primroses. Surrounding the largest rocks were thorny gorse bushes, filled with sweet-scented tiny golden blossoms, and star-shaped, purple-blue spring gentian. Nearby were blackberry bushes just beginning to flower in white.

At the edge of the shade cast by the oaks and willows were pink blooms of foxglove, long and slender. Beneath the oaks, in the deepest shade, were little violets of purple and blue and white.

As a backdrop to the flowers were masses of dark green, three-leafed clover with clusters of tiny white blossoms. All of it made a lovely contrast to the grey rocks and grey-green sea.

Brendan looked down once more on the massive rings of the dun. "Flowers and clover, cattle and sunshine, and a fortress home where all can live in safety and contentment," he said. "It is the same at Dun Bochna. And for the same reason, I am sure."

"What reason would that be?" Muriel almost smiled. He was certainly a grand talker, if nothing else.

"Why, its king, of course!" He turned his brilliant smile on her as they walked, his gold-brown hair ruffling in the wind. "King Murrough's land reflects his own character, his own virility, his own justice. King Galvin's land does the same."

Muriel turned away from the bright light of his smile and made herself look only at the grass where she walked. "Of course," she agreed, and meant it. "It is always so. A king's land is like his queen. If he serves it and protects it and cherishes it– with his mind and his body and his heart– it will bloom beneath his hand."

Brendan nodded in agreement.

"But if he is false, or disfigured, or weak…"

"His land will become the same. As you say, Lady Muriel, it is always so. No one knows this better than I, a man who will be king of his own land someday."

She glanced up, beginning to smile again. It was almost too easy to hold him at a distance, to keep him in his place. "Yet I see nothing of a king about you. Or a prince. You have no fine clothes or good iron weapons. There is no tanist's torque around your neck. No king's

43

gold on your wrists or fingers. All you have are boasting words and fanciful stories."

Muriel thought he would stop and frown at her, and give her some indignant response; but he only laughed and spread his arms and went on walking.

"Some men might need such things for others to know them as a king. I am one who does not! Each time I set out, the warrior men follow me. Each time I return, I bring more cattle and more wealth. Everywhere I walk, the land blossoms under my feet.

"You can see this from the flowers which surround us now. Surely even you can agree that I must be a king, when such things happen wherever I go!"

Muriel did laugh this time, shaking her head. Anyone else saying such things would simply have been an insufferable braggart, but Brendan was so good-natured that it was difficult to hold his boasting against him.

Difficult– but not impossible. She must not begin to allow him so close. She reminded herself again that she did not know if was really a prince or just the grandest liar she'd ever met... and she made herself still the longing that had begun to rise in her heart and, instead, think only with her head.

They came to a high open spot where lush grass rippled in the wind. Brendan gathered a few of the yellow primroses and dandelions, and the two sat down together on the soft, thick grass.

For a time there was only silence between them. Muriel was more than content to simply gaze out at Dun Farraige and at the sea beyond, enjoying the warm sun and the fresh sea breeze and the scent of thick greenery and springtime blossoms. She found that it helped to keep her heart from pounding– and her breath from quickening– if she looked at anything else but Brendan.

I will be the one to control my feelings, not you. Muriel took a deep breath and deliberately looked away from him, out at the glittering bay.

"This is indeed a lovely place," said Brendan. "Now, out there, straight across the water to the north, is the land that I am from."

Muriel followed his gaze to where the mountainous land was visible as a hazy outline. "You are fortunate today that we can see it at all. So much of the time it is hidden in the mist."

"I have found that many things might be hidden in the mist... but you need only wait for the sun to come out and burn it away, and then all will be revealed to you." He grinned, and Muriel could not decide whether he was serious or merely trying to bait her again.

Brendan turned and pointed off to the east. "There, past our sight, at the closed end of the bay, is the place where Odhran overthrew a king."

"And where you sent a tanist to his death." Muriel watched his face this time, wanting to see if he would laugh or boast or perhaps even do both.

But he did neither. His shining eyes grew serious and his voice became quiet. "I had no wish to kill him. I had no choice, either, if I wanted to live. But I had no wish to kill him." He fell silent and looked out toward the open sea.

Muriel watched for a moment, waiting for him to continue; but he said nothing more.

"I often come up here in fine weather to do the spinning or the sewing," she offered, brushing a strand of black hair from her face. "It is a favorite place of mine."

He turned back to her and his smile returned. "Do you come up alone?"

It was as if she saw nothing else but that beautiful smile. "Sometimes," she said, looking down to pick a few blades of grass. "At other times Alvy comes with me, or, on the best days, perhaps a few of the other women. But most often they prefer to stay closer to home. When I am alone here, I find this a place of great beauty and peace."

"I am not surprised that you would enjoy looking out towards the sea," said Brendan. "Straight down the bay, nearly at the place where the ocean begins, is my home. Dun Bochna. You have been looking to me all this time, Lady Muriel."

She turned her head very slowly to stare at him. "And when you looked out from your shores, do you mean to tell me that you were looking at me in turn?"

He looked a bit surprised, and before he could answer she smiled coolly and turned away again. "I thought not."

"But I *was* looking to you." Brendan reached for her fingers, but she moved her hands beneath her cloak. "I knew you were out in the world somewhere. I hoped to find someone like you before–"

"Before you exhausted yourself with all the other women you encountered?"

"Before I had to take my place as king," he finished patiently. He got to his feet and stood very tall, forcing her to crane her neck to look up at him. He still held the bright yellow primroses and dandelions he had gathered. "I will need a queen. And I have not yet found one."

"Your speech is well rehearsed," Muriel said, frowning. "You must have used it many times. It seems

46

strange to me that such a fine and handsome man as you– as I am sure you will be happy to remind me– can find no woman who will have him."

She waited for his response, but he merely turned and walked with long, graceful strides towards the nearby rocks. The wind stirred his golden brown hair around his face as he paused in front of the gorse bushes.. "You misunderstand me." He broke off a little branch of gorse, heavy with golden blossoms. "There were plenty of women who would have accepted me. I have not yet found one that I myself would accept."

"Oh. Oh. Now I see. Well, Brendan, I suppose you will simply have to keep on searching."

"Perhaps," he said, and added a few stems of spring gentian to his collection. Arranging the blossoms carefully, he walked past the rocks to some blackberry brambles. In a moment, a slender cane of tiny white flowers joined the primrose and dandelion and gorse and gentian.

"You are forgetting what King Murrough just said," Muriel told him. "You may never leave Dun Farraige. You could very well stay here and live out your life as a slave."

Brendan smiled back at her, carefully adjusting his bouquet to avoid the sharp thorns of the gorse. "If that happens, perhaps I could persuade you to be a servant, and live alongside me. It would be a simple life but a happy one, so long as we were together."

Muriel watched him as he worked with the flowers… and as she watched, it seemed to her that he no longer wore his fine black leather and soft grey wool. Instead she saw him in the rough, undyed garb of a slave. There was no shining brooch at his shoulder now, only a couple of long heavy thorns pushed through the fabric. And he seemed cold and despondent and underfed, nothing like the strong young man who had stood above her a moment before.

A cold shock ran through Muriel. Her face grew hot and her hands felt cold. "Being a slave is nothing to laugh about," she whispered, fighting to keep the tremor from her voice..

He walked to her and leaned down, trying to catch her eye. "My lady, that possibility is so unlikely that the only thing I *can* do is laugh about it."

Still, she could not look at him. "The king's men leave in the morning for Dun Bochna. It will not be long until they return. Then we will know the truth."

"You already know the truth, for I have told it to you. I am the tanist of my father's kingdom. In time, I will be its king."

The fresh breeze blew over them again. Muriel took another deep breath and firmly reminded herself that this Brendan was an unknown, a mystery, as insubstantial as the mist and as shadowy as they grey cloak he wore.

He was the last man she would ever want to know… much less marry.

II. MARRY A KING, OR NO ONE

Brendan walked away from Muriel, this time towards the willow trees. From the edge of the shade he took blooms of the foxglove, long and slender and deep pink. Then he moved to the deepest shadows beneath the trees to pick a few tiny violets, all blue and purple and white.

He walked back to Muriel and sat down in the grass beside her, toying with his bouquet. She waited for him to give it to her, but the idea seemed not to occur to him. "I have told you all there is to know about me," he said. "I would like to know more about you."

She shrugged. "There is little of interest. I have lived here all of my life. I am the daughter of a warrior who served the previous king of Dun Farraige and died in his sixtieth year. My mother's life ended some ten years after my birth. I was left in the care of Alvy, one of the king's servants, and she has cared for me ever since."

"And there is no man in your life? Aside from me, of course."

"There is no man in my life at all. Including you."

He frowned, but she could see the merriment in his eyes. "It is hard to believe that no man of Dun Farraige, or anywhere else, has wanted to make you his wife."

"Perhaps they have, Brendan. That is not something you would know. But I will tell you this: I will be the wife only of a king, or I will be no man's wife at all."

His eyebrows lifted in surprise, but he grinned all the wider. "I see! Well, Lady Muriel, I cannot fault you for wanting only the best in a husband. I suppose it would limit your choices somewhat, but no matter. You can marry me! I am going to be a king. I am already the tanist–"

"As you have told us many times. But a tanist is not a king. I am waiting for a king."

"And you have not considered any other men?" Brendan cocked his head. "Has there never been a good man who was simply a warrior, unlikely to be chosen king? Was there no well-spoken bard or learned druid who loved you and wanted to make you his wife?"

He smiled. "I could never believe that any man who saw you would not find himself drawn to you, just as I am."

Muriel tried to answer, but her voice caught. All she could see were his strange shining eyes and all she could hear were his flattering words. "There have been others," she said at last. "But I knew the fate which awaited me if I allowed myself to love them. I kept well away, good men though they were."

"You kept away, even as you do with me." He gazed at her, and his expression grew thoughtful. "Many women hope to marry a king, but I have never known one who insisted she would have no other. Yet I see by your eyes that you are quite serious. Tell me: Why have you come to such a decision?"

She turned away. "I have my reasons. But they would not interest you."

"Oh, but you are wrong! I am more than interested. And I will wait until you are ready to tell me." He leaned over and picked a handful of three-leafed clover, adding it to his collection of flowers and carefully arranging it to his liking.

Muriel stared at his hands as he worked. "Then you shall wait until the day I learn you truly are a king... or you will hear nothing from me."

"I am indeed the next king of my people," he continued, working the clover in and out among the bright yellow primrose and gorse and the blue and purple violets. "And you forget that even if– *if* I had not already been named tanist, I still carry the blood of kings. My own father rules at Dun Bochna. Even if I were only a nephew or a cousin of his, I would still be one who could be named king by the free men of my tribe."

Brendan glanced up again. "There are not many who stand eligible to be a king, whether or not they are ever chosen. Is this not enough for you?"

"It is not," she said quietly. "Only a true king will I consider. Only a man who already wears the torque of kingship and has been chosen and accepted by his people. A tanist is not a king. It can be no other way."

"No matter. You will soon learn that not only am I to be a king, I am exactly the kind of man that a woman like you has need of." He looked up at her and grinned, as though he expected her to smile back.

Instead she got to her feet and began walking down the path to the dun. "Farewell, Brendan. The next time I notice you heading for certain death on the rocks, I will send a school of codfish instead of a pair of dolphins."

"Wait! Please wait!" She heard him get up and hurry through the grass behind her. "I am sorry. It *is* the truth that I am to be king, as I said. But it is also the truth that I am a better fighter than I am an artist... and

51

can sometimes be as crude with words as a poet would be with a sword."

Gently he touched her shoulder. "I would like to give you this."

She turned around. Brendan held out the lovely bouquet of flowers he had made. It was as pretty a gift as any she had ever received, though she was determined not to let him know that.

Muriel folded her hands, held her head high, and briefly eyed the bouquet. Then she tilted her head to study him. "I am offered gifts all the time. Why should I be impressed with yours?"

He considered her words, but his strange eyes were bright with something like mischief. "You need not be impressed with them at all, Lady Muriel. You need only carry these flowers and enjoy their beauty and their sweet scent. They are simply a small emblem of my gratitude to you for rescuing me from the sea."

"I see. Yet I did not do it for thanks."

"Of course not. Ah, I understand now!" he grinned. "You need no gratitude. Well, then! I will throw these flowers into the sea– the place where I would be right now if not for you."

Her eyes widened as she watched him walk towards the cliff. There was nothing but deadly rocks and pounding sea far below. "Brendan..."

He turned, his face questioning, and stood patiently waiting for her to speak.

"I will accept your gift, if you wish to give it to me."

Smiling, he walked back to her and held out the colorful bouquet. A bit of clover fell to the grass as she took it, warm and damp from his hand. "I thank you," she said. "I suppose if I could rescue a stranger from the sea, I could do no less for such pretty flowers."

"I am very glad that you have rescued both." He looked at her in genuine curiosity. "If I promise not to offend you again, will you tell me why you will marry no man but a king?"

She ran her fingers over the soft petals of the flowers. "Perhaps I will tell you. Very soon you will either be a slave or you will be gone, so I suppose it does not matter."

He smiled. "It matters to me. Please tell me why you will have none but a king."

She glanced at him, and then turned to stare out to sea. "Did you not wonder how it was that I was able to help you last night?"

He paused. "I suppose not. I suppose I was merely grateful that you saw my boat when it came ashore on the beach, and that you brought the men to lift me out and take me to your fortress."

Muriel turned back to face him. "Do you think I spend the dark and rainswept nights alone on the shore, anxiously waiting for boats with men in them to land at my feet?" She pushed her dark hair back from her face. "I was safe inside my house. So how did I learn you were out there, tossing on the rough sea with your death only moments away?"

"I must confess… I do not know."

Muriel folded her hands around the stems of her bouquet of flowers and stared down at them. "I have a water mirror. Do you know what that is?"

He nodded slowly. "I have heard of such things. A dish of the finest bronze, or even of gold, is filled with pure water and placed where the moon can light it."

"Some of the most powerful work solely by the light of the stars. But mine is a basin of bronze that takes the cold water of the sea and stirs to life when the moon shines down. It shows me things that are important... things that are worth knowing."

"And your water mirror revealed my little boat coming ashore?"

"Your little boat did not come ashore, Brendan. It was headed straight for the cliffs."

"Then... how..."

"I called out to two friends who live in the sea. If I am able to draw strongly enough on the power of the water, those friends will hear me and do my bidding if they can. Last night I asked them to go to your boat at the foot of the cliffs and bring that boat to the beach instead."

"Dolphins," he whispered. "Dolphins brought me ashore."

"They did. And I am grateful for their help."

"As am I." He smiled. "Then your powers are not limited to the mirror."

"They are not." Now it was her turn to walk a few steps to look out over the sea.

Brendan followed. She could feel the heat of his presence as he moved close behind her. "Please, Lady Muriel," he said quietly. "Tell me about these powers of yours."

She took a deep breath, and wrapped her purple cloak more closely around her shoulders against the sudden chill of the wind. "It is the power of water," she said, after a moment. "Especially the water, and the creatures, of the of the sea. Only rarely will any other sort of water respond to me. By far, the greatest power lies with the sea."

He took another step, and then he was so close she could feel the fire of his body at her side. "My own powers are those of sword and spear," he said. "I have spent little time on the subtler arts. But I do know that a water mirror shows nothing to most who try to use it. Only someone who possesses an inborn magic, and the skill of long practice, can see what the mirror displays."

Brendan paused. Somehow she was aware that he was smiling. "I knew you were no ordinary woman when I saw you reach for me where I lay in that wreck of a boat… but now I see that you are even more special than I knew. How is it that you come to have the power of the sea and its creatures, and the wisdom to use a water mirror?"

Muriel turned a little, facing the wind and keeping watch on Brendan from the corner of her eye. "My mother had this power," she said. "My two sisters had it, too. I am simply one more of my family who has a little of the old magic."

He nodded again, looking closely at her; but still she kept her gaze out on the distant whitecapped waves. "You said that they *had* this power, as if they no longer do," Brendan said. "You already spoke to me of your mother's passing. But what of your sisters?"

Her gaze flicked to him. There was genuine curiosity in his blue and brown eyes, and sympathy in his gently curving mouth. "You are quite right. My sisters did have this power once, as I do, but no more."

"What happened? How is it that the power left them?"

She started to speak, but then halted. "Come with me, if you truly want to know. I will introduce you to my sisters… and then you will understand."

* * *

It took a bit of searching, but at last Muriel found her two sisters. They walked barefoot in the cold wet sand of the narrow beach, each carrying a basket. They kept their eyes down, searching for small shelled creatures and fresh strands of seaweed with which to fill their baskets, and held their plain brown and grey skirts up out of the surf.

As the high grey clouds drifted in from the sea, Brendan paused at the rocks above the shoreline while Muriel walked ahead to greet the two women. "Moreen! Moina!" she called, and they paused in their work to look up at her.

He studied them, as he might study any attractive women. Both were slender and fair, as Muriel was, with the same noble features and long dark hair. Yet there was something very different about these two.

It was not just that they were older than Muriel, though it was clear that she was the youngest. Muriel's hair fell back from her face in shining black waves, while theirs hung down their backs in dull, tired braids.

Her skin was flushed and fair and vibrant, while their faces looked so pale they were almost grey… as if half the blood had been drained away.

And the eyes. Muriel's eyes were of deepest blue and as lively and flashing as the sea on a clear and windy day. But the eyes of her sisters were so quiet, so somber, so grey, that there was scarcely any life in them at all.

As Muriel stood between the two women, Brendan slowly walked towards them. Clearly the three of them were related by blood. But what could have happened to cause the two older sisters to be so very different from Muriel?

"Moina. Moreen," she said, placing a hand on the arm of each. "This is Brendan. He is– he is a guest of the king. He would like to meet my older sisters."

Brendan walked to them, standing tall and smiling politely, and bowed to each one. "It is an honor to meet you. An honor to meet this lady's sisters."

He glanced from one woman to the other, trying to catch first Moreen's eye and then Moina's. "Each of you is as lovely as the other. I would be quite content to set out yet once more in my little broken curragh, if it meant meeting Muriel and her sisters."

He gave them his warmest smile. The two women only regarded him with a kind of empty silence. "Our husbands are waiting," said Moina, with a glance at Muriel.

"We will leave now," added Moreen.

"Of course." Muriel stepped back to let them go, holding the trailing ends of her rectangular purple cloak out of the rushing waves. "Give my greetings to your husbands, as always." She watched them as they walked back up the steep and rocky path to the dun, lifting their heavy baskets with one hand and holding up their long skirts with the other.

They never looked back. In a few moments they were gone.

Brendan turned to Muriel. "What is wrong with them?" he demanded. "Are they truly your sisters?"

She walked towards him, climbing up on the higher ground towards the rocks. "They are."

He shook his head. "You are as filled with life and strength and beauty as a young dolphin flying through the surf. But they have none of your vitality, your energy. It is as though all the color of life had faded away and left them empty, somehow. Have they always been that way?"

She shook her head, still gazing after them. "They have not. Both were lively young women of excellent wit and unsurpassed beauty– far more beautiful than ever I could hope to be. Moina was a skilled mistress of the water mirror. Moreen could speak to the creatures of the sea whenever she wished, and they would answer."

"What could have happened to them?

Muriel turned to meet his gaze. "They got married."

"Married?" Brendan gave a short laugh. "I have certainly heard of marriage causing distress to some. But Lady Muriel, you cannot be serious about marriage being the cause of your sisters' despair and emptiness."

"I am very serious."

He only shook his head. "I should be surprised if your two older sisters, who would surely have at least some of your beauty and spirit, had *not* found husbands. But it is clear to see that whatever spirit they had has somehow been drained away from them, taking their beauty with it." He continued to gaze up at the distant hilltop. "It is a troubling sight. Are you truly telling me that they became this way only after they married?"

"I am."

"How is that possible?"

Muriel folded her hands and walked a few steps past him, away from the sea, looking down at the sand and shells and scattered seaweed as she considered what to say. At last she turned and stood among the rocks, closing her eyes and listening to the rushing of the waves.

58

"It has always been so for the women of my family," she began. "Long ago, so long that none of us knows exactly when, one of the girls was renowned as a great mistress of magic. The water mirror, the creatures of the sea, even some foreknowledge of the future– all these were hers to command, and more. And though she had such powers, she was a good and noble woman who helped her people when she could and never used her magic to harm anyone."

"As you, too, use your magic only to help those who need it." Brendan sat down near Muriel on one of the boulders. "But what of this lady who was your distant ancestor?"

Muriel nodded slowly, gathering her thoughts. "She met a man, the story goes, a strong and handsome man… a man whose beauty turned her head and whose voice and words filled her thoughts. She found a stronger magic than her own: the magic of a man who wanted her, a man whom she loved in return.

"Though he was a stranger, and her father and mother begged her to wait until they better knew his home and family, she would have none of it. She would marry her handsome warrior without delay, fearing that he might find another if she waited. So marry they did, and he took her away to the fortress of his own king far across the countryside.

"So she married in haste," said Brendan. "Did she not know her husband as well as she thought?"

"She did not," answered Muriel. "Her husband was indeed a handsome and powerful man, but he was only a warrior. He was a fighter and little more. There was no room for gentleness or courtesy in his heart, and only the smallest of kindnesses. He considered his wife to be well treated as long as she had sufficient food and woolen gowns and a cloak to keep the chill out, and the opportunity to share his bed each night– or whenever he chose."

"He did not love her," said Brendan, his voice quiet.

"He knew nothing of love. And had no care to learn."

"Yet she, too, must have been resourceful and strong, even as you are. Why did she remain with such a man?"

Muriel smiled a little. "As you might imagine, it was not long before she knew she would have a child. No one could blame any woman for staying with her husband at that time... even a husband who thought of her only as a servant and bed partner, and not as the woman he loved.

"She tried to use her magic to persuade him, just a little, to allow something like love to enter his heart. But this only enraged him when he learned what she had done, and he told her she was forbidden to use her magic ever again.

"To keep peace in her house– and to protect her child– she agreed to do this, for nothing is more important to any woman than her children. In time she found herself the mother of five daughters, all of whom were as beautiful as she and who also had the power to command the sea and the rivers and the rain.

"Then, one terrible night, her husband and a few friends spent an evening with too many skins of blackberry wine and decided to race each other in their curraghs. There was a storm just offshore and the waves were rising, but they thought it would only add to their sport. And so it was that this woman saw her husband, the father of her five children, smash onto the rocks in the bay in his little leather boat.

"Without hesitation, she ran into the sea and threw herself into the surf, calling on the waves to become quiet and calling on the dolphins to come and save her drowning husband. And as she struggled against the storm and the cold, the waves near the rocks did lessen. The dolphins did come and bring her husband safely to the shore.

"But by the time the creatures could return to rescue this woman, even her great strength and powerful magic had reached their limits. The waves threw her up on the rocks where the dolphins could not reach her. It was nearly dawn before the storm lessened enough for the men of Dun Farraige to go and retrieve her broken body from the rocks.

"To their shock, she still lived. But as they lay her on the soft sands of the beach and her weeping daughters gathered round, the druids told them she would not be among them for long.

"With her last breath, my ancestor placed this curse upon her family: that no woman of her line should marry an unworthy man. If she did, she would find that she no longer had any power of magic at all. None of them, she swore, would end up as she had, wasting her life and her magic on a man who had neither love nor respect for what she was.

"She commanded her daughters to marry only kings, for she hoped that a king could not hide the mistreatment of his wife the way another man might… and being a king, perhaps he would possess enough truth, enough justice, enough strength on his own, to let him cherish his wife's magic as much as she herself did. It was the best hope that she could give them.

"The years passed by. Of her five daughters, the four eldest did not heed their mother's words. As women so often do, they chose their mates solely with their hearts and not their heads. They married the first men who kindled the flames of attraction within them; men who were not bad, but who were not good, either. They treated their new wives well enough but even so, it was not long before the women found their magic starting to fade.

"Soon these four young women, once so lively and strong, had no magic at all. They spent their mornings and their evenings bent beneath the weight of endless wooden buckets of water, and the nights suffering at the hands of their husbands."

Brendan closed his eyes. "And they lived out their lives in this way? It is a very sad story."

"There is a bit of hope. The youngest daughter, remembering her mother's words and seeing what happened to her sisters, did wait until she could be the wife of a king. Her powers remained, as did her beauty and liveliness; and it has been so ever since among the women of my family.

"Only those who marry kings retain their youth and spirit and magic. The others– those who marry ordinary men, or worse– become as my ancestors became. As my sisters have become."

There was silence between them for a time. Then Brendan stood up and walked around to her, and took hold of one of her hands. Gently touching the side of her face, he said, "Such a fate will never be yours, Lady Muriel. That I can promise you."

"I have already promised it to myself," she said, looking into his blue and brown eyes.

The wind blew cool and damp as they returned to the dun, just as the rain began to fall.

* * *

When the sun began to set, Muriel walked alone to the edge of the sea and peered up at the sky. It was as clear as an evening was likely to be in Eire, with just a few high clouds drifting off to the north and none to be seen on the western horizon.

She felt great relief at the simple knowledge that the sky was clear and the nearly full moon would soon be rising. There was nothing she wanted more right now than to use her water mirror to learn a very important truth, and there would be no better time than tonight.

Muriel dipped her leather bag into the edge of the sea, allowing the rush of the surf to fill it with cold water. Then she crossed the beach and made her way back up the cliffside path until she reached the dun, where she went into her house and shut the door.

* * *

Alvy snored softly in her warm nest in the rushes, but Muriel had not even tried to sleep. She sat on a bench beside the stone border of the central hearth, working by the glow of the fire and a flat seashell lamp with a little rushlight burning in it, and tried to pass the time by spinning a basket of fine wool.

Perhaps she would attempt to dye this lot in the purple-blue color that was her favorite– the same color as the spring gentian flowers that grew among the rocks– but it was difficult to keep her thoughts on such ordinary things as spinning thread and stitching pretty gowns.

The flame in her lamp flickered and went out, for it had burned its tallow-soaked reed all the way down to the bed of sand in the shell. Muriel got another reed and used the embers of the fire to light the lamp again.

She glanced over her shoulder at the window, but saw only black sky and stars. Never had the moon traveled so slowly. It dawdled in the east, shining down only on the land, forcing Muriel to wait and wait as it made its slow journey across the clear night towards the sea.

Never, it seemed, had she spun such a great amount of thread as she had on this night.

When her lamp burned out again, she lit another. And when it went dark a third time, she got up and walked to the table beneath the window.

The high white moon was just beginning to show itself. The black sky around it was sprinkled with bright stars. Muriel reached below the table into the heap of rushes, pulled out her water mirror and her damp leather bag, and poured the seawater into the polished bronze basin.

Before the water had even settled, she held both hands over it and lowered her fingertips to touch its cool surface. As she did, the moonlight filtered down so that it shone directly through the window, casting a faint blue-white glow over the basin.

She let the water become still around her fingers. *Brendan,* she called silently, closing her eyes for a moment. *Brendan.*

Muriel gazed down at the mirror and slowly lifted her hands. The water quivered and then became still, shining in the moon's glow… and then the images began to form.

She saw a misty grey cloak in the darkness, moving softly as a tall man made his slow and aimless way around the inner wall of Dun Farraige. Apparently she was not the only one who could not sleep this night.

Muriel waited until she saw him walk out of the shadows and move across an open grassy space, a space that was lit by the radiant moon.

Brendan, she called to him again.

This time he slowed and stopped.

She placed her hands beneath the basin, feeling the cold of the seawater through its etched bronze sides. *Show me who you are,* she said in her mind, and stayed perfectly still as the moon shone down on both him and the water in her mirror.

A new image formed: Brendan's face in the summer sunlight, framed by golden brown hair that was well past his shoulders. His one blue eye and one brown eye shone as he laughed. As he swung up onto a big grey horse, Muriel saw that he wore a heavy golden torque around his neck. There were golden bands and rings at his wrists and fingers, all gleaming in the light of the sun.

Now his cloak was brilliant blue; now his tunic was blue and green and yellow and cream; now he wore a fine iron sword at his hip. He galloped away on that powerful horse, followed by twenty men who were equally well dressed and armed.

Now he looked like a prince... if not a king.

The image faded as the men rode off into the mists. Then she saw Brendan's face again.

This time he was pale and exhausted, chilled and soaking wet, his hair cut short and dripping with water. He looked as he had when she had found him on the storm-wracked sea, dressed in rags like a slave.

A slave.

Her fingers shifted slightly on the cold sides of her bronze basin. *Show me who you are. Show me what you are!*

Again came the image of Brendan as he was right now, all in grey and black, standing motionless as though held in thrall by moonlight and magic. Then the vision wavered and dissolved into the form of a crying infant no more than a few months old, lying on a heap of worn straw in the corner of a rough shelter… a baby dressed only in a tattered square of undyed wool that was tied around him with an old rough cord.

In a moment the infant was lifted up by a woman who was clearly a slave of the lowest class. She wore only the poorest and roughest dark wool and had rusted iron bands around each wrist. The child rested its head on her shoulder and quieted… and then opened its eyes.

Muriel saw one brown eye and one blue eye staring straight at her.

She jerked her hands away from the bronze basin. The water inside wavered and darkened, and the images vanished.

Eventually, the moon settled towards the western horizon and the sky in the east began to lighten with the first touches of dawn.

Muriel was still standing at her mirror when she heard the thunder of hooves outside. As if waking from a deep sleep, she closed the wooden shutters of her window and hurried to throw open the door of her house.

She was just in time to see five of the king's men gallop out through the open gates, out into the morning light and onto the path that would take them to Dun Bochna. There they would learn the truth about Brendan once and for all.

But it would be at least a fortnight until they returned– fourteen nights of wondering whether Brendan was the prince he claimed to be, or whether what the mirror had shown could possibly be true.

* * *

The days were at once the longest that Muriel had ever known, and not nearly long enough.

Within the walls of Dun Farraige, Brendan was quartered in a house with three other men. All of them were craftsmen, workers in iron and bronze and wood. As such, they were neither servants nor nobles; they were men who lived just as King Murrough had ordered that Brendan should live until they knew for certain what he was.

The craftsmen's day began early. Brendan served as a mere helper to them, hauling loads of wood for their fires and carrying buckets of seawater for quenching hot metal. But he must have found time to slip out each day before the work began, for every morning when Muriel stepped out of her house she found a bouquet of wildflowers on the stepping stone in front of her door.

Always the flowers were newly gathered from the hills above the dun, always still damp with dew. Some days there would be bright yellow primrose and gorse; others might bring the pink of foxglove and violets; still others would deliver pretty combinations of blue gentian and purple violets, or white blackberry canes with white violets set off by deep green clover.

In the afternoons Brendan would often come to sit with her as she worked at her spinning and sewing. They might stay in the hall with the other women if rain threatened; but would walk out to sit on the grassy hilltops if the weather was fair, there to enjoy the warm summer sun and cooling sea breeze.

She would sew, and he would talk, and so many times she would find herself laughing more than working. His stories were varied and wonderful, but consisted mostly of Brendan's heroics and Brendan's bravery and Brendan's great victory in stealing half of King Odhran's cattle. He would walk around her gesturing and talking and acting out each part, and she would watch, and smile, and laugh.

Muriel knew the chance she took whenever she spent time with him. On each successive day, he became more a part of her life and it became more difficult to hold him at arm's length. Yet again and again she allowed him to stay at her side. Again and again she told herself that it was only for a short time, that soon he would be gone and she could safely forget she had ever known him... just as he would no doubt forget about her.

Late in the afternoon of the fourteenth day, as the shadows began to lengthen, Brendan finished yet another tale and came over to sit down close beside her. "Tell me, now," he said, a little breathless as she worked at stitching together a fine white linen gown. "You have watched me and listened to me all these many days. Do you still believe I am only a slave?"

She set her mass of white linen down on the grass. Brendan sat near enough to touch, his golden brown hair and grey cloak blowing in the wind and his blue and brown eyes shining.

For the first time, she reached out her hand to him. He stayed very still as she brushed a strand of sunlit hair from his eyes. Her hand lingered near his brow, and she drew her finger lightly down the edges of his hair and onto the smooth warm skin near his left eye– the eye that was blue. She paused for a moment, stroking the skin again and marveling at how very soft it was.

"Have you never touched a man's face, Lady Muriel?" he asked peering up at her. His eyes were bright with laughter.

She froze. "I have not," she said, and started to take her hand away.

But he caught hold of it lightly, gently, and brought it close to his chest. "I am glad to know this," he said, and bowed his head to touch his lips to the back of her fingers.

The world around her seemed to grow misty and disappear. She saw only his closed eyes and gentle face, felt only the heat and surprising softness of his mouth as he caressed her skin.

Off in the distance, far below near the gates of the dun, came the faint sound of galloping hoofbeats. It seemed of no consequence to Muriel, who found that she was no longer capable of moving; her entire body had gone warm and soft.

But Brendan opened his eyes and looked up past her shoulder, and then sat back.

Muriel blinked as the light of day intruded on her once again. As she watched him stand up and take a step towards the fast-approaching hoofbeats, she knew without having to look that King Murrough's riders had finally returned from Dun Bochna.

* * *

Brendan raced down the path, finally having to let go of Muriel's hand. She could not bring herself to move any faster than a walk, for she found herself feeling terribly sad. But he ran for the open gates and dashed across the lawn, quickly disappearing among the scattering of houses.

She hurried a little to catch up to him. At last she found him standing with his hand against the wall of one of the houses, staring at the closed doors of the King's Hall. Seven horses were being led away as Muriel walked up to stand beside him.

"They're already in the hall, waiting for the king," Brendan said, still watching the doors. "I didn't get a chance to talk to them."

Muriel took a deep breath. "Did any of the men from Dun Bochna come with them?"

"They did! I saw Darragh and Killian, two of the best fighters and two of my closest friends." He grinned down at her. "Nothing but the best for me! Isn't that true, Lady Muriel?"

She closed her eyes. "You say you know them. but even the lowest slave at Dun Bochna would know who they were. Here is my question for you, Brendan: Did *they* know *you?*"

He stared at her. "Of course they will know me. They have come all this way just for me."

Muriel stood up on tiptoe to peer over his shoulder. "So, where are they? Surely they would have been quite excited to see you. Why are they not here, talking and laughing with you?"

"They have not yet seen me. They were taken directly into the hall." He tried to smile. "I did not think I should shout out to them when they were on their way to see your king."

"I see." She drew a deep breath. "So whether they saw you or not, they have not yet recognized you."

He frowned, confusion evident on his face. "As I told you, they have not yet seen me. When they do, they will know me. Just as I said they would." His face brightened. "Ah, now I think I understand why you are so gloomy. You fear that if they don't know me, I'll be proved a great liar. But if they do know me, then I will have to return to my home and leave you here."

Her eyes widened as she stared up at him, feeling something like shock at hearing Brendan put her feelings into words. She looked away towards the King's Hall, and squared her shoulders.

"Either way, Brendan, you will be gone from me. You will vanish into a life of servitude, working with the slaves and the lowest of servants; or, you will return to your fortress very far away and become the king you claim to be. Have you forgotten that?"

There was the lightest of touches at her fingers. She glanced down to see a little bunch of white blackberry blossoms being offered to her.

"Do you see these flowers?" he said. "They, too, have become part of your life, for I make certain to have them waiting for you each morning. They are there for you as soon as you step outside, for it gives me pleasure to place them in your hands whenever I can get them for you.

"Listen to me, Lady Muriel. Whether I am servant or king, I promise you this: I will find a way to be part of your life, now and always, just as these flowers have become part of your life."

She could not bring herself to take the blackberry canes. "Yet once you walk through the doors of that hall– no matter which way it goes– there will be no more flowers for me."

"Ah, but you are wrong about that," he countered, pressing the white blossoms into her hand. "There will always be flowers, my lady. One way or another, there will always be flowers."

* * *

There was nothing to do now but sit and wait. Muriel knew that, as always, the two visiting men would be seated on cushions in the clean rushes of the King's Hall, offered fresh water and good wine and plates of hot food, and then left in peace to eat and rest until they felt refreshed and ready for conversation with their hosts.

The sun was sinking into the sea when the doors of the hall finally opened and one of the druids beckoned to them. Brendan leaped to his feet and hurried inside, almost pushing past the startled druid and leaving Muriel to follow alone.

She forced herself to step inside, blinking in the dim light. At the far end of the hall, King Murrough sat on his bench surrounded as always by his warriors and his druids; but standing in front of him were two strange men dressed in bright wool cloaks and tunics and trousers. They both had wide gold bracelets around their wrists and slender torques of twisted gold around their necks. Each of them carried a fine sword and dagger at his thick leather belt.

But it was difficult to see the strangers now. Brendan had all but leaped into their arms, shouting at them and clapping them on the back. "Darragh! Killian!" he cried, as though he were their long-lost brother. "You're here! It's so good to see you!"

"We knew that if anyone could survive exile, it was you," said Darragh, grinning as he reached down to clasp Brendan's wrist.

"Though we feared we might not see you again," said Killian, reaching out to do the same.

"I will admit, that thought did cross my mind while I was out on the sea with nothing but wind and rain and darkness for company," Brendan agreed, releasing them at last. "But thanks to this lady, I am still here in this world to greet you."

All three turned and looked towards Muriel. She could only watch as Brendan stood with the two warrior men who were who were so clearly his friends and equals. It was clear to her that he had told the truth and was exactly who he said he was– a prince, a warrior, the second son of King Galvin, and the tanist of Dun Bochna.

A man who was next to be king... and who would have to rejoin his people very soon.

Never had Muriel felt so torn. Part of her fairly sang with the knowledge that Brendan had told the truth, that he had indeed been chosen to be the next king of Dun Bochna. He truly was, apparently, a man whom she might marry without fear of losing her magic.

And another part of her knew that his being a prince did not necessarily mean that he would love her, or even want to have her as his wife.

Since the night of his rescue he had been as charming and kind to her as any man could be; but Muriel had been his only companion in this strange place where everyone doubted who he was. It was not surprising that he might wish to stay close to her while he was here. It could be a different story when he returned to his own home, to his own people, and no longer needed her.

And even if he did become a king and did love her and did want to make her his wife, there was still the supremely troubling vision that the water mirror had shown her: the image of Brendan as the child of slaves.

How such a boy could have grown up to be a prince was a mystery, for no man born a slave could ever be a king; but she did not know how she could ever learn the truth.

Muriel gathered her fine cloak a little more closely around her, for the sun was gone now and the warmth seemed to have left the hall. She felt only a chill and an emptiness in its place as she closed her eyes and held her little bunch of white flowers very tightly.

* * *

The men in the hall went on talking and laughing for a long time, and then got down to making the arrangements for Brendan's return to his people.

Darragh took a large, soft leather bag from his belt and turned to King Murrough. "We have, of course, brought you the ransom for our prince." He held out the bag, which one of the druids accepted, and after looking inside he showed it to the king.

Murrough leaned over to look inside the bag and then nodded. "A beautiful torque. Very fine gold work. We will accept it. Although..." He glanced up at his druid. "I should think that this gold torque alone is not enough to ransom the tanist of a tribe."

Murrough's druid looked at Darragh. "It is not enough," the druid said. "The ransom requires fifteen milk cows as well, or thirty heifers, in addition to the gold that you have brought."

"Of course," Darragh said. "We left so quickly, racing to get here, that it was not possible to bring down the cattle from the mountains and take them with us. I am sure you can understand how anxious we were to see our tanist again, after having reason to think he was dead."

"That is understandable," said King Murrough, and motioned the druid away. "Brendan. I know King Galvin well. You may return to your home now and

74

send the remainder of your ransom to me, or you may stay here as our honored guest until it can be brought. You are the son of King Galvin and the tanist of Dun Bochna. I am giving you a choice. What is your wish?"

Brendan turned and smiled at Muriel. "I would consider it no hardship to stay."

But Darragh and Killian looked at him, and their faces grew serious. "You must come now," said Killian. "It will take another two fortnights to get the cattle safely here. You cannot wait that long."

"Why not?" asked Brendan, his eyes still flicking to Muriel. "Perhaps I will stay and see how this lady likes me."

"You must hear us," said Darragh. "King Galvin wants to see you. Your father wants to see you with his own eyes. Now."

Before it is too late. Muriel could hear the unspoken words.

It seemed that Brendan heard them, too, for his face grew serious. "I understand," he said quietly. "We will go in the morning, as soon as it is light enough to ride. The cows will be sent." He looked over at Muriel and his eyes were full of apology.

Muriel knew that in the morning, Brendan would be gone. She tucked the white flowers beneath her cloak and left the hall, walking in silence back to her house.

She could not bear to look at him again.

* * *

It was the darkest night Muriel had ever known, for there was no moon, and the heavy clouds rolling in from the sea had turned the sky into a solid wall of blackness.

She stood in her house beside the empty water mirror, running her fingers over its cold bronze surface. The basin would be of no use to her on this night. Even if she had been able to set it up, what could she have asked? It had given her no clear answer to her first question, the one that would not leave her: whether Brendan had actually been born to a low servant– to a slave.

There seemed to be no doubt any longer that he was what he said he was. His men had greeted him as a prince and a brother and a friend. So why had her mirror seemed to show the image of Brendan, when he was just a few months old, with a woman who was herself a slave? Muriel had never known her mirror to be wrong before. Its message might be difficult to decipher at times, but she had never known it to be false.

Muriel knew that she should go to her bed and try to sleep. She was exhausted and the dawn would come much too soon. But she was consumed by a kind of restlessness that she had never experienced before, and finally she walked quietly to the door of the house, opened it, and stepped out into the night.

As Brendan had done some fourteen nights before, she paced through the torchlit grounds of the dun. It seemed that she was searching for something but did not know what it was. She told herself that she would walk in the night air for a time and then go back to her house and sleep.

Soon she found herself standing and gazing at the house where Brendan stayed.

In the morning he would be gone. He would go back to his own people, where he was a prince, where no doubt he had more than one lady waiting for him.

Muriel would never see him again. Standing here, beside the house where he slept, would be the closest she would ever come to him again.

She started to go to the house, just to place her hand on it, but stopped herself. Instead she bowed her head and looked away.

I will not weep! Not now. Not ever. Not for this. Not for him.

"Muriel."

Instantly she turned. Brendan stood behind her in the shadows, his grey cloak stirring gently in the night breeze.

"I could not sleep," he said, walking towards her. "And I see now that I am not the only one. I thought to go to your house and stand outside it, to place my hand against the wall where you lay sleeping... but when I left, I saw you walking here. And now we are alone together, each of us wandering in the night unable to rest."

Brendan reached for her hand. "I regret I have no flowers to give you. I have not yet gone outside the gates."

"I need no flowers from you," she whispered, unable to look away from him.

His fingers closed around her own and he drew her a step closer. "What do you need from me, Lady Muriel?"

She turned away, searching for words. "I... I need nothing."

"Oh, my lady... it is no crime if you do want something from me." He let go of her hand and gently took her by the shoulders, turning her around so that she faced him. "Nothing would give me greater pleasure than to give you whatever you wish to have, whether that is one small violet from the woods or a kingdom with borders so wide they reach beyond your sight."

He moved a step closer, and then another. He seemed so very tall as he stood before her beneath the cloudy night sky. Looking up at him, all she saw was his shadowy form with his soft hair blowing in the wind... and then he leaned down to kiss her.

Muriel shut her eyes and pulled away, and then took several hurried steps to the massive earthen wall of the dun. She leaned against it with one hand, trying to think only of the packed earth and damp grass against her fingers even as Brendan moved to stand beside her once again.

"Muriel," he whispered, reaching out to touch her arm.

"And if I did want something from you, Brendan, what would it matter? It serves me not at all to want anything from you. After tomorrow you will be gone... and I will not see you again."

"Ah, but you are wrong. I must leave in the morning to see my father the king, it is true; but I will return."

She jerked her head around to look up into his eyes. "And what if you do return? What will I do then, if you are– if you are–"

If you are indeed the son of slaves, as the mirror says! What good will it do me to love you then, if I must trade all that I am to do it!

"If I am what?" Brendan looked down at her with a baffled expression.

She tried to take a breath. "If you are– bound to another," she finished, turning away. It was a weak response, but the only one she could think of besides the truth.

78

Muriel did not have the heart to tell him what she had seen in the mirror. She had no other proof and neither did he. There was really no choice but to keep her doubts and fears to herself, and wait to see what the future might actually bring.

"Bound to another?" There was real confusion in his voice. "I have told you, there is no other. There is only you. And I promise you, I will return."

"Words are easy," she whispered. "I can only wait to see what you will do. I wish you a safe journey, Brendan of Dun Bochna."

She caught up the hem of her skirts and hurried back to the shelter of her house. If she had to stand and watch as he turned his back and went striding away with his grey cloak floating out behind him, she would never be able to let him go… and would use whatever magic she possessed to make him stay.

* * *

The dawn came. Muriel sat down on a boulder beneath a grey sky on the flower-covered hills above the great dun. She pulled her cloak up around her head against the wind, for it still carried the chill of the night.

As she watched, three men rode out through the open fortress gates. Brendan, Killian, and Darragh galloped their horses along the path and up to the top of the hill, past the place where Muriel sat hooded and silent among the rocks.

She expected that they would simply race on past, shouting and happy at the thought of going home. All thoughts of a woman named Muriel would be long gone from Brendan's mind. But as they rounded the curve at the top of the hill and came upon her, Brendan brought his horse to a sudden stop and his companions quickly did the same.

79

"It is so cold out here in the early morning, Lady Muriel," Brendan said, as his horse danced about. "Though I will tell you that I am glad to see you one more time before I go."

She looked up at him and the cloak fell back to her shoulders. Once more she saw his strong young face, his fair skin touched with color from the cold sea wind and his one brown eye and one blue eye shining down at her.

Muriel looked away and closed her eyes. "I merely came up here to watch the sunrise," she heard herself say. "I did not know that you would be riding past."

He began to laugh. She stole a glance at him. "The sun rises behind you, my lady. You are facing the sea!" he cried, and laughed again as she turned her face away from him once more.

Brendan turned his horse to go. "I will come back for you, Lady Muriel," she heard him say. His voice was clear and steady and he was not laughing now. "Think hard on marrying a prince. For what is a prince but a king, in a few years' time?"

Muriel kept her face impassive and once again gazed out at the sea. "Go, Brendan," she said. "Your companions wait for you."

He hesitated, but then started his horse trotting along the path. "Will you marry a prince?" he shouted, twisting to look over his shoulder as they galloped away.

Her breath caught as they disappeared over the crest of the hill. "Perhaps," she whispered. "Perhaps… if that is what you truly are."

* * *

The journey home to Dun Bochna took a few days longer than it otherwise would have, for Brendan and Darragh and Killian had to turn inland and ride far to the east to avoid the lands controlled by King Odhran. And though they rode only on the outskirts of Odhran's borders, the things they began to see filled them with increasing concern.

It was not yet midsummer, but already the oak leaves were beginning to wither and turn yellow. A few had dropped off and blew dry and rattling across the pale grass. There were no flowers anywhere in sight; only a few dead blossoms scattered among the dead leaves.

Strangest of all, no birds called from the trees. The forest was silent, its branches half bare.

"How can this be?" asked Darragh. "The land looks like it's beginning to die. Yet it is far too early for things to sleep in winter."

"And I have seen not one bird, and not one sign of a single animal, since we rode past the borders of Dun Camas," added Killian. "How is that possible?"

Brendan shook his head. "All my life I have heard the tales of such things happening. Now, I think, we are seeing it for ourselves. Dun Camas is a land which has a false king– a dishonest, unjust king by the name of Odhran.

"The land is like a wife to the king," Brendan went on. "If he does not care for it and protect it– if he takes it unjustly, if he is not worthy to have it– the land will begin to die. It will become dry and lifeless and barren, and all who are forced to live under his rule will suffer. As the king goes, so goes his land. That is what is happening to Dun Camas."

The three men glanced at each other, and rode on. It was not long before Brendan spotted a plume of black smoke rising up into the sky ahead of them– a plume too large and too thick to come from an ordinary hearth or campfire. The men urged their horses on and in moments reached a clearing where a herdsman's rath stood.

A rath was like a smaller version of the great fortresses. This one was a single high earthen wall encircling a little round house and a couple of sheds, and it was quickly turning into a smoking, flaming inferno.

Fire broke through the old straw roof and began eating away at it, sending sparks flying on the wind to land on the empty wooden sheds nearby. Even the earthen wall showed smoldering lines of smoke as the sparks took hold of the dry grass and weeds growing out of it.

Frantically trying to put the fire out, using battered wooden buckets dipped into the nearby stream, was the herdsman and his wife and their five sons.

Brendan and his two companions swung down from their horses and raced to help, but the family dropped the buckets and hurried into the woods the moment they spotted the three strange men running towards their home.

"Wait!" Brendan cried, running after them. "We will help you! Come out and speak to us! What has happened here?"

The old herdsman leaned out from behind a tree trunk and glared at Brendan. "I don't know you," he answered, glancing at his family's burning home. "Who is your king?"

Brendan stood as tall as he ever had in his life. "We are from Dun Bochna. I am the son of King Galvin. How did this happen? Is anyone hurt?"

"None are hurt. But I wish they were," growled the old man. "It was Odhran and his men who did this."

Brendan looked at Darragh and Killian. "We knew that Odhran displaced King Fallon and took over these lands. Why would he burn out those who serve him?"

"Serve him?" The old herdsman spat on the ground. "We do not serve Odhran. Why do you think they did this to us? He and his champion and a few of his followers rode out to see their new lands, and when they found us they demanded we swear our loyalty to him. When we would not, they did this– and rode away laughing."

"They could not have gone far," Brendan said, already running back for his horse. "Save what you can. We will deal with Odhran."

* * *

Brendan, Darragh, and Killian galloped their horses through the forest directly to the west, straight towards the fortress of Dun Camas far away on the coast. Brendan was sure that Odhran and his men would be headed home after inspecting the farthest reach of their newly stolen kingdom– and so they were.

Just ahead, Odhran, his champion, Aed, and four other fighting men walked their horses as calmly as if they were out for an enjoyable afternoon ride.

"Odhran!" shouted Brendan. "Odhran! Come back and face men with swords, instead of herders with sticks! Or do you not have the stomach for a match with real warriors?"

Instantly the six riders halted and turned. Then four of them drove their mounts straight at the newcomers, roaring in rage and slapping their horses with the flat sides of their swords.

"That's Aed who stays behind with Odhran," said Brendan. "Leave them to me." His companions nodded

83

and then all three drew their swords and galloped out to meet the enemy.

As Brendan had expected, Odhran remained with Aed, his champion and guardian, for a king was too valuable to risk in battle. Even the boldest fighters would retreat if their king was struck down. A king would lead his warriors to the battlefield but then stay on the sidelines and let his champion do his fighting for him, unless circumstances forced him to do otherwise.

Which was exactly what Brendan had in mind for Odhran.

The sword felt good in his hand. He'd not had a chance to use it since the last time he'd faced Odhran's men. Now he galloped his horse at full speed straight into the shoulder of the first man's horse, using his animal's momentum and weight to drive the other horse nearly off its feet.

The unexpected tactic caught the other man by surprise. Brendan swung hard at him as the other horse staggered. It was a clean blow and the man fell heavily to the ground. As his horse recovered its balance and bolted away the man got to his feet, but a growing stain of red covered his side and he could barely lift his sword.

He would be no threat to anyone else today.

Brendan swung his own horse around to face Odhran's other three men. They were trying to take on both Darragh and Killian at once, but were having a difficult time. One of them fell with a terrible wound to his arm, and then his own horse's hoof struck him in the head as the panicked animal turned and ran from the fight. The man did not move again.

The other two saw that the numbers had suddenly changed and now they faced three attackers.

Brendan raised his sword and charged the nearest one. The warrior fought back with his own sword, but with a powerful blow Brendan knocked the weapon out of his hands and sent it spinning across the dry grass.

"Where is your champion?" Brendan cried. "Bring him on! None of you is a match for any of us. Where is your champion? Where is your king?"

The two men looked over their shoulders— and suddenly realized that Aed and Odhran were gone. In an instant they forced their horses around and galloped off the way they had come.

Brendan's laughter filled the silent forest. "Hurry back! We will not wait long! Bring your champion. Bring your king!"

Killian laughed, too. "I don't think they're coming back!"

Brendan peered deep into the woods. Killian was right. There was no sign of any other riders. All they could see were the tails of the last two riders' horses as they swiftly disappeared among the bare and dying branches of the trees. Odhran and Aed were already long gone, well before them.

Darragh snorted. "They've run away. Odhran is as cowardly as he is cruel."

"That is why his kingdom dies." Brendan turned his horse away and set out once again for Dun Bochna, his home, where flowers bloomed on the high cliffs and birds rode high on the fresh winds from the sea. His friends followed closely.

* * *

Brendan and his men kept their horses moving at the fastest possible pace; and seven nights later, they arrived at the high stone walls of Dun Bochna.

It was one of the largest fortresses ever built, sitting high on the cliffs on the westernmost part of the great island called Eire. But instead of circular walls like most of the other strongholds, this place was built with two enormous half circles of dry stone– half circles because the far side of the fortress ended at the sheer precipice of the cliffs overlooking the sea.

Only the birds could approach Dun Bochna from the west.

The three riders galloped through the gates and onto the wide expanse of green grass in front of the largest of the scattered round houses. Brendan slid down from the horse and tossed the exhausted animal's reins to a servant, just as the door of the house swung open.

Two men stepped out to greet them. One was young and dressed only in a long simple tunic, while the other was white-haired and bent but wore the heavy gold and weapons of a king.

"Father!" Brendan ran to the white-haired man and clasped him by the wrists– but then found himself steadying the older man instead of embracing him. "Father. It's good to be home."

"Brendan." King Galvin reached up to touch his son's shoulder, with a faint trembling in his hand. "So many thought we would not see you again. But I never doubted it."

For a moment Brendan could not speak. He was shocked to see how much his father had changed in the days since he himself had been away. The man's hair was whiter, his skin was paler and more deeply lined, and his touch was frail and old.

Brendan glanced at Killian and Darragh, who nodded slightly. So this was why they had insisted he come back immediately. Age was rapidly overtaking his father and it would catch up to him soon... though it would not happen today.

"Colum! I am happy to see you, too," Brendan said, turning to embrace his older brother.

"Welcome home," said Colum, returning the affection. "You are just in time to hear the new poem I have created."

"And it is all about me and the bold adventures I have had? Good! I look forward to it."

Colum grinned. "That would be such a long poem that no bard in Eire could remember it. You'll have to settle for the shorter one I made, along with the music of my harp, while you eat."

"I suppose it will have to do," said Brendan, with a laugh. "Though I have so much to tell you that you will never again be without a story to create!"

"Come inside, all of you," said the king, taking a careful step up inside the house. "When you have eaten, Brendan, you will tell us of these adventures of yours. I'm sure they are many."

"They are," agreed Brendan, walking inside with his father. "And I will take all the time I have to tell you all you wish to hear."

"Do not take too much time, my son," said King Galvin. Then together they sat down on the leather cushions placed on the rushes of the floor.

* * *

The sky had turned black and the plates of food were long since cleared away by the time Brendan finished telling his story. Colum played gentle notes on his harp as the rest of the men relaxed on their cushions.

"You are a fortunate man," said King Galvin, taking a sip of honey wine from his small gold cup. "I am happy that you are still among us. Now, if you will,

87

tell me more of this lady who rescued you from the storm."

"Ah," said Brendan, taking a drink from his own gold cup. Setting it down, he gazed at its finely worked surface shining in the soft firelight and let his thoughts travel to the fortress far across the wide bay. "That was the Lady Muriel."

Galvin smiled. "Muriel, *bright as the sea*," he murmured. "A lovely name."

"A lovely and secretive lady to whom I owe my life, as I have said. And in the days that I spent in her company at Dun Farraige, I came to know that I wanted to marry her."

"Marry?" The old king regarded him, and smiled. "Now, that is not a word I ever thought to hear you say. She must be very special."

"Oh, she is! She–"

"Then bring her here, Brendan. Let me see her. Bring her to your home."

"I would like nothing better! But I am not sure that she will have me. She is determined to marry no man but a king… and never hesitates to remind me that I am not a king yet." He smiled a little and shrugged his shoulders.

His father raised his eyebrows. "Only a king? You will be a king in good time, my son, but I would like to meet this lady before then. Go to her and ask her to marry you. Then bring her here. Go to her and bring her home."

III. THE SON OF A KING

For nineteen days after Brendan's departure, Muriel made herself get up each morning and dress herself, and made herself eat a few bites of the oatbread and baked eel or boiled crab with butter that Alvy always left out for her. She would then go about her daily tasks as she always did, though it seemed to her that the world was somehow different now.

On this particular afternoon she carried a basket of fabric and good wool thread out to the hilltops overlooking the bay, where she had often talked with Brendan. She sat down and began to piece together a new gown, this one of heavy wool dyed a dark blue. Though it was summer now, the cold days would be here soon enough.

After a time she glanced up to look out over the water. Thoughts of winter seemed to have affected the way the world looked to her today. The sky was a solid grey, and it seemed that the land and the sea and even the grass had taken on that same shade of grey. The waves now seemed dull and monstrous, and the wind had lost the warmth it should have had with summer.

Muriel paused in her sewing. The bone needle hovered above the linen fabric as she stared down at it. She raised up one hand and studied it, looking to see if it still held its warmth and color or whether it, too, was becoming faded and worn and grey the way the world seemed to look on this day... the way her mother had become, the way her sisters were now.

Instantly she clenched her hand into a fist and hid it within her sleeve. She had been so determined to keep from marrying a man who was not a king, but was it enough to simply avoid marrying at all?

89

If she had begun to fall in love with the wrong man– one who might well be a prince but was still not a king– would that alone be enough to drain her magic and leave her with a cold and empty world?

Muriel bowed her head, and then raised it again so that the wind from the sea struck her full in the face. Brendan was gone. She had no doubt he had forgotten her the moment she was out of his sight. There was no danger of his taking her love and, with it, her power and her magic.

There was no reason for her to think of him ever again.

* * *

On the morning of the twentieth day, Muriel opened her door and started to step outside– but then paused. A little bouquet of flowers rested on the flat stepping stone in front of the door.

For a long time she could only stand and look at them. They seemed to be violets, carefully tied together with a strip of fine blue linen, their tiny purple and white petals fluttering in the sea breeze. Then, slowly, she reached down and picked them up, holding them close and studying them as though she had never seen violets before.

Quickly she closed her eyes. She feared to look up, fearing she would see him walking across the grass and smiling at her with the dawn light gilding his hair, see his fair face smiling down at her, see his one blue eye and one brown eye shining as he held out his hand to her.

But with a sigh, Muriel raised her head. There were only a few of the servants moving about the dun, carrying wooden buckets for hauling water or armloads of feed for the animals.

Brendan was not here.

Of course he wasn't. How could he be here? He had ridden away and forgotten her long ago. Someone was playing a little trick by leaving a bunch of violets on her doorstep. Perhaps it was Alvy, in a misguided attempt to cheer her up.

She took the violets back inside the house, placed them on the sealskin furs strewn on her bed, and walked outside again. Just as she tried to close the door, a shadow fell across it and blocked out the light.

"Good morning, Lady Muriel."

Blinking, she looked up at a tall, strong figure backlit by the early morning sun. Golden brown hair ruffled across his face and the deep blue cloak across his shoulders moved and stirred in the sea breeze.

"Brendan," she whispered.

He stepped forward, and now she could get a better look at him. His tunic was a soft plaid of grey and green and was made from the finest wools. His long blue cloak was so wide that it had to be folded several times over his shoulder and was pinned in place with several heavy gold brooches through the folds.

Black leather trousers and folded boots, no doubt the same ones he had received here at Dun Farraige, completed the outfit. She saw gold rings on the small fingers of his hands and a wide gold band around the muscles of his bare upper arms.

And there was a heavy gold torque at his neck, a torque capped with the heads of sea dragons at each end. Only a king– or a tanist– would wear something like that.

But most of all, those strange and otherworldly eyes shone down on her once again. They were eyes with the colors of water and of earth, of blue and of brown, the strangest and most beautiful eyes she had ever seen.

Muriel smiled back at him, which set him to beaming. "I did not expect to see you again."

"Why, I cannot believe you would say such a thing! Did I not promise that I would return?"

"You did. But I know how rare it is for men to keep promises made to women they have only just met."

"Yet I have told you, I am not an ordinary man. I am–"

"Oh, a king, a king, as you have indeed told me many times. And I will admit that on this day, you do look like one." She smiled up at him again, for one moment allowing him to see a little of her happiness at finding that he had indeed returned. "Yet as I have told you just as many times, a prince is not a king."

He sighed, though his eyes still sparkled as he gazed back at her. "Lady Muriel. Please tell me what I can do, once and for all, to convince you that I am worthy of you."

She turned away and carefully arranged the folds of her deep blue gown, smoothing the lightweight wool and inspecting it for any flaws. "Why, Prince Brendan, I was about to ask the same question of you. I was about to ask what you can do to convince me that you truly are– or will be– a king."

Muriel peered up at him again, pleased at the somewhat disconcerted look on his face. "Even my old serving woman tells me that I should take no chance. She says that I should not consider your offer of marriage– if indeed you make one– until after your kingmaking, whenever that might be."

He cocked his head. "Are you certain that I will wait that long for you? There are others who would have a prince, and gladly."

Muriel nodded. "I see. Well, that is all that I need to know. Good luck to you, Brendan, in choosing but one of the great crowd of young women who simply cannot wait to be your wife. Good morning to you."

She turned to go back inside the house, but a firm hand on her arm made her pause. "Please. Do not go," he said. "I have only just arrived. And you are right; though I could no doubt find another to marry, there is only one whom I truly want at my side. That is why I have come back to you this day... and why I have brought this."

Muriel turned to see what he wished to show her. From his black belt he untied a soft leather bag, opened it, and poured out the contents into his hand.

She saw a collection of beautifully worked objects in gold and copper and bronze. There were brooches and rings, armbands and beads, all of them gleaming and new. "Never have I seen finer work," she whispered.

Brendan smiled and seemed very pleased. "These I intend to offer to King Murrough to secure your contract. I have come back to ask you to return to Dun Bochna with me... there to become my bride."

Bride.

The word echoed in Muriel's mind. She turned to meet Brendan's gaze, and saw that he meant what he had said.

She had a decision to make.

"Brendan... you already know my story. You have seen my sisters. You know why I fear to marry any man but a king."

"I know all these things. But do I know whether you love me?"

He stepped close to her and placed his hands on her shoulders, bending his head down to look directly into her eyes. He was so close that she could sense the warmth of his body in the cool morning air, feel the heat of his hands through the fabric of her gown, and see the gleam in his eyes and the warm color spreading through the fair, smooth skin of his face and throat.

"Brendan of Dun Bochna!"

There was a flash of movement and then strong hands grabbed his arms from both sides, pulling him away from Muriel. He clenched his fists and started to fight back, but then kept still.

"What is this?" he demanded, looking from one captor to the other. He twisted about to look at the little group of warriors who stood behind the two who held him, but kept still when he saw that they all had their swords drawn.

"You are a prisoner here."

"Prisoner? I am no prisoner! I am the tanist of Dun Bochna, and the guest of your King Murrough!"

Brendan's two companions, Darragh and Killian, came running to his side; but the men only took a firmer grip on their captive. "What is wrong here?" cried Darragh. "What has he done?"

"He is a hostage with an unpaid ransom," continued the first warrior. He nodded to the men who held Brendan. "Take him to the hall, place him in one of the rooms, and bolt the door." With a shove they started him walking in the direction of the King's Hall.

"What do you mean, an unpaid ransom?" cried Muriel, hurrying after them. "These two companions of his brought the gold when they first came here for him. I saw it myself, as did you! What are you talking about?"

"The gold was only part of the ransom. Cattle were due as well. Fifteen milk cows, to complete the honor price under the law for a tanist."

Darragh and Killian looked at each other.

"Cattle?" Muriel stepped in front of the first warrior and held up her hands in front of him, forcing him to stop. Brendan's captors halted, too, but kept hold of their prisoner. "Surely his men can return to Dun Bochna and fetch a few head of cattle, if that is all that is needed!"

"Lady Muriel," said Brendan, his voice formal and calm, "I thank you for your concern. But these men are right. The remainder of the ransom was never paid. I thought only of returning here to you and nothing else entered my mind."

"Listen to me," said Muriel, catching the warrior by the arm. "In the leather bag at Brendan's belt, there is gold and bronze and copper enough to ransom any prince. Ask the king if he will accept that instead of milk cows. Ask him!"

"Muriel. I will have your king do nothing of the kind," said Brendan. "That is your bride price and it will be used to secure your marriage, or I will throw it into the sea. I thank you for your offer," he said, smiling at her, "but now I must apologize to your king. Then it is for him to tell me what I must do to make the situation right again."

"That is true," said the warrior. "It is the king who will decide. Now, Lady Muriel, please make way. The king awaits us."

They took Brendan to the King's Hall and walked him inside. Then the doors shut tight and Muriel could only wait outside, alone.

* * *

The day wore on. Muriel shut herself up in her house with the largest basket of clean combed wool that she could find, spinning the wisps of wool into fine, smooth thread wrapped around long wooden spindles.

The simple work occupied her hands, but it could not keep her from thinking the same tormenting thoughts over and over again. She tried to push those thoughts away, tried to tell herself that she was calm and unconcerned, but knew that she was fooling no one–certainly not Alvy.

"Please, dear one, don't worry for him," the old woman said, combing out more wool for Muriel to spin. "They wouldn't think of harming him. He's just being held for the ransom he's worth. They'll put him in a fine room and feed him enough for three strong men and make sure he's well and happy. He wouldn't fetch much of a ransom otherwise! He'll be back with you before you even have a chance to miss him."

Muriel kept her eyes fixed on her work. "I know he is safe. It's just that– that I am so unsure myself of what he is."

"Unsure?" Alvy sounded quite confused. "Isn't he the tanist of Dun Bochna? Their next king? That's why King Murrough is being so careful with him. A tanist will bring a very nice price. Murrough would be a poor king to his people if he did not get what this Brendan is worth!"

"Brendan says he is the tanist. But he says many things."

"Ah! You are unsure of his words." Alvy laughed, pulling her comb through the masses of wool that she, too, was spinning. "Then I suppose I am happy, dear one, for you have learned a thing or two! No young woman with a mind to call her own would believe every little thing a handsome man says."

Muriel smiled a little. "I have listened to you for many years." Then her face grew somber again. "No matter how many times Brendan tells me he is a prince and will one day be a king… no matter what fine clothes he wears or how much gold gleams at his shoulder and on his arms and on his fingers… the only way I see him is as a prisoner."

"A prisoner? What do you mean?"

Muriel looked away, gazing into the softly burning hearthfire as her thoughts drifted back to when she had first found Brendan. "I discovered him as a half-drowned outcast, an exile thrown to the storm to die. Then he was a mysterious visitor dressed in grey, not a guest but not allowed to leave, who might or might not have been what he said he was. Now he is again an outsider, a prisoner dragged into the King's Hall and locked into a room."

"I see," Alvy said, nodding her head. "But everyone else confirms the story he tells. Why do you doubt him? I am sure you would not, unless you had good reason."

"The mirror," Muriel said quietly. "You are right. Everyone does confirm his story. Only the water mirror seems to say otherwise."

Alvy set down her wool and leaned in close. "What does the mirror say?"

"Perhaps I am not understanding it… but it seems to show Brendan as the child of slaves."

"Slaves." Alvy leaned back again. "I've never known the mirror to be wrong– not when you used it, or your mother, or your sisters. But Muriel, I don't understand. How could the tanist of Dun Bochna be the child of slaves?"

Muriel shook her head. "I want to believe him. I know that he himself believes what he told me. I know he does not lie about that. But though my heart wants to take him at his word, there are still many questions left unanswered about who– or what– this Brendan really is."

* * *

The afternoon wore on. The sun barely moved in the sky. Then Muriel heard the sound of galloping horses, horses heading across the grounds of the dun and towards the open gates.

She dropped her wool and her wooden spindle into the rushes as she dashed outside, flinging the door wide open and not bothering to close it. "Brendan!" she cried, as she saw the three riders approaching the gate. "Brendan!"

Muriel thought he could not possibly hear her. But his grey horse slid to a halt and his two companions halted as well. Brendan twisted around in the saddle to face her as she ran to him.

"I'm sorry," he said, as his horse moved restlessly beneath him. "I did not mean to leave without a word for you, but I did not want you to worry."

She reached out and touched his horse's neck, and the animal quieted. "You are leaving?" she asked. "I thought the king ordered you to stay until the rest of the ransom was paid!"

"He did. I convinced him that the best one to bring back the cattle was none but myself."

"You? You mean to say that King Murrough is allowing you to ride all the way to Dun Bochna, and then all the way back here again, to bring back your own ransom?"

He grinned again. "Not so far as Dun Bochna. Only to the hills above Dun Camas, where King Odhran's cattle graze. I have promised to bring back not just the number of cattle owed for my ransom, but twice that number."

"Twice?" Muriel was truly baffled. "How can you hope to do that with only two men?"

"I do not rely on hope, Lady Muriel. This will allow me to take care of two tasks at once," he said. "Not only will I be paying the lawful ransom for myself as a hostage prince, but I will be able to convince you– once and for all– that I am worthy of being your husband, even to you, the lady who will have none but a king."

"And– and why would King Murrough agree to such a thing?"

Brendan sat back, and his horse began stepping about impatiently once again. "Because he knew that there was no one else who could accomplish such a feat!"

Muriel stared up at him. "Or because he knows you will be killed!"

Brendan only laughed. "No one but a king can defeat another king. That's the real reason why he's sending me to face King Odhran. Take care, Lady Muriel, and I will be back in three nights. Watch what I will do to win my lady!"

He reined his grey horse back towards the gate and then, with his two companions, Odhran galloped away towards King Odhran's lands and the certain fierce battle that awaited him there.

* * *

For two nights and three days, Muriel went about her normal life and tried not to think about Brendan and the unbelievably risky attempt he was making. But it was impossible to avoid hearing about it, for it seemed that the people of Dun Farraige talked of nothing else.

Working at a loom beside the other women in the King's Hall, Muriel kept her eyes on the fabric she wove but could think only of the conversations floating through the air all around her.

"Dun Bochna's tanist means to steal thirty head of cattle from a vicious outlaw king?"

"How can he think he will get close to those herds?"

"They will be guarded by half of Odhran's warriors. And the tanist himself rode out with only his own two men!"

"King Murrough will have to send out yet another party to find what is left of him."

"Ha! Our king has no reason to send out anyone to search for this Brendan and his men. He is little better than a fugitive, so far as our laws are concerned."

"That's right. No matter how you look at it, none of them are any part of Dun Farraige."

"But this Brendan might just succeed. He might return with his ransom."

"If he returns empty handed, he'll simply be a prisoner again in a room in this very hall. Perhaps I will favor him with a visit and take him some honey wine."

All of the weaving women laughed. "Or maybe he won't come back at all. Maybe he'll just flee back to his own kingdom, happy to be alive and nothing more!"

Muriel closed her eyes as their laughter started up again. Brendan would never turn away from the task he had been given, for that would only make him a figure of ridicule and satire for years to come. She knew very well the amount of pride he took in being the tanist of Dun Bochna, to say nothing of his own personal pride in himself.

She wished, now, that King Murrough had indeed kept him a prisoner, just as she had seen… for if he were a prisoner, he would be safe, and he would be alive. Brendan would never flee back to his home without keeping his promise to bring back the ransom he owed. Only death or capture could stop him. He would come back victorious with King Odhran's cattle, or he would not come back at all.

* * *

The sun set again. The waning moon rose. But there was no sign of Brendan and his men.

Muriel was long past telling herself that she should not be concerned with his life, or that he was nothing to her but a strangely handsome man who had chanced to come into her life one wild and stormy night… a man with romantic intentions he would almost certainly never fulfill.

In the darkness she filled her water mirror and carried it outside, placing it on the earth in the shadows of the house. Then she sat down in the grass before it.

Muriel placed her fingers on the surface of the mirror's cold water. The moon was losing its power now, at this part of its never-ending cycle, and high white clouds from the sea obscured its light from time to time. Seeing anything would be difficult this night, but not half so difficult as sitting back and not trying anything at all.

101

Muriel gazed into the bronze dish, feeling only the cold seawater on her hands and the soft night wind on her face. "Brendan," she whispered. "Now."

Faint rings appeared on the surface of the water. The pale shadow of a cloud passed over it. And then the water cleared and Muriel saw the image of Brendan, riding with his two men in the darkness, sweeping past a herd of bawling cattle high on the mountaintop pastures with a whole crowd of shouting, torch-bearing men riding after them.

Her heart pounded. The battle had begun. But which way was it going? It was impossible to tell. She saw only a wild stampede of men and horses and cattle in the darkness.

She raised her fingers clear of the water and then touched them to its surface once more. "Brendan," she repeated. Again she saw him. This time the cattle lumbered across the moonlight hilltop with Brendan and his men driving them on.

Hope surged through her. He had the cattle— he and his men had somehow gotten control of them and were herding them away. Now that they had the animals, they would leave Odhran's territory and return to Dun Farraige were where they would be safe.

Where Brendan would be safe.

The images faded. Once more Muriel raised her fingers and dipped them into the water. "Brendan," she whispered a third time through clenched teeth, fighting to maintain a calm and patient mind. *"Brendan!"*

Only brief images came: Brendan and his two men and their cattle overtaken by the torch-bearing riders of King Odhran. Men and women hiding in the trees and watching— men and women dressed in the rough garb of slaves. Attacking riders swarming over

Brendan and his men, drawing their swords and shouting as they swung and slashed their iron blades.

Then the heavy clouds took away the images, leaving the water dark and still. Muriel tried again and again to see Brendan, caressing the water and calling his name, but it was no use.

Only shadows remained.

* * *

The two days that followed were perhaps the longest of Muriel's life. The worst part was realizing it could well be a very long time before she knew what had happened to Brendan. Her mirror could show her nothing again until next the moon was full.

She would have to wait until word came to them somehow, from someone who knew something at King Odhran's court... or worse, wait until a party came galloping to Dun Farraige to take their revenge for a failed cattle raid, bringing with them the severed heads of those they had defeated.

Either Brendan would return, or he would not. There was nothing more that she could do for him now.

* * *

The sun rose yet again, though on this fifth day after Brendan's departure it soon disappeared into a heavy grey wall of cloud. Muriel sat in the King's Hall among the other women and worked at her embroidery, listening to the rain and to the soft voices and laughter of the others, but most of all she listened for the sound of approaching hoofbeats.

The rain grew stronger. From time to time a little flicker of lightning appeared outside the hall's windows and through the opening in the roof above the firepit. Thunder rumbled in the distance and then faded again, though after one bright flash the roar seemed to roll on and on and did not fade.

Muriel looked up. That was not thunder. That was the sound of horse's hooves.

She got up and hurried across the hall, unpinning her purple-blue cloak and dropping it to the rushes as she ran outside, not caring that the cold rain soaked her hair and beat down on her face. Grabbing up the hem of her gown, Muriel raced across the muddy grounds, straight to the enormous herd of black cattle pouring in through the gates, straight to the three horsemen riding close behind them, and straight to the man who was the last to come through the gates– the man who sat so very tall and proud on his big grey horse.

* * *

All of the people of Dun Farraige gathered together that night in the bright torchlit King's Hall. Since the thatched roof of the great rectangular building was open in the center to allow smoke to escape, steady rain fell hissing and steaming into the flames of the firepit below. But the sound was largely lost in the laughing and talking and singing of the revelers inside.

In the shadows on the far side of the pit, Muriel and Alvy had taken on the task of directing the servants who worked to prepare the very large feast.

"Muriel, there is no need for you to watch the servants do their work!" Alvy scolded, as she dropped freshly caught crabs and lobsters into a bronze cauldron of boiling water. "You could have sat beside Brendan tonight, instead of getting your hands greasy back here!"

"I do not mind," Muriel said, carefully spooning some of the dun's precious store of salt from a leather bag into three small golden bowls. Not so much as a single grain spilled onto her plain green gown. "I am not sure I want to sit with him just yet. I want to see what he will do on his own before the king and queen. If I am not there, will he ask another to sit in my place?"

"Dear one, I have taught you well," Alvy said with a chuckle, and tossed the last of the lobsters into the steaming cauldron.

Muriel put the salt away and turned her attention to the rest of the feast. Some of the servants turned great sides of beef on spits; others pulled codfish wrapped in clay out from beneath hot ashes where they had been baking; and still others saw to the chopping of fresh seaweed and cress, ready now for a brief plunge into the water and salt and beef fat now boiling in the cauldrons. Everyone else who could be spared worked to prepare endless pieces of flat round oatbread.

On the other side of the firepit, well away from the bustling preparations, a long line of polished wooden slabs lay end to end in thick dried rushes. On each slab was a sand-filled seashell with a rushlight burning in it. On either side of those slabs rested straw-stuffed cushions made of grey sealskin and black cowhide, and in front of each cushion sat a gleaming gold plate and cup.

Muriel caught her breath and smoothed her damp hair back from her face. All was ready. Brendan's own kingdom could doubtless do no better.

Then, as three of the servants came out with heavy skins of honey wine to fill each golden cup, Brendan and his two companions from Dun Bochna entered the hall. They were closely followed by a large group of King Murrough's warriors and druids, each with his wife– or with the lady who was his favorite if he had no wife.

All of them looked especially strong and proud and handsome tonight. But Muriel found she had eyes for no one but Brendan.

If she had never seen him before, she would think him a prince just from the way he was dressed. His plaid tunic was woven from blue and cream and yellow wools, with a wide blue cloak pinned in folds over his shoulder with an enormous golden brooch.

She could not help staring at the brooch for a moment. It was one of the most beautiful she had ever seen, circular like most others but overlaid with a leaping, arcing dolphin also in gold.

An iron sword with a bone handle hung in a scabbard at his hip. His skin was fair and glowing, and his damp golden brown hair shone in the soft light of the hall. All the other men seemed dull and faded and ordinary next to him.

Muriel stayed back in the shadows as the guests moved to their places beside the cushions. The hall fell silent as everyone stood waiting for the king and queen.

In a moment King Murrough appeared at the door with his wife, Queen Orla, at his side. The music of harps and drums filled the hall as they walked to the far end of the wooden slabs. The royal couple sat down on their own cushions, which were covered with the softest white fur. The rest of the company settled comfortably at their own places, with Brendan across the corner from the king and both of his own men sitting right beside him.

The music quieted as the king raised his cup and held it out towards his guests. "Brendan of Dun Bochna," he said. "No longer are you a prisoner, or a hostage. You are my guest on this night, as are your men Killian and Darragh. You are welcome here."

"We all give you our thanks for your hospitality, King Murrough," Brendan called; and all of them raised their cups and drank deeply of the honey wine.

Muriel hurried back to the servants and sent them out to serve the first course of the feast. The king, the queen, the druids, and the most favored warriors received lobster. The rest were served crab, all with steaming cress and heaps of seaweed alongside. The strong and delicious aromas of the food wafted through the hall.

It was not long before everyone had been served. But just as they got down to the business of eating, Brendan sat back from his plate and looked over at the king.

"What is wrong, Brendan of Dun Bochna?" inquired King Murrough. "You are my honored guest tonight, yet I have seen you taste only a single bite of lobster before sitting back. Will you tell me why you do not eat?"

Brendan nodded politely to his host. "The food is magnificent," he said. "And I am especially grateful for the company here this night in this beautiful hall. But as I look about me, I see that one guest is missing."

"Missing?"

The music fell silent. The king glanced from Brendan to Queen Orla to his druids, and then back again.

"I do not understand," King Murrough said, with a slight frown. "Both of your men sit here beside you. All of my wisest druids and most honored warriors are here to offer counsel and conversation. The best of my bards play their harps for you now and will entertain you with their poems after we have eaten. And none but the most skilled of my servants are preparing this meal. So

107

tell me, Brendan: Who could be missing from my hall on this night?"

Brendan smiled. "It would be my honor if the Lady Muriel, who saved me from the sea not long ago, would share this feast with me tonight."

Muriel stood very still. The steam from the nearby cauldron drifted over her hair, leaving it damper than ever. The rain made a steady pattering and hissing as it fell into the firepit. "Go to him. Go to him!" Alvy hissed, nudging her. "He has asked for you, just as you wished."

Still she hesitated. "I don't–"

"Go, go!" Alvy said. "It's not for a marriage. It's just for a meal! Enjoy yourself for one evening. Wipe your hands and go and sit beside him."

He has asked for you…

Muriel smoothed back her hair, dried her hands on a clean cloth, and walked with all the dignity she could summon towards Brendan.

For her work tonight, she had put on the oldest and plainest of her gowns. It was rather worn and dyed in a dull shade of green. There was no gold or bronze at her wrist or shoulder or throat, no touch of rowan at her lips to redden them. Yet as she sat down beside Brendan on the soft cushion, Muriel felt as though she were dressed in her finest linen gowns and glowing with every piece of gold that was hers to wear.

"Does my hall now hold all the guests that you could wish, Brendan?" asked the king, his voice sincere.

"It does. And I thank you." He smiled at Muriel and took her hand, and this time she returned the gentle pressure of his fingers as she smiled up at him in return.

The music started up once more, and all of the guests made short work of the lobster and crab. More wine was served, and then the next course came out: great, thick cuts of beef with baked codfish and hot, flat oatbread alongside.

But instead of trying the meat and fish, Brendan drank deeply of his wine and once again turned to the king. "King Murrough– the food in this hall has been some of the finest I have ever enjoyed. This honey wine is beyond compare. The plates and cups gleam, the cushions are soft as clouds, the rushlights glow. And yet... as before, I find that some item, some thing of beauty, is missing from this hall."

The king sat back. This time he regarded his guest with amusement in his eyes and seemed to be enjoying Brendan's game.

"All of my best possessions have been brought in for the enjoyment of my guests," Murrough said, with a wave of his arm. "The most polished of the wooden flats, the softest of the furs, the largest and cleanest of the shells to hold the best of the lights, and the most beautifully worked of the golden plates and cups.

"Tell me, Brendan. What thing could be missing from my hall on this night?"

Brendan started to speak, but then hesitated. "It is better shown than said. If you will allow me, I will go and fetch it."

The king smiled this time, and did the queen and all of the warriors and druids gathered at the table. Brendan was providing them with some entertainment and they were curious to see what he would do next. "Go, Brendan. Bring us whatever my poor hall is lacking. We will wait to try our beef and bread until you return."

Muriel looked up at him as he rose to leave, but he never spared a glance for her. He simply went

109

striding across the rushes and straight out of the door, into the rain and into the night.

The music played and more honey wine was brought out; but even as the food began to grow cold on the plates, there was no sign of Brendan's return. The guests drained their cups and the servants refilled them.

Brendan's own place remained empty.

Muriel played with her own cup. She could not bring herself to look up at the king, or at anyone. It was as if all of this were somehow her fault. The feast was delayed yet again while they waited for Brendan to do something for her.

She wished that the guests could go on eating, but the king had said that they would wait for Brendan and he would not go back on his word. He spoke to one of his druids and in a moment a pair of bards stood up beside the tables.

The bards began to recite the story of a hero and the lady he had loved and nearly lost, for he had believed she was a goddess and had to fight for her until at last she took him with her to live forever in the Otherworld. It was a pretty story, but Muriel could not enjoy it now. She only felt more angry and embarrassed as the night wore on.

What could Brendan possibly be doing? How could he think to humiliate her this way? Why would he play with her so, in front of the people, in front of the king? Had he taken his horse and gone home to Dun Bochna, leaving her to wait for him here as some sort of monstrous joke? Had he–

Brendan walked int the hall just as the bards' poem ended. He held a large bouquet of flowers still wet from the rain, a beautiful and colorful gathering of yellow primroses and white violets and fresh green clover. He walked behind Muriel, set the flowers down before her, and calmly sat down at his place again as though nothing at all had happened.

The hall was silent. Muriel peered up at the king and queen. King Murrough looked vastly amused and Queen Orla was smiling. "I should say that the hall's decoration is now complete," remarked the queen, and she caught Muriel's eye and gave a small nod towards the flowers.

Slowly, as if not certain they were safe, Muriel picked up the bouquet. "Thank you, Brendan," she said. "Though you need not have gone to so much trouble."

"It was no trouble, Lady Muriel."

"Please go on and continue with the feast," said the king. "I agree with Queen Orla. Such beauty was worth waiting for."

All of the guests began eating once more, not seeming to mind too much that their food had gotten cold. When they were finished with the beef and fish and bread, and the plates had been cleared away, King Murrough glanced at the servants. Alvy quickly set them to assembling the last course.

In a few moments the last dish was set before the guests. It was a sweet made of boiled dried apples mixed with crushed hazelnuts, with drops of honey scattered over the top.

"This is good, very good," commented the queen. "But I will be so glad when the autumn equinox is here. The second harvest is always my favorite one, I will admit."

Muriel smiled. "The harvest of fresh fruits," she said. "I miss them, too. I think everyone does. But I will agree. This is delightful." She started to take another bite, but then realized that Brendan had not touched his own plate and sat gazing at the king once again.

The king cocked his head. "What is it now, Brendan?"

"King Murrough," he answered. "I have eaten until I can eat no more; drunk honey wine until I can barely lift my cup; admired the magnificence of your hall until I know that I will never see its equal; and so enjoyed the company of all who are here that I know I will never encounter any better. And yet–"

"And yet again, you feel that something is lacking." The king remained in good humor. All the others leaned forward at their places, waiting to see what their guest might do next.

"Yet again," Brendan sighed, and then glanced down the table at his men. "Darragh," he said to the first one, and Darragh reached into a small leather bag at his belt. He handed something to Brendan, who placed it beside the flowers before Muriel.

She saw a circular golden brooch in the shape of a leaping dolphin. It was made like the one Brendan himself wore, only this one was a little smaller– suitable for a lady's hand to work. Muriel looked up at him, but again he had turned the other way.

"Killian," he said, and now Killian took something from his belt and handed it over. Another bright object joined the dolphin brooch beside the flowers. This time it was a wide, flat, curving bracelet made of gold. On its shining surface were etched the phases of the moon, with the breaking waves of the ocean underneath them.

Like the brooch, the bracelet was breathtaking.

Now Brendan reached into the bag at his own belt and drew out a small and slender torque, clearly intended for a woman's slim neck. It was made of thin gold rods twisted together and shaped into a circle, but left open a little at the ends. Capping the ends were the heads of sea dragons, those ancient and powerful creatures which were well known from the many stories told of them.

It was a smaller and finer version of Brendan's own torque.

Muriel stared down at the three shining objects before her. "What is this, Brendan?" she whispered, though she knew very well what it meant.

In answer, he lifted the flat leather case from his belt, untied its wrapped cord, and carefully poured out the contents on the wooden flat in front of Muriel.

In a moment the brooch and the armband and the torque were lost beneath a heap of shining gold and bronze and copper objects– the same rings and brooches and armbands and beads Brendan had shown to her upon his arrival, before he had been taken prisoner once more.

He stood up and turned to the king and queen. "This lady, Muriel, is the one who has my life. Were it not for her, I would have been claimed by the storm and banished forever to the depths of the sea. She gave me my life, and now I would like to give it to her… if she will have it."

Muriel sat very still. Brendan reached down to her and very gently took her hand, and then raised her up to stand beside him. "Lady Muriel… I want to offer you both my love and my life. Will you return to Dun Bochna with me, there to be my bride?"

She started to speak. But her breath was coming fast in this warm, close room, and staring into his blue and brown eyes she could say nothing at all.

Now she must make her decision. He had offered gold and bronze to the king as her bride contract, and offered to her three of the most beautiful golden pieces she could ever have imagined.

Brendan had returned for her, as he promised he would, and he had given her gifts that only a prince– or a king– could give. If she turned away from him here, in front of all the people of her tribe, she would never have a chance to change her mind at some later time. He would have no choice but to return home with his offer of marriage publicly refused.

Muriel knew that he could never make her another.

"Muriel of Dun Farraige," he said again. "Will you come with me to my home and become my wife? Become my queen?"

King Murrough stood up, his gold cup in hand. "What say you, Lady Muriel?"

"I say…" she began in a whisper, but her voice caught. She was aware of the silence in the hall, and of the suspense, and of the many eyes staring at her. And she was also aware, across the firepit, of the shocked and disapproving face of Alvy.

Do not, do not! He is not a king yet. Do not!

Still looking into one blue eye and one brown eye, still feeling the warmth of his skin and breath, Muriel heard herself make a whispered response. "I say… that I will go with you to Dun Bochna, Brendan, and I will be your wife."

Brendan grinned, and leaned forward to give her the softest of kisses.

"Drink to Brendan, tanist of Dun Bochna, and his bride, Lady Muriel!" shouted the king.

114

"Brendan and Muriel!" cried the guests, and this time Muriel returned his gentle kiss.

* * *

Seven days later, Muriel rode a small bay mare through the late-spring afternoon with Brendan at her side on his prancing grey. Behind them rumbled a four-wheeled wooden wagon pulled by a team of large black oxen. Two servants walked alongside with long switches to keep the slow animals moving.

The wagon was piled high with wooden boxes and leather bags holding the many bride gifts that the people of Dun Farraige had give to Muriel. There were plates and cups of gold, wooden buckets for water, sealskin furs and black cowhides, woven woolen cloaks, many linen and woolen gowns, soft folded boots and leather belts, golden brooches and bracelets, bronze cauldrons, an assortment of iron utensils for the hearth, leather pillows stuffed with moss and horsehair, and even a dismantled weaving loom.

All of this was Muriel's *tinnscra*, a collection of household objects that were hers and hers alone. She would be allowed to keep them even if her husband should leave her. The custom meant that no woman would be left without a home and means of caring for herself and her children, though not all displays of *tinnscra* were as extensive and fine as this one.

At the front of the wagon sat a druid, Bercan, whose task it would be to make the final delicate negotiations of the marriage contract.

And high atop the wagonload of treasure rode Alvy, balancing herself among the furs and pots and wooden boxes. It was as though she had appointed herself its guardian and must prevent the items from falling at every bump and jiggle.

Following the wagon was a small herd of bawling black cattle. This was the rest of Muriel's wealth, given to her along with the household goods as wedding gifts from her sisters and their husbands... though she knew that none of them would attend her wedding.

Behind the cattle rode Killian and Darragh, along with five warrior men dispatched by King Murrough to accompany them. The men worked to keep the cattle together and moving along the path to Brendan's fortress home.

Muriel rocked along with her mount's easy strides, comfortable on the padded leather saddle as her feet dangled at the horse's sides. It seemed to her that her day– her life– could not get any happier than this. She was on her way to be married to a handsome young man who would one day be a king, a man who loved her, and she was going to his home with a magnificent *tinnscra* of goods along with a dowry of fine cattle.

She had all she could ever wish for, all she would ever need. It seemed so perfect... perhaps too perfect. Muriel tried not to hear the small voice at the back of her mind that kept whispering to her. *He is not a king yet... he is not a king yet.*

* * *

On the evening of the second day of the journey, the group made a comfortable camp beneath willow trees not far from a stream. The two servants kept close watch as the hobbled horses grazed among the cattle on the rippling grass. Soon the black cows and the bay and grey and chestnut horses all faded into hazy shadows as darkness fell.

Muriel sat on a leather cushion beside her loaded wagon. Before her, a fire crackled nicely in the stone-ringed pit that Brendan had built. On the other side of the flames, Alvy tended to a newly killed hare cooking in a small bronze cauldron.

"Just a bit longer now. It's nearly ready," Alvy called, and then held out a wooden bowl. "Muriel, would you walk down to the stream and find a bit of watercress to go with the meat? Take this and fill it, if you can, and there will be a fine meal for all of you."

Muriel quickly stood up. "Of course I will," she said, smiling as she reached for the bowl.

"Oh, but it's dark down there. Go with Brendan. Have him take a torch for you."

"I'll ask him." But before she could call his name, Brendan stepped out of the darkness with a heavy stick of wood that had a grease-soaked scrap of old linen wrapped around it. He touched it to the flames, glancing up at Muriel as he held it. "You wished for a torch, my lady?"

"I did." She walked to him and rested her hand on his arm. "And some watercress as well."

"Then come with me and you shall have both." He raised the smoldering stick and breathed on it so that a little flame took hold. Arm in arm, Brendan and Muriel walked into the darkness of the trees and moved towards the sound of the cool running stream.

* * *

Brendan went first, holding the glowing torch out ahead of them and moving carefully down the nearly imperceptible path. Muriel followed closely. She tried to use both the flickering light of the torch and the pale, distant glow of the stars to find her way, but the glare of the torch blocked out the faint stars and it was difficult to find her way.

117

As she walked, Muriel stepped on a twig. It cracked in the darkness and caused a sudden rustling in the bushes somewhere off to one side of the path.

Brendan stopped, raised his torch, and peered into the darkness in the direction of the sound. But after waiting many moments, the only sounds were the breeze high in the trees and the soft rushing of the stream far ahead in the darkness.

"Just an animal of some sort," said Brendan, continuing on. "Most likely otters or hares, frightened of you and your snapping twigs."

Muriel watched his strong shoulders as he walked ahead of her. "I'm sorry," she said. "I'm not well accustomed to the forests. I've spent all my life at the edge of the sea, and that's where I am most at home."

He glanced back at her. "And in just a few nights, you will again have a home by the sea– this time at Dun Bochna. I hope that you will come to love the place as much as I do."

Muriel stepped close to him as they walked, feeling the strength of his body as he led the way down the ever steeper path. "I already do, Brendan. It is your home and so I–"

There was another rustling and a small crash in the bushes, this time on the other side of the trail.

Brendan halted so abruptly that Muriel found herself pressed up against his back. He lowered one arm and braced her with it. "Stay still," he commanded.

"I stepped on no twig this time," she whispered.

"I know. Stay still."

Again they listened. Again there was nothing. "Most likely a deer come down for water and startled by the sight of us." Brendan started off again, holding the torch a little higher and moving it from side to side.

"The watercress must be quite good here. It's a popular place we've come across."

They continued on. When they reached the edge of the cold running stream, Muriel gathered her skirts and crouched down beside the water to search for the cress while Brendan stood guard with the little torch.

In the faint and wavering light, she worked as quickly as possible to pick the clumps of wet, shiny green leaves, careful to leave the fine white roots so that more would grow. "Brendan, please hold the torch steady! I cannot see–"

The light jumped wildly as he whirled around. "Brendan!" she cried, and instantly he reached down to pull her close beside him. Her wooden bowl tumbled to the muddy bank of the stream, spilling out the watercress as it fell.

"Shhh," he warned her. "We are surrounded." Brendan pulled his iron sword and stood waiting with his guttering torch in one hand and the blade in the other. Muriel stayed very still and tried to look past the glare of the flickering little flame, but the darkness lay heavy on the trees and bushes around them and she could see nothing.

Then came a steady rustling of leaves and a breaking of twigs. First it was off to one side; then it was to the other; then it was in front of them. Muriel pressed close to Brendan as a line of people moved out of the dark forest to stand in front of them.

She took a step back, nearly stumbling into the water as she waited for Brendan to go on the attack... but he did not. He stayed very still as the little group of people took one step towards them, and then another.

Brendan held his torch high and moved it left and right. Muriel caught her breath as she was finally able to see what it was that had been following them.

She had expected to see warriors, most likely the men of Odhran's kingdom come to take the cattle, rob them of their goods, and force them all back to Dun Camas as prisoners.

But these people staring back at them were not warriors.

Muriel saw pale and staring faces half hidden behind the bushes and the branches of the trees– the faces of people dressed in plain dark wool so old it was hardly more than rags. Their tunics were tied around them with old pieces of coarse rope. Their boots were simply old scraps of leather and wool held together with the same worn rope… those who had boots at all.

They carried no weapons that she could see; not even the smallest dagger. Counting carefully, Muriel saw that seven of them were men along with four women and three children. And all of them looked like nothing more than the lowest of slaves.

Brendan lowered his sword. Muriel moved out from behind him and stood close beside him. "Who are you?" she asked, as gently as she could. "Why do you follow us?"

One of the men found the courage to move forward a few steps, pushing aside the thickly growing bushes to stand on the path in front of Brendan and Muriel.

He looked to be tall and broad-shouldered and strong in the manner of those subjected to a lifetime of hard work, though a bone-weary exhaustion was evident as well. His face was hidden by a worn woolen hood and by a strip of old leather tied around his head so that it

120

covered his left eye. Staring in tense silence at Brendan, he suddenly reached out to him with one hand as though Brendan were someone he knew.

Brendan gripped the hilt of his iron sword. Instantly the man let his hand drop. "We are here to be your slaves," he said, and looked down at the damp earth again.

"Slaves?" Muriel stared hard at the hooded man and tried to make out his face. "It appears that you are already slaves. How is it that you are out here alone in the forest at night, following us like outlaws?"

The man looked up at her, though she could still see little of his half-covered features. "We are not outlaws."

"Then why do you hide yourselves and stalk travelers who pass by?" asked Brendan. "Will I have to fight to get past you?"

The hooded man stood very still for a moment, and then stepped back into the shadows of the trees. "We fight against no one. We have only come to offer ourselves to you."

Brendan sheathed his sword and stepped forward to stand right in front of the man, who was nearly as tall as he was. Holding up the torch, he inspected the stranger's rough clothes, worn-out boots, rusted iron collar, and iron wristbands. The dirt and grime and sweat had plainly been with him for a very long time.

"You are Odhran's slaves," said Brendan.

The man nodded and glanced back towards his companions. "Escaped from the mountaintop when you and your men came for the cattle. We've hidden in the woods since then."

Muriel took a deep and silent breath. So, these were the slaves she had seen in her water mirror on the night of Brendan's successful cattle raid. She had never given a thought to what might have happened to them, merely assuming they had gone back to Odhran's dun and the endless toil that was their lives.

"We have no slaves at Dun Farraige," she told them, speaking up at last. "Servants, but no slaves. I recall seeing only two men in my life who wore the iron collars and chains of slaves, and they were paying the price as required by the law for crimes they had committed."

"We have no slaves at Dun Bochna, either," said Brendan. "So no you must tell us what crimes you have committed, to be forced to serve as slaves for Odhran."

The tall man raised his chin, though his face remained hidden by the darkness and the hood and the old leather strip. "None of us as ever done any crime, except to be born as rock men– as the simplest people of the land. A man like Odhran considers us to be less than the cattle that graze on his mountaintops. He can do whatever he wants with us– work us, chain us, starve us, put us to death. It's all the same to him."

"And so you hide in the woods rather than go back to Odhran." Muriel took a step towards the hooded man.

He turned his head in her direction, and it seemed to her that he smiled. "We would rather live alone on the poorest land that go back to Odhran. But we are not hunters. We have no weapons. There are children among us and we have little in the way of food or shelter."

"There would be a place for you at Dun Bochna," said Brendan. "It is my fault that you are alone and starving."

"No fault of yours, Prince Brendan. We are grateful to you for giving us even the smallest chance to live. If you want us, we will go with you to Dun Bochna and work for you there."

"Come with us if you wish, but it will be as servants and not slaves. The work is hard, but the food is good and has no limit. The roofs leak only a little and will keep you dry in a bed of soft rushes on most nights."

"It sounds like a life good enough for a king. If you'll have us, we will live and work only for you."

"Then come this way." Brendan raised his torch and started up the narrow path with Muriel close after him.

Behind her she could hear the hooded man and the others whispering to each other. "We're going with Prince Brendan!" the mothers told their children. "There will be food. A warm bed in the rushes. We're going with the prince! We're going home!"

* * *

A few days later, as the sun shone high in the sky, Muriel and Brendan rode side by side through the gates of Dun Bochna. Following them were a wagonload of goods, a small herd of sleek black cattle, and a ragged group of men and women and children who now had something like hope in their eyes.

Muriel sat up tall on her horse, trying to take it all in. She knew that the walls of this fortress were only half circles and that the far end of the dun dropped away in a sudden sheer cliff straight down to the sea. She could scarcely imagine such a thing but was anxious to see it anyway. Like everything else in her new life, it was strange and frightening and wonderful all at once.

The people of the dun began to gather round, eager to see their tanist and his bride and to see the rough newcomers they had brought with them. Servants came to take the horses and see to the wagon and the cattle.

As Muriel dismounted, she turned to look at the silent group of former slaves. They had all gathered close together, aware of the many eyes staring at them, and looked at no one. "Wait here," Muriel said, with what she hoped was a reassuring smile. "Someone will come for you soon."

"Father!"

Muriel turned at the sound of Brendan's happy voice. She saw him run towards a grey-haired, red-cloaked man walking slowly in their direction, his warriors close at hand.

The two men embraced. Muriel could not help but notice how Brendan towered over his aged, grey-haired father… and how Galvin had a round face and grey eyes, while Brendan had fine-cut features and eyes like no one had ever seen before.

But she pushed all such thoughts aside as Brendan stepped back from the king and reached out to her. "Muriel, come and meet my father, King Galvin," he said. "Father, this is the Lady Muriel of Dun Farraige, come home with me to be my bride."

He took her hand and drew her forward to stand before the king. Galvin stepped forward to kiss her gently on the cheek. "Welcome, Lady Muriel. I welcome you home as my daughter."

Muriel smiled back at him, genuinely touched by the sincerity of his words and by the affection shining in his old eyes. "Now," he said, "come with me to the hall, where food is waiting. You can eat and rest and then tell us of your journey."

"I would like nothing better," Muriel said, smiling at Brendan. They set out for the King's Hall but it was a slow procession, for they followed in the hobbling footsteps of King Galvin.

Muriel was struck by just how frail and bent the king of Dun Bochna really was. One leg clearly pained him, and he moved with both the stiffness and the weakness that came with great age. More than once she saw him angrily shake off the hands of the warriors who tried to help him.

A chilling thought came to her as they followed his slow and painful steps. How much longer could he hope to serve his people as their king? Any man who wore the torque of kingship knew, in the back of his mind, that a king could no more be infirm than he could be blind, or maimed, or false.

The land required that any man who ruled her be as strong and as vital and as life-giving as she herself was… and if the day came when he was not, it was a true king's duty to do what must be done to make way for the new young king who would replace him.

Yet this, too, she pushed from her mind. She and Brendan were here at a time of great happiness, the eve of their marriage, and it seemed that everyone's spirits were as bright as the summer sun which shone down upon them. This was not a day for serious thoughts, which, she knew would come all too soon anyway. But not on this day. Not on this day!

Inside the shadowy hall, Muriel found a row of polished wooden slabs set in a neat row on the clean straw of the floor. The wooden slabs were set with shining gold plates and cups and laden with wooden bowls of steaming crab and lobster, plates of fresh wheat flatbread, and dishes of rich golden butter and dark sweet honey.

As Muriel and Brendan settled down on the furs to begin the meal, waiting politely until King Galvin was comfortably seated, she glanced around the long rectangular hall. It was much like the one at Dun Farraige: servants worked along the back wall and at the central firepit, preparing food and cleaning up afterward. A few women sat together at the far end of the building, working at embroidery and smiling and whispering about the noble gathering before them.

Then Muriel caught sight of two other people sitting quietly together in the farthest and darkest corner.

They appeared to be an aged man and woman. She had nearly white hair and his was iron grey. The woman sat combing a basket of dark brown wool to smooth and clean it, and then passed the combed pieces over to the man so he could spin them into neat lengths of thread.

These were the tasks of servants. Yet this couple did not appear to be servants at all. Even from a distance Muriel could see the fine clothes they wore, the good linen dyed in bright blues and greens and even purples, and catch the gleam of gold at the man's fingers and at the woman's wrists as they worked.

She touched Brendan's arm. "Who are they?" she whispered. "They do not appear to be servants."

He followed her gaze, and then smiled, but there was sadness in it. "That is King Fallon and his queen, Grania. They came here after being forced out of Dun Camas by Odhran."

"King Fallon..." Slowly, Muriel nodded. She remembered Brendan's words when he had told his story back at Dun Farraige.

The king was blinded with the same pin Odhran uses to fasten his cloak... and now lives quietly in the shadows with his queen. He remains alive only for her sake, and I can tell you that when she dies, he, too, will be gone before the sun sets on that day.

"I am glad to see that they are safe here," Muriel said. "Dun Camas bloomed like a spring primrose under his rule. It is a terrible thing that happened to him and to all who lived there."

"It was." Brendan glanced at Fallon and Grania again. "Would you like to speak to him?"

"I would. Oh, I would. To both of them."

"Then wait here." Brendan got smoothly to his feet and helped Muriel to stand. After bowing to King Galvin, they walked across the hall to the corner where the aged man and his wife sat peacefully at their simple work.

"King Fallon. Queen Grania. I am here with my lady. Her name is–"

"Muriel." The old king stood up and faced them. "Lady Muriel, who is to be your bride. I am honored and happy to meet you."

Muriel's heart broke at the sight of his ruined eyes. Only the skill of King Galvin's druid physicians had saved his life after such terrible injuries. He was alive, but she knew that it was not much of a life any longer.

"And I am happy to meet you, too," said Grania. There was still a sparkle in her gentle blue eyes, and it was clear that she had not been defeated even by the tragedy that had befallen her and her husband and their kingdom.

Muriel smiled at the queen and reached out to touch Fallon's hand. "I would like to ask you both to come and sit with us at our feast."

Brendan paused, but then he smiled, too. "We would be honored if you would join us."

Fallon raised his chin and faced Brendan, as if he could see him perfectly well. "Prince Brendan," he said. "Lady Muriel. Surely you both know that I no longer have any place among the nobility. My wife does, and could return to her family far away at Dun Cath if she wished; but she stays here with me in the shadows and no longer resides in the place of honor she deserves."

"You will always have a place of honor among all who know you," Muriel said. "Please. Come and sit down."

But neither of them moved. "My lady," Fallon said. "We appreciate your courtesy. But did Brendan not explain our plight to you?"

She hesitated. "He did. And yet–"

"And yet, there is no amount of courtesy that can make me whole again." Fallon stood very still. "No amount of kindness that can give me back my kingdom. The land demands that her king be as whole as she is, that he be missing nothing lest she, too, become lacking and incomplete. I am missing my eyes… and so I am no longer worthy of being a husband to the land I once ruled."

"Fortunately, I am not so demanding," Grania said. She smiled up at her husband even though she knew he could not see her. "I would rather sit in the shadows with this man than rule all of Eire beside any other."

Fallon took her hand and held it close to his heart. "There can be only one king at this fortress, or at any other, Brendan. Again, I think you for your courtesy, but I will stay right here with my lady while you go back to serve the rightful king."

Fallon and Grania nodded politely and then walked back to their benches in the corner, picking up their wool and returning to their work as if nothing had happened.

Muriel looked up at Brendan, and then took his arm as they returned alone to the feast which awaited them.

IV. GAMES AND DIVINATIONS

Some days after her arrival, late in the afternoon of the summer solstice– the longest day of the year– Muriel walked out through the gates of Dun Bochna with six of the loveliest young women who lived there. All of them were dressed in their most brightly colored linen gowns, and all of them wore all the gold that was theirs to wear.

Next to Muriel walked Bercan, the druid who had accompanied her from her former home. And hurrying close behind, anxiously making sure that the hem of Muriel's newly made purple linen gown and long grey linen mantle stayed out of the damp spots, was Alvy.

Following after them were five of the King Galvin's warriors. They were all dressed in gleaming leather armor with swords at their sides and flowing woolen cloaks at their shoulders.

The little party followed the path that led away from the great cliffside fortress and its two enormous half circles of stone. After a long, gentle rise up the windy hillside, the path ended in a wide grassy space at the highest point overlooking the sea.

Muriel paused, for the sight took her breath away.

The very center of the space was covered with sand and ashes and an enormous stack of wood. Muriel realized that this was where the people of Dun Bochna built their bonfires at the time of the festivals. This one would be lit tonight to mark the summer solstice.

She could understand why this place would be used for sacred ceremonies. It was higher above the world than she had ever imagined she would be, much higher than at Dun Farraige. A cool and gentle breeze constantly blew in from the sea, whose vast and endless waters were broken only by a few small rocky islands some distance from the shore. Beyond those uninhabited bits of land, Muriel knew, no boat had ever ventured. They were truly standing at the edge of the world.

Waiting for them in the grass beside the mountain of wood was Brendan, his dark blue cloak blowing wide in the breeze over his grey tunic and black trousers and boots.

Next to Brendan was Lorcan, the druid who would recite the marriage contract. Close by was King Galvin, leaning on the arm of one of his warriors, along with Brendan's older brother, Colum. All around them was a crowd of warriors and druids and their ladies.

Brendan reached for Muriel's hand. She offered it at once, feeling both peace and excitement at the same time as his fingers closed strong and sure over hers.

But just as she took the first step with him towards the waiting druid, the heavy golden brooch at her shoulder– the dolphin brooch that Brendan had given her– pulled free of the soft grey linen mantle and dropped with a thud to the damp grass-covered earth at her feet.

She released Brendan's hand and caught at her mantle before the wind could blow it from her shoulders. Alvy hurried to pick up the half-buried brooch and wipe the little clots of mud from it with the hem of her own skirt.

The gathering waited patiently while the old woman refolded Muriel's grey linen mantle and forced the sharp pin of the brooch through the fabric, fastening it again as securely as she could and turning the brooch so that the pin could not slip again.

At last Muriel turned back to Brendan with a brave smile, embarrassed over the small mishap just as her wedding was to begin. But he reached for her hand once more and together they turned to the druid Lorcan. He nodded to them and then began reciting the contract of marriage.

"Standing before us are Muriel, a lady of Dun Farraige, and Brendan, tanist of–"

Just as the druid spoke the word *tanist* Brendan flinched and slapped at his neck, just below the gold torque that was a symbol of his rank. As Muriel looked up at him, she saw a crushed honeybee roll off of his shoulder and drop away. A red welt quickly appeared where the insect had stung him and Brendan shifted the heavy torque in obvious discomfort.

But he took a deep breath and turned back to Lorcan. "Please. Continue."

The druid glanced from one of them to the other, cleared his throat, and began again. "Here before us is Muriel, a lady of Dun Farraige, and Brendan, the tanist of Dun Bochna." He watched the two of them carefully for a moment, and when all remained quiet he went on.

"She has brought with her the following of her own property: five milk cows, eleven heifers, one bay mare, three bronze cauldrons and– and–"

Now it was the wedding party's turn to stare in amazement at the druid. Lorcan stammered for a few moments and tried to continue, but his mind had simply gone empty. He could remember nothing of what he was supposed to say.

After a few moments of paralyzing silence, Brendan quietly turned to Bercan. "Please. Could you assist him with the recitation of the contract?"

Glancing from Brendan to the strangely mute druid in front of them, and then back again, Bercan stepped up to stand beside Lorcan. Haltingly he picked up where the other man had left off, watching and waiting for him to step in and continue once more. But Lorcan remained silent, his face reddening with humiliation, and so Bercan went on and finished listing the terms of the contract as quickly as he could.

At last it was over. The property owned by each of them was accounted for, and Muriel's bride contract was deemed acceptable by both King Murrough of Dun Farraige and by her own family, which now consisted only of her two sisters and their husbands.

Though Muriel was happy at being married, she was also worried over three such strange incidents marring the occasion. Such signs should not be ignored–not when they happened one right after they other at such an important event.

But such things could happen, she told herself, and still mean nothing. All she could do was go on through the day.

Muriel walked with Brendan and the others back towards the gates of Dun Bochna. She brushed the remaining bits of mud from her shining brooch and glanced up at the red welt beneath Brendan's golden torque. "Does it hurt?" she whispered to him.

"Does what hurt?"

"That sting. It looks angry."

"That is the last thing I am thinking of right now." He smiled down at her and stopped just in front of the gates of the dun. "I am looking at my wife... my queen... my lovely Muriel. I may never think of anything else ever again."

She looked up at him, standing on the threshold of her new life, thinking of how strange it was to feel both the greatest joy and the most painful doubt all at once... joy that Brendan was now her husband, and a nagging doubt that she might not have truly done the right thing by becoming his wife.

Together they turned and walked across the boundary separating the outside of the dun from the inside; but as they stepped over, Muriel felt as though the earth itself had suddenly clamped itself to her foot. She fell down hard across the entrance and her hand was ripped from Brendan's grasp as she fell.

In an instant he had lifted her to her feet. "Muriel! Are you hurt?" The others gathered close to see what had happened, and she could hear the steady murmur of *what is wrong? Is she hurt?* from all around her.

She reached down and shook out her fine new skirts, trying to get the grass and dirt out of them even as Brendan continued to hold her in a tight grip. "I am fine. Truly, I'm fine," she said, taking a deep breath as Brendan eased his hold. "And I am so sorry. Please, let us all go inside."

He looked closely at her, gently running his hands over her arms and face and satisfying himself that no harm was done. Then he took her by the hand and the crowd of people made way for them as they walked to the King's Hall, where the wedding feast awaited them.

* * *

The wedding celebration began. At first it was all that Muriel had always hoped it might be. She was surrounded by crowds of happy, laughing, colorfully dressed people sitting on furs and cushions along the boards, with the last of the summer sunlight filtering in through the high thatched roof and open windows.

Musicians played harps and drums and wooden flutes. Endless amounts of the finest food and blackberry wine were brought out. She and her new husband were the honored and beloved guests at this lively party where everyone ate and drank and shouted and laughed, and wished them all the best in their life to come.

And then Muriel looked down to see that her sleeve was on fire.

She jerked back her arm just as Brendan grabbed it, slapping out the flames with his bare hands as Muriel stared in shock. Holding up her hand, she looked at the scorched and tattered remnants of the sleeve of her gown– the beautiful purple linen gown that she had made herself for this day of her wedding to Brendan.

He pulled back the sleeve to her elbow, examining the skin and running his fingers over it, and breathed a sigh of relief when he saw she was uninjured.

Again he held her, trying to steady her even as her heart pounded and her hands trembled with shock. He clasped her fingers tightly. "I am so sorry about your gown, but very glad that you are not hurt. There will be many other gowns. I will see that you have all you could ever wish for."

She could only stare back at him, realizing that he did not understand this the way she did.

Then he leaned close to whisper into her ear, his soft golden brown hair brushing her lips. "Though perhaps on this night you will need no gown at all."

Muriel drew back, looking away from his blue and brown eyes as her heart began racing again. "Brendan," she said, reaching for her cup of honey wine. "Did you not see what happened today when we stood

135

before the druids? When we walked through the gates? When I sat here beside you at our wedding table?

"First a honeybee stings you from the air. Then I fall hard to the earth. Then my gown goes up in fire." She shook her head and took a long drink of the wine. "And that is aside from how my brooch fell from my mantle and how a learned druid forgot what he had memorized. Too many things. They are a warning, Brendan. Too many things!"

"Muriel," he said gently, and took hold of her arm to steady her. "Such things happen at any ceremony. Now, look here. Look at what is real." He placed his hands on top of her own and then leaned down to kiss her on the lips, and a warm thrill ran through her. "Even after a few small mishaps on our wedding day, we are here together, are we not? That is real. That is what matters.

"We have been through far worse together. Nothing was able to keep me from finding you: not your king and his warriors, not an evil man like Odhran, not even the mighty sea itself. Kiss me, dear wife, and let me kiss you in return, and tell me you will not think of these things again."

She closed her eyes and kissed her husband, and finally could not resist smiling. "I am sorry. I cannot bear the thought of anything going wrong, of anything coming between us."

Brendan kissed her again. "Nothing will ever come between us. I promise you that. I will wait while you finish your food and wine, and then I will take you to the home that is now yours."

"The home that is now ours," she added, smiling again; and drank the honey wine from her cup until there was no more left.

* * *

The wedding feast went on, and there were no more mishaps. As usual, most of the women eventually gathered near the central firepit to talk and gossip and laugh, while the men stayed at the boards to finish their beer and blackberry wine. The merriment ended only when King Galvin got up from his cushion, helped to his feet by two of his men.

"Good night to you, Brendan and Muriel," said the king. As they quickly stood up, he moved slowly on trembling legs to stand before his son's wife.

"A more beautiful daughter I could never wish for," he said, in a voice whispery with age. "And a finer queen Dun Bochna could never want." With great care he kissed her on the cheek.

Turning to Brendan, the man rested a hand on his son's shoulder and smiled. "You have a lovely bride. See that you always take care of her."

"I will do that, and much more. Good night to you, Father."

Walking slowly with his men, the king left the hall. As soon as the doors closed behind him, the music stopped. The servants began to gather up the plates and the food and the wine, and blew out the small burning rushlights on the boards.

Brendan took Muriel's hand and placed it on his arm. "It is time for you to go to your home," he said. "To our home."

She looked up at him and started to speak, but the words seemed to catch in her throat. Instead she gave him a slight nod, held tight to his arm with her fingers, and walked with him out of the door and into the heavy air of the summer night.

The sky was not entirely dark. Beyond the stone walls of the dun, out on the sand and ashes high up on the mountain where this day they had made their marriage contract, a great orange ball of flame rolled and billowed in the night. Sparks flew upward from it as the huge logs burned through and went crashing down into the heart of the flames.

"There is no mistaking when the summer solstice comes around," said Brendan, looking up at the brilliant light high on the cliffs. "Everyone in the kingdom can see that bonfire, whether it burns at midsummer, or Lughnasa, or the autumn equinox, or any of the other festivals that make up the wheel of the year."

Muriel nodded. "It was the same at home. The great fires are lit across the country so that everyone knows when an important day is hand– especially this one, the longest day of the year."

Her husband turned her around so that she faced the other way, and pointed to the south. "Look there, across the bay. All the way across. Do you see it?"

Far out in the darkness was a small orange dot, and she caught her breath as she realized what it was. "Oh," she said. "That is the midsummer fire of Dun Farraige!"

Brendan nodded. His hand was warm on her shoulder. "So many times I have seen it burn, never realizing it was your home and the light I saw was yours... and now I am watching it here beside you. I hope that we will always watch these fires together, for as long as we live."

Muriel smiled and reached up to press her hand against his. "Over the years, I, too, have watched this same fire that burns here now, as you have watched mine at my home across the bay."

This time Brendan turned her to face him. "Yet this place is home now. Yours and mine." He bent close to her, and his soft hair brushed her cheek as his lips found hers. Her husband kissed her, gently and for a long time, and then they walked together to the house that was now their own.

Brendan's dwelling lay on the far side of the fortress, between the King's Hall and the flat open space that led to the sheer cliffs overhanging the sea. Muriel had stayed in a room in the hall upon her arrival, and so, on this night, she was walking into her own house for the very first time.

Her husband held the heavy wooden door for her. Carefully she lifted the hems of her skirts as she stepped over the threshold and onto the thick cover of clean dried rushes. The round house was softly lit by glowing coals in the central hearth, and by two seashell lamps sitting on shelves on either side of the room.

"Here is your home, my lady wife," Brendan said, walking inside and pulling the door closed behind him. "Take your time and look around. See that everything is in its place and all is to your liking. "If there is the smallest thing that you might wish for, you have only to ask for it."

She smiled up at him, and her heart beat faster at the thought that she stood in a house that was hers to arrange however she wished... a house that was entirely hers and Brendan's. She was alone in her own home with the man she loved, the man who was now her husband.   Muriel took one step onto the rushes and then another. This house was much larger than the one she had shared with Alvy back at Dun Farraige. That dwelling had been a bit crowded at times when her two sisters had been there with her, in the days before they had married.

They had been three lively young women sharing a crowded and cozy space, laughing and working and living side by side together, year after happy year, until first one married and then the other... and then the laughing stopped.

Muriel continued her slow walk along the curving wall. It was in perfect repair, white and smooth with new clay. And so much space! It was take the rest of the night to make the circuit of it, so large did it seem.

All of the things she had brought with her, it seemed, had been carefully arranged throughout the house. There were iron tongs and hooks for preparing meat. Bronze cauldrons shone in the hearthlight. And there were plates and cups of polished wood for everyday use, and gold ones for special occasions.

Tall leather screens, framed in wood, created a separate room at the back of the round house. She peered past these screens and saw that a third seashell lamp rested high in a niche set into the wall, casting its soft and wavering light over the thick furs and cushions heaped on the wide sleeping ledge.

Past the screens were three large wooden chests. One was for Brendan; the others she had brought from her former home, filled with her own neatly folded cloaks and gowns and good leather boots and belts. All of her golden jewelry was stored there, too, including the sea-dragon torque Brendan had given to her. That would wait until the day of his kingmaking, for it was meant as a queen's torque and she was not yet–

Muriel willed herself to keep moving. In a moment she found herself at the smooth wooden ledge beneath the open western window, where her mater mirror sat waiting. The bronze basin was dry and empty now, cold and dark in the shadows of the house.

She touched the tip of her small finger to its cool, dry rim, running it lightly over the metal edge and listening to the faint singing of the bronze. She could still hear it, as she always had; the singing told her that the mirror was alive and in tune with her, even now at the dark of the moon.

For a moment she felt a small touch of relief. She had listened to her heart and married Brendan, who was not a king yet, and she still possessed her magic. But then a cold realization struck her: She had married him by legal contract, but nothing more.

Not yet. She would not truly be his wife until she gave herself to him, all of herself, here in their house in the candlelit bed that awaited them against the far wall.

Muriel backed away from the water mirror until stopped by the central hearth. Reaching back until she could feel the cool stone beneath her fingers, she stood consumed by the rising beat of her heart and her swift intake of breath as Brendan slid the heavy bolt to bar the door and walked towards the back of the house.

He moved the screen aside, unfastened the gold dolphin brooch at his shoulder, and allowed his dark blue cloak to slide off his back until it dropped to the sleeping ledge among the furs. Reaching for his thick leather belt, he untied it from its golden ring and wrapped it around the scabbard that hung from it, placing both the belt and sword in the rushes on the floor.

"And how do you find your house?" he asked, walking back to her. He stood close, reaching out to brush a strand of soft dark hair away from her face with one finger.

She closed her eyes at the gentle touch of his hand on her cheek. "It is a beautiful house," she whispered, her eyelids fluttering a little as he began to stroke her cheek. "A perfect house. And I thank you for it."

Brendan's finger left her cheek and followed the curve of her neck to the hollow of her shoulder, brushing away her hair once more and coming to rest on her back. He stepped closer, and in the warm glow of the hearth she saw his young and gentle face with its strong jawline, and smooth fair skin, and eyes of light blue and dark brown.

She reached for him in return, running her fingertips over the side of his powerful neck and marveling at how the skin was as soft as the petal of a flower even while the cords beneath were strong as iron. Now it was his turn to close his eyes and breathe deep, to lean his head against her hand and softly kiss her fingers with his lips.

"Brendan..."

He stepped towards her, and then she was held close in his arms, his broad chest pressed against her own and the hard strength of his thigh locked firmly against her hip.

"Muriel," he whispered, into the dark cloud of her hair. "I am the man who loves you. and now that I am your husband, I am free to show you that love... all of it. Let me show you the love I hold for you and for no other... let us show each other."

Brendan lifted her up in his arms and held her close as he carried her past the hearth to the waiting bed.

For a moment she clung to him as he walked, hearing only his boots breaking the rushes underfoot and his quickened breath as he held her close. But as he

142

lowered her down to the furs on the bed, she suddenly stiffened and moved away from him, pushing herself to the far side of the bed to sit with her back against the cold clay wall.

Brendan sat down on the edge of the bed, hands folded in his lap, and smiled patiently at her. "There is nothing I would like more than to stay here with you this night, and share with you the love that a husband shares with his wife. Yet... we will have many more nights like this one. If you are not yet ready, I will wait for you until you are."

She could only stare at him from the shadows, seeing his graceful form on the edge of the bed with one foot down in the rushes and the other pulled up so that his knee rested on the furs. His soft hair shone in the glow of the seashell lamp. He remained quiet, his hands folded together, waiting with great patience to see what she wished to do next.

Muriel sighed, and then eased forward a little, away from the wall so that she sat near the center of the bed. "I am sorry," she said, looking away from him. "It is not you that I fear. You are the man I love and you are my husband. I wish... I could do this, but I am not sure I ever can."

He moved slightly, and the low light revealed a look of confusion on his face. "I can only tell you, my lady Muriel, that this is not the type of thing a husband would like to hear from his wife on the night of his wedding."

"I understand, Brendan. But you must understand this: It is not you that I fear. It is the thought that I may have made a terrible mistake."

She got up from the bed and walked away from him, around the far side of the hearth, until she reached the ledge beneath the open window where her water mirror rested. Brendan, too, got up and walked over to stand behind her.

"What mistake could you have made?" he asked, placing his hands lightly on her shoulders and trying to keep his voice light as well. "Are you not certain you have done as well as you could have in choosing a man?"

He laughed a little. "I will introduce you to a few of my cousins and you can see how I compare. I am not so gifted with words as Lasairian, nor as handsome and golden-haired as Ailin, nor the possessor of as many gold wristbands and brooches and young bulls and heifers as Conaire... but perhaps you could learn to accept me after all, and not think our marriage a mistake."

She turned to him. "It is not you who is the mistake. I have never known any man as handsome or a strong or as kind as you are. There would be nothing easier for me than to walk to that bed and give you my love in the way I have longed to do almost from the first day I met you."

He shook his head in confusion. "Surely there is nothing to stop us from doing so, then. We have married each other; there is no reason why we should not–"

Muriel abruptly stepped away from him. "Here is the reason, Brendan." She touched the cool rim of the wide bronze basin, staring at its dark surface. "I told you of my sisters."

"You did."

"And you saw them."

"I saw them." He placed his fingers on her cheek, gently turning her face so that she looked at him. "Do you still doubt me? You must have believed, today when

144

we stood before the druids out there on the point above the sea, that I was the king you wanted to marry. Surely you would not have been there otherwise! Why do you doubt me now?"

She turned away again. "I did not doubt you before the ceremony began. But I cannot forget what happened all throughout the day, from the moment we arrived at the mountaintop."

He frowned slightly in disapproval. Quickly Muriel went on. "At the first touch of your hand, my dolphin brooch slipped from my shoulder and dropped to the mud. While trying to recite the contract, the druid lost his memory. At the mention of you as the tanist, the honeybee left her sting in your neck– right beneath your tanist's torque.

"Then I fell hard to the earth just as I tried to walk across the threshold of the fortress that was to be my new home. At my wedding feast, the sleeve of my gown went up in flames."

Brendan sighed. "As I said at the feast, such things happen from time to time. They can happen to anyone."

"But never all at once. Not as they happened today." She shook her head. "I have learned never to ignore the instructions of the natural world. Just one omen can tell you far more than all the wise druids in Eire... and there was far more than one such omen on this day."

Her husband was silent for a time. Then he glanced from Muriel to the empty water mirror. "You have married me," Brendan said. "Do your powers of magic remain?"

She took a deep breath and stared down at the mirror. "I have no way of knowing whether they yet

145

remain or not. There is no moon this night, and the water mirror comes to life only when the moon shines down upon it. But even if the moon were full and the sky were clear..."

Muriel closed her eyes. "We are married only according to the laws that men created. We are not married in the true sense of a man and a woman, according to the laws of the natural world. It is not a marriage according to the natural laws. Not... yet."

He stood close behind her and embraced her, resting his head against her own. "Then come to me now, and we will make a marriage such as will leave you no doubt... and you will find that not only do your powers remain, but they are twice, three times what they were before, so true and so strong is the love that we will find in each other."

She closed her eyes tightly. "Brendan, I cannot! If I had not married you this day, if we had simply given ourselves to each other for an evening's warmth and little else, my power of magic might remain unaffected.

"But I married you under the law, and when I did every sign told me that I had married a man who was not a king and would never be a king. And now, though I love you, I am afraid. Afraid I will lose what I have, afraid to become what my two sisters have become. And at this moment, I do not know what I should do."

He released her, and slowly moved back to sit down on the stone ledge surrounding his hearth. "My lady, I do not want you to be afraid. If nothing else, you must know that I have never spoken anything but the truth to you in all things and at all times. If you are certain of nothing else, I hope you are certain of that."

Muriel nodded. "I do understand. I though all would be well, for I knew that you told the truth when you returned for me. That was when I saw for myself that you were indeed the tanist of Dun Bochna, one day to be its king. But that was before I saw the signs that appeared before, during, and after the wedding ceremony itself."

She turned away and began to pace again. In a moment she found herself moving past the tall leather screens and standing near the sleeping ledge, staring down at the sealskin furs that covered it. With some hesitation, she reached out to touch their softness. Then there was a rustling behind her and another touch at her arm.

"Muriel." Brendan's voice was low and soft. "I must ask you this. Would it matter so much to you if I were not a king? Are you saying that you can love me only if I have the power and wealth that go with kingship?"

She raised her head but looked only at the flickering lamplight on the wall above the bed. "I loved you when none of us knew whether you were king or slave, when you had nothing at all to give me save a few bright flowers gathered from the cliffs.

"It is not a question of whether I can love you, for I know that I can, and that I do. It is a question of whether *you* can love *me.*"

Brendan turned away from her again. When he spoke she could hear the anguish in his voice. "I stopped at nothing to bring you here, to have you for my wife, because you are the one I love! What else would you have me do? What else can I do to prove to you that–"

She turned to face him. "You saw my sisters! You saw what happened to them when they married men who were not kings. Would you have me become as they have become? Is that what you want in a wife? A woman who has no power, who has no magic, who has lost herself, who is hardly more than an empty shell?"

"Of course I do not. She would make no queen, nor would I want a woman like that for my wife in any case. You, Muriel of Dun Farraige, are filled with power and with magic and with the tides of life. That is how you will remain, at this moment, and all through this night, and tomorrow when the sun rises, and on all the days after that."

Muriel closed her eyes. "I wish I could know that. I wish I could be sure. I wish–"

"You wish that I were already the king and not merely the tanist."

"I cannot become like my sisters," she whispered. "I cannot become like my sisters."

Brendan reached out and held on to her with one hand firmly on each of her arms. "If I must, I will wait for you," he said, giving her a little shake.

She could hear the truth in his words, though she also heard the tension and frustration in them. "If it will ease your mind, and help you to know for certain that I married you for love and for no other reason– then you will sleep alone in this house until the day that I am made a king."

Silence fell between them. Muriel stared up at Brendan, her breath coming fast as she looked into his strange eyes. She saw him look back at her, even as his hold on her tightened and he drew her ever closer... even as he slowly bent down until his lips were almost touching hers.

His breath warmed her face. The scent of his skin filled her nostrils and went straight to her head. Her lips parted and she started to embrace him, but she could not for he still had her arms in the iron grip of his hands.

Forcing her to keep still, he whispered, "Good night to you, my wife. In the morning I will return."

Muriel half closed her eyes as his lips touched hers, touched them so lightly that she could barely feel it; yet she knew when they had met because of the warm thrill that ran through her body. It left her knees feeling as though they would give way and let her fall, and made the flickering lamplight waver until it was swallowed by the darkness.

She was aware that Brendan still supported her. At last he slid his hands around her shoulders and pulled her close against his chest, where she was held fast by both the strength of his arms and the weightless caress of his lips upon her own.

Now Muriel's own arms came up to clasp his broad back, and she raised her mouth to kiss him in return. The weakness left her knees and a flash of sudden urgency ran through her body, leaving her strong and determined and pulling him close to her, drawing him in with embracing arms and demanding lips.

Suddenly he wrenched back and held himself still, though the tension vibrated through him. He stared down at her and Muriel knew he was awaiting her response.

"Don't go," she whispered, into the flickering light between them. "Oh, please, do not go."

Brendan kissed her again. Her eyes closed. He reached down to catch her up in his arms, and then lifted her up and placed her on the fur-covered bed.

There were no more words between them. He continued to kiss her, sitting on the edge of the bed and clasping her hands so that only their fingers and lips were touching.

149

The hearthfire burned ever lower. The flame in one of the seashell lamps went out. Brendan bent down to kiss her once again– but as he did, Muriel abruptly sat up. She slid her hands out from his grasp, swinging her feet down along the side of the sleeping ledge and standing up in the rushes. Her breath was ragged and quick.

"Muriel." Her husband's voice had become a rough whisper. "I must go now, or I warn you, I will not go at all."

Standing before him, she reached for the dolphin brooch at her shoulder and turned it release the clasp. Then she pulled the long slender pin out of her mantle and the length of grey linen fell away to the rushes. Last of all she dropped the shining brooch within its folds.

Her boots and belt soon lay beside the mantle. Carefully she slipped her arms from the sleeves of her purple gown and allowed it to fall atop the linen and the brooch. Beyond the leather screens, another of the lamps flickered into darkness.

She started to reach for the neckline of her white linen undergown, but then paused. "Brendan," she said, reaching out towards his shadowed figure. "Brendan…"

Instantly he stood and caught her hand. After a kiss on her fingers, he let her go, and then quickly stripped away his own soft grey linen tunic and black leather trousers and boots.

Now he stood before as the goddess had made him, silent and noble in the low light of the remaining seashell lamp above the sleeping ledge.

Muriel stretched out one hand to him, reaching up to touch his neck beneath the heavy golden torque, running her finger slowly over his throat and down his

150

broad chest and the soft golden brown hair that covered it... down to his slim waist and long narrow hip...

He stepped closer. Taking her face in both of his hands, he kissed her gently. Then he took top of her white linen gown and eased it down over her shoulders until it, too, fell to the rushes.

Now it was his turn to begin a slow tracing of her body, though he used both of his hands and ran the tips of his fingers gently over every curve, every rise, every fall, every secret place of hers that no man had ever seen or touched.

Muriel could only close her eyes and steady herself with her hands on his sides, sliding them up over his chest and shoulders as he leaned down to kiss her... and then bending down until his hair fell across her own shoulders, and then easing himself down on one knee so that he could touch and kiss and caress every part of her.

Finally the lamp above the sleep ledge wavered and went out. It seemed to Muriel that she was melting into the darkness, as though it whirled past her and drew her in... the way the power of the sea held its victims fast and carried them away.

Brendan lifted her up and laid her down on the soft furs of the bed, and then stretched out close and warm and strong beside her. Together they rode the tides that their love for each other had created, again and again, until at last they lay exhausted and sleeping in each other's arms.

* * *

When the dawn came, it brought a pale grey sky and a warm wet breeze from the ocean.

Muriel was the first to open her eyes. She lay cuddled against her husband with her head pillowed on his chest. The steady and reassuring beat of his heart had

151

comforted her while she slept. One of her legs was drawn up over his hip and the two of them lay pressed together, leaving his skin and hers warm and damp in the midsummer dawn.

Daylight filtered in through the straw roof and the small, high windows, and brought with it the familiar seaweed smell of the ocean and the rushing sound of the waves.

And then Muriel became aware of something else.

It sounded as though a large group of people walked slowly across the grounds of the dun. She could hear the low murmur of their voices and the steady tramp of their footsteps, as well as the slap of leather and the ringing of metal on metal as they walked.

It sounded like a group of warriors on the march.

She sat up on one elbow, pulling a sealskin fur up over herself. "Brendan," she said, but he had already stirred at the sudden feel of the air on his damp skin. "Brendan… do you hear that?"

He opened his eyes and smiled up at her. With one fluid move he rolled over and took her back down to the furs to lie across her, kissing her as though there had been no interruption from the night before.

Muriel began to respond, kissing him in return and holding him close, stroking the smooth skin at the back of his neck and shoulder; but then he raised his head and looked towards the door.

He was listening to the sound of the marching outside.

With a quick kiss for her, Brendan sat up and swung his legs over the side of the bed. He pushed the leather screens to one side and went striding across the

152

rushes to the door, unbolting it and pulling it open just enough to get a look outside.

Muriel counted her heartbeats as her husband stood there for several moments– and then, to her relief, he quickly closed the door again. "Muriel, please get dressed," he said, and then hurried back to the sleeping ledge and caught up his trousers and boots from the floor where he had dropped them the night before.

"What is it? What is out there?"

"I don't know. I must go and find out, and quickly." Brendan pulled on the leather trousers and threw on his boots, whipping the cords around his ankles and tying them fast. "My father is on the march with all of his men."

* * *

With her husband's blue cloak wrapped tightly around her, Muriel hurried to the doorway. She stood watching as Brendan raced to catch up to King Galvin, and the warriors and druids who walked with him, as they moved towards the heavy wooden gates of the dun.

"Father!" Brendan cried, struggling to pull on his grey tunic and fasten his thick sword belt around his waist. "Father! Where are you going?"

The old king stopped. Slowly he turned around, his heavy red wool cloak swinging from his rounded shoulders. He held a shining bronze sword in his trembling hand, but the weight of the weapon dragged his arm down and it was clear that he could barely lift it.

"Brendan," Galvin said. Muriel could see him smile behind his beard and heavy mustache. "Why are you out so early on the morning after your wedding? Should you not be with your bride?"

"Father, you are the one who is out early. And with all of your men?" Brendan made a final wrap of his leather belt and tied it off through the bronze ring at one end. "Why you are out, and where you are going? What is so urgent as to take you away from your bed, from your rest?"

King Galvin took a few slow steps forward. The tip of his bronze sword almost dragged on the ground. For a moment he stood and gazed steadily at his son, saying nothing.

At first Muriel thought the king was offended by Brendan's words. But then she saw the gentle smile and the look of peace in his eyes, and felt a strange and rising apprehension.

Galvin reached up and touched Brendan's face. "You have been as fine a son as any man could have hoped for," he said. "You will be as fine a king as Dun Bochna has ever had. And you have brought home a gentle and beautiful queen to help you serve your people. All of my pride goes with you."

Brendan shook his head in confusion. "I thank you for your kind words, Father," he said. "But I still do not understand why you are marching out with your men on this day. Has something happened? Was there a raid? Did Odhran–"

Galvin stepped back and gripped his bronze sword with both hands. Muriel blinked as she saw a look of piercing anger come into his old grey eyes. "It is the waves," he answered, his voice low and growling.

"The– what?"

"The waves!" shouted the king. With shaking arms he raised his sword until its wavering tip was pointed towards the sea. "They offend me with their ceaseless noise! I will have peace. I will stop them!"

Quickly Brendan reached out and caught his father's arm, just as the sword point fell down to the

154

ground. "What are you talking about? This sounds like some kind of madness. The waves have always been here! Why would they anger you now?

"Come with me," Brendan said to him. "I will take you back to your house, back to your bed. Come with me, now."

But with all of his strength, the old king pulled away from his son. Holding his sword out before him, he turned around and walked– slowly and lamely but with great determination– past his men and towards the gates of the fortress, which swung open for him as he approached. "I will stop them! I will stop their noise! I will stop the waves!"

Muriel shut the door of the house and raced for the bed, throwing on her clothes and tying up her boots as quickly as she ever had. In moments she was out the door and running after Brendan, who followed King Galvin and his warriors on their slow journey to the waiting sea.

* * *

Muriel soon caught up to them, for the royal party moved at the slow and hobbling pace of their aged king. It took a long time to travel the winding path down the face of the cliff until at last they reached the narrow strip of wet, sandy beach.

She stood with one hand resting against a large grey rock and the other against her heart, greatly fearing that she understood what was about to happen but Brendan did not. Not yet. She could only wait and watch, knowing that an age-old drama was about to unfold before her eyes.

The crowd of warriors and druids stood at the edge of the sand while King Galvin slowly made his way down to the water. But when he was halfway there,

Brendan started to go after him again. "Father! Come away from there! This makes no sense. Come back with me. Let me–"

The flat of a blade, placed on his shoulder silenced him. Brendan turned to see an older grey-haired man, one who looked much like Galvin, gazing down at him. "If the waves offend him, he must be allowed to deal with them as he sees fit," warned the man. "He is the king."

Brendan looked at the warriors and the druids. They all stood together in silence at the edge of the beach. Their manner was quiet and respectful, in the way of guardians at some sacred ritual.

Then he saw Muriel standing by the rock. She could only look back at him with an anguished expression.

Muriel understood, as all the people standing on this beach understood, that a weak and infirm king could neither serve nor protect the land he ruled. If the land was to keep its own fruitfulness and vigor, it must have a king who was equally possessed of life and strength… and Galvin knew that as of this day, that king was Brendan.

Yet Muriel could also understand how difficult it would be for Brendan to stand and watch his own father carry out this last ritual.

"Fergal, surely you will not allow this!" cried Brendan, looking at the old man who restrained him– the man who was his uncle. "You must know what he means to do!"

When he got no response from Fergal, Brendan turned to the other men on the beach. "How can all of you stand back and allow this?"

Fergal gazed after his brother, who was making his slow and painful way alone down the beach. "We do this to allow him this final dignity– this final act that is his alone– even as you must allow it. I say this to you as his brother who loves him, and who loves you as well."

For a time the only sounds were the rushing of the waves and the calling of the gulls. Then Brendan turned and walked with his uncle back to the waiting warriors and druids, and he stood with them and kept his silence along with them.

King Galvin continued his hobbling journey to the edge of the sea. The tip of his bronze sword hung lower and lower until it trailed after him, leaving a line in the wet sand. But as the foam rushed in to surround his boots, he managed to raise the weapon again and hold it high overheard in both hands.

"Silence! Silence!" he shouted to the waves, his face red with fury and with effort. "Be silent. Be still. Or else you will face me in single combat!"

The sword wavered above his head as he gasped for breath. The waves continued to rush and roar at his feet, and one of them splashed up to his knees by way of further insult.

The old man's grip tightened on his sword. "Face me, then!" he shouted, and with the last of his strength he waded out into the sea.

King Galvin struck once at the first wave that leaped up to meet him, gouging out a spray of water from its smooth, rolling surface. Again his sword slashed down as a second wave attacked him, and though he staggered in the chest-high surf the old king remained on his feet.

But then another mountain of surf rolled towards him, higher than any of the others. Its foaming white edge broke over him just as he swung his sword for the third and final time, and then the old king disappeared beneath the water.

* * *

The men of Dun Bochna stood patiently at the edge of the sand, their long bright cloaks whipping in the wind, as they waited for the sea to give up the body of their king. After a long time they saw a gleam of gold among the white foam breaking on the beach, along with the dull shine of wet leather and bronze.

Brendan and eight of the men started down the beach. Muriel followed at a respectful distance, not wanting to intrude but unable to stay away while her husband suffered this ordeal.

No one made any objection.

At last the little group reached the place where King Galvin lay, his sword still gripped in his right hand. Brendan, Fergal, and five other men lifted the body from the sand, and then held it still while two of the druids moved to their places on either side of the king's shoulders.

With great care they pulled apart the open ends of the heavy, twisted gold torque around Galvin's neck and worked it free. One held it flat in his open hands and showed it to Brendan.

It was a large and beautiful piece of heavy gold, made with sea-dragon heads even larger and more intricate than those on the tanist's torque that Brendan wore. "The king's torque will remain in our keeping until the kingmaking is done at Lughnasa, when all can gather, some forty-two nights from now."

Brendan nodded, and then looked across the body of his father to Muriel. "Well, my lady wife," he said quietly, in a voice that caught only a little. "None can say that I am not a king now."

All of them turned and carried the body of King Galvin up the cliffside path to Dun Bochna. The only sounds were the crashing and roaring of the waves, and the calling of the distant birds.

* * *

The following day, another procession left Dun Bochna. This time it headed away from the sea and out towards the open grass-covered hills above the fortress.

First walked the king's three brothers. All of them wore full armor with their best wool cloaks. Gold ornaments shone at their necks and wrists and fingers. Behind them came seven warriors bearing a wooden platform draped with a great red cloak, and atop the cloak lay the body of King Galvin.

The dead king's long wooden shield had been placed over his face and body. His bronze sword lay close by his side. Like his brothers and those who carried him, Galvin wore all of his armor and gold– all except the king's torque. That piece was now carried by Colum, himself a druid and Galvin's oldest son. Colum held the gleaming gold torque flat in both hands as he walked in silence directly behind the body of his father.

Right behind Colum, walking before the crowd of all the remaining warriors and druids and highborn men and women of Dun Bochna, was Brendan, with Muriel at his side.

Brendan moved in silence. He kept one hand placed casually on the hilt of his sword and it seemed to Muriel that he was at peace. From time to time he would glance out towards the sea, which was a spectacular sight from this great height. But most of the time her husband simply kept his gaze straight ahead and followed the men who carried the body of his father.

They continued across the grass until the sea disappeared from sight behind them and they reached the edge of the forest.

In a place of deep shade among a thick stand of hazel trees, a wide rectangle had been dug in the earth. It was as deep as a man was tall and nearly twice as long, and lined with rocks both large and small. A great heap of stones and a pile of earth remained a short distance away.

The seven warriors bearing the king stood on either side of the rectangular pit, holding the king over its dark open space. Another seven men moved to the edge and vaulted down so that they were inside.

Brendan and Muriel stood with Colum beside the grave. The three of them watched as each of Galvin's three brothers moved to the end of the long dark rectangle and then handed down an object to the waiting men below.

One produced a dagger. Another gave an ax. The third handed down a spear. All of the weapons were made from iron and bone and rowan wood, and all were of the very best work.

Now the rest of the men and women of Dun Bochna began to file past the end of the grave, and each one handed down whatever he had brought for his king.

First the warrior men and the druids offered beautiful objects and ornaments of lustrous gold: plates, cups, wristbands, and finger rings.

They were followed by the women, who handed down leather skins filled with blackberry wine, small golden cups of honey, a basket of bread topped with butter, and a gold plate bearing a heavy cut of roasted beef.

The men in the grave took down the objects as they were offered and placed them all around the edge of the rectangle. They leaned the weapons against the stone-covered sides and arranged the food and plates and gold jewelry all at one end of the pit.

When at last all was ready, they caught the hands of the men at the surface and climbed out. Then they stood back as the seven warriors slowly and carefully lowered the body of the king into its final place of rest.

The druids unrolled two long sheets of leather and allowed them to drop into the grave, so that the king and all his fine possessions were now hidden from sight. The seven warriors used wooden spades to throw the damp, heavy earth back into the grave from where it had been taken. They worked in silence, unashamed of performing the menial task because it was done in service to their king.

With the grave filled in, Colum stepped forward to stand beside it. He faced the gathering and held out the king's sea-dragon torque in both hands.

"People of Dun Bochna," he said. "This day you have taken the body of your king to rest in the forest. You have given him the things he will need and the things he will desire in his next life, and he will reside in the Otherworld until such time as he is reborn in this one.

"He served us well in this life. You have served him well in his death. Now do this last service for him and we will return home with Brendan, his son, the chosen tanist of Dun Bochna."

One by one the men and women walked to the great pile of stones nearby, took one in each hand, and tossed the stone atop the newly turned earth of Galvin's grave. Soon all of the stones had been moved to the grave and formed a cairn above it.

"King Galvin lies safe and protected," said Colum. "Now it is for us to return to his hall and celebrate his life." He looked to Brendan, who started on his way with Muriel beside him.

But then Muriel heard a gasp from behind them. She turned around to see Colum stagger, half leaning on the arm of one of Dun Bochna's warriors as though he had just stumbled– and then the heavy gold torque of kingship fell from Colum's hands and clattered across the rocks of the newly made cairn, coming to rest partway down the side.

It was the final addition to the grave of the old king.

Bravely Colum reached down to pick up the torque, but he turned pale as it caught on the heavy rocks. For a moment it seemed that he would not be able to free it; but at last he lifted the golden torque and carried it away.

In silence, the procession continued down the path which led back to the fortress.

* * *

That evening Muriel sat beside her husband at the feast, listening to the merry music and to the laughter of the others at the tales of King Galvin's heroics. She found herself enjoying, along with everyone else, the happy memories of a strong king and a life well lived.

Everyone, it seemed, but Brendan. He was far more subdued than Muriel had ever seen him. She rested her fingers on his arm and leaned down to look at him. His strange eyes were somber now, almost unreadable in the shadows of the lamps.

"So many fine tributes to your father," she said. "And to see the best one of all, you have only to look at the faces of the people gathered here tonight. Each one shows peace and gratitude at having lived under the rule of Galvin."

"Most have never known any other." Brendan took a long drink from his golden cup. "He was king for many more years than I have been alive. Life will not be the same without him."

"It will not," Muriel agreed. "But this place will be as safe, and as happy, and as just, under the rule of King Brendan." She held his arm a little tighter, and he set down his goblet and turned to her to take her hand. Still, his face was somber and serious.

"King Brendan," he murmured, and then shook his head. "Now it is my turn to tell you, Muriel, that I am not a king yet. I, too, saw the king's torque fall from Colum's hand and come to rest on Galvin's cairn… and I am not ashamed to tell you that the sight of it left me cold."

He tried to laugh a little. "Before that, I was the one who tried to calm your fears. Now I am the one who saw a sign that has unnerved me." He glanced at her with a faint smile. "I am surprised that you have not."

She placed her other hand atop his. "I saw what happened. I never fail to take such signs to heart, as you well know. And yet…"

Muriel paused, gazing out over the lamps where the people laughed and applauded the bards' stories of their old king. "And yet I can also see what is plain and true and undisputed. The old king is gone. The tanist has been named, and that tanist is as loved and respected as was his father. The people look to him with the same love and trust."

She smiled, and smoothed the warm skin of his fingers. "Even I, always the first to worry, can find little cause to worry now."

He looked at her, and she could see the doubt that remained in his eyes; but then he shrugged and looked away. "Well," he said quietly, "Colum never was known for his agility."

Muriel covered her mouth with one hand, but it was too late. She and Brendan put their heads together and laughed. "There, you see?" Muriel said, sitting back. "Some signs are not really signs at all. Sometimes they are just a bit of clumsiness."

Brendan grinned and leaned forward to kiss her cheek. "I hope you are right," he said. "I do hope you are right."

But soon his face became serious again. He held his cup and went on staring at nothing, paying no heed to the music and the storytelling across the great hall.

Muriel touched his arm. "If you have no ear for the poetry tonight, perhaps you would play a game of fidchell with me."

His face brightened a little. "You can play fidchell?"

"Of course. It is more than only a game. It can also be used for divination."

"So I have heard." Brendan set down his cup and got to his feet, reaching down to help Muriel get up. "A game of fidchell it will be, then."

* * *

They sat down together on a bench a little space apart. A servant brought them the fidchell board and the large wooden box of playing pieces. Brendan placed the board between himself and Muriel and began to set it up.

The board was a flat oaken square with seven rows of seven holes. Muriel opened the box and began unwrapping the playing pieces from their protective squares of linen. Each one was a large, heavy oak peg capped with various designs in either gold or bronze.

She set the pieces before Brendan. "You play the king and his defenders. Somehow it does not seem right for anyone else to play the king."

He grinned. "I'll play the king, but tremble in fear at the thought of you being the attacker."

Brendan picked up the king peg, which was capped with a gold sea-dragon's head much like those on his own torque. He placed it on the center square and surrounded it with the defenders, which were just a little smaller and capped with the golden heads of dolphins.

Muriel took the attackers and arranged them along the sides. These pegs were capped with bronze hawks with outstretched wings. "I'm told the attacker goes first. Is that how you play?"

"It is. Go ahead."

To begin, Muriel moved her bronze pieces along the rows in an attempt to surround the golden king. Brendan tried to get his king safely moved to one of the corner holes. They battled back and forth, arguing, laughing, playing their best, until at last Brendan seemed to have the win right in front of him.

"Well, my lady wife," he said with a laugh. "You said that fidchell was a divination as well as a game. What do you make of my great victory?"

She laughed as well. "I should say that this game has given you a very good sign. Perhaps we should play it often."

"We should. And we will. But first..." He lifted up the king by its gold sea-dragon head to make the winning play.

The peg dropped off of the head and clattered to the board below. Brendan was left holding the heavy head in his fingers. In shock he let go and it, too, fell to the board.

Muriel caught her breath. Quickly she reached out to grab the broken pieces, and saw that the heavy gold sea-dragon head had left a deep gouge in the polished wooden board.

"That board has been in my father's family for many generations," Brendan whispered. He touched a finger to the damaged spot. "Look what I have done to it."

"You have done nothing to it," Muriel said. "The cap is loose. Do you see? It fits back onto the peg. It simply needs a craftsman's attention. No doubt it has been so for a long time."

She began wrapping up the pieces in the linen squares and replacing them in the boxes. "It was a great victory. And I do not often lose at this game! Come, Brendan. Help me put it away and we will return home. I cannot think how tired you must be after these last few days."

"I will look for no more signs," he said. "No more signs." He made no move to touch the pieces or the board. "And I may never play this game again."

He stood up. "Please. Leave that for the servants to put away. I want only to go with you to our home. Tomorrow I want to think of nothing but preparing for the kingmaking at Lughnasa. I want no more of signs or messages or magic, and certainly no more of games of fidchell."

Muriel tried to smile. "I will do anything I can to help you."

"Just come home with me and love me, and stay always by my side," he whispered.

"Done," she whispered in return, and together they left the King's Hall.

* * *

Beginning the very next day, and for many days thereafter, Brendan threw himself into the role of king. Each morning he would say the same thing to Muriel: "I cannot wait for a ritual to make me king. I cannot wait until Lughnasa. I must begin now, so that there will be no doubt in anyone's mind what I am. Not in my mind, or in yours, or in anyone else's."

Muriel could only nod and reach up to kiss him. "Everyone knows that you are a king," she would say, and then smile. "Even I am convinced. No one doubts you, Brendan of Dun Bochna."

"Do they not?" he would ask, and she would see the uncertainty that lingered in his eyes. But then he would kiss her in return and go off and do all the things that a king might be expected to do, making every effort to do them twice as well.

The first task of any new king was to make a complete and thorough inspection of his lands. He must present himself to all who lived within his borders and see for himself everything that he was responsible for guarding and protecting.

Brendan started the tour of his own lands close to home. He began by walking through the dun and inspecting the great King's Hall and the armory and the horse pens and the cattle sheds and every one of the houses. He would direct the craftsmen to repair the thatching on one house or add to the smooth white clay on another, or set to work making more wooden and iron buckets since the old ones were beginning to wear out.

But he quickly moved on to matters outside the everyday concerns of daily life in the dun. Muriel could see that he was anxious to range farther out in larger and larger circles, determined to see every man and woman and child and tree and rock and flower and blade of grass with his own eyes– which were now the eyes of a king.

He wanted to speak to all of the farmers and herders and their families living in the raths, those small isolated ring-forts just large enough for a family and their livestock. They must all be told of the death of Galvin and that Brendan's king-making would be done at Lughnasa. They must all see for themselves that they had a new king.

"Go to them, Brendan," Muriel said. "I can see to the repairs and the work that must be done here. You already know about the thatching and the shortage of buckets. I have noticed that some stones have fallen from the outermost ring and need to be replaced. I will see that it is done."

He grinned, looking as happy as she had seen him since the night of his father's wake. "Together we will make this a kingdom like no other," he said. "Though I wonder... should a queen concern herself with buckets and stones?"

She smiled back at him. "I am sure that being a queen is not all gold cups and fine embroidered gowns. Go, Brendan. See to our farmers. I will see to things here."

He kissed her once more. "Keep my love while I am gone. I will return to you as soon as I can."

Muriel watched as he rode away with four of his men, and tried not to wonder when she might see him again.

* * *

As Muriel left her husband at the gates and walked back inside the dun, she followed the curving inner wall past the cattle pens. She wanted to get back to the King's Hall, for her mind whirled with ideas and plans for the many tasks she hoped to complete before Brendan's return.

But when she passed a wooden shed at one end of the cattle pens, something made her stop.

A single black cow lay resting in the shed, chewing her cud. In the corners, on worn piles of rushes and greying straw, a group of people– a group of slaves, she realized– shared chunks of old bread and passed a wooden cup of water among themselves.

Muriel paused. Then she walked to the wooden fence rails, placed her hands on the top, and leaned in to peer beneath the shed's roof. She looked from face to pale and dirty face, and recognized the fourteen slaves that she and Brendan had found hiding in the woods on their wedding journey from Dun Farraige to Dun Bochna.

The seven men, four women, and three children been here for the past several days, for as long as Muriel herself had been here; but with all of her time taken up with first preparing for her wedding and then with the death of King Galvin, Muriel had not seen these people at all.

And since her arrival here, she was ashamed to admit, she had not thought of them, either.

"Why are you in the cow shed?" she asked. "Were you given no other place?"

169

They all looked up at her and froze. Eventually two of the men got to their feet, but stayed where they were. The women gathered their children close.

"The craftsmen said they would return and give us our work for today," said the tallest man, the one with the hood half covering his face.

"We have worked for them each day since we got here," said the second. "They told us to stay here and eat first."

"Of course." Muriel folded her hands across the rail. "Do not hurry yourselves. I meant only to ask why you have been forced to stay in such a place. Do the servants here not sleep in the King's Hall at night, or in one of the houses, as my own servant does?"

"My lady," said the hooded man, from where he stood in the shadows. "The roughest shed is a finer home than any we have known before. The smallest crust is a better meal than any to be had at Odhran's fortress. We will stay here. Servants may sleep in the King's Hall, but not slaves."

Muriel could only stare at them, seeing a lifetime of suffering in their gaunt faces and thin and weakened bodies. Her fists tightened. She had told Brendan she would take care of things within the dun. There would be no better place to begin than right here.

"Tell me your name," she said, to the hooded man.

He hesitated. "Gill," he said at last. "My name is Gill."

Muriel looked at him again. This was the same man who had spoken to her and Brendan on that night when they had discovered these slaves hiding in the forest. As before he kept a hood up over his head, leaving only a few wisps of white hair showing around his face. He still had the old piece of narrow leather tied over his brow so that it covered his left eye. He was taller than any of the others, and looked strong and broad-shouldered in spite of his age.

For a moment he seemed to remind her of someone she knew, or had once known; but she could not imagine who that might be. She was did not know anyone who had ever been a slave.

"Gill." She smiled at him, and at all of them. "Tonight you will all make your beds in the clean rushes of the King's Hall. It is dry. There is a fire to keep out the evening chill. And in fact..."

She glanced at the children finishing the last of their stale bread. "I would like you to go there now. The rest of the servants have got fresh bread with butter, along with dried apples boiled in milk. There is enough for you, too."

The men and women all looked at each other, sitting as they were in the cowpens. "My lady. We are slaves. We wear the iron collars and wristbands of slaves. We are not–"

"Gill," she broke in, and he fell silent. "There is one thing you must learn about Dun Bochna. We have servants here. Not slaves. Go, now. Go to the King's Hall and get your share of the food. Find my servant Alvy and tell her I sent you. When you have eaten, go to the armorer's house. I will tell him to remove the iron bands from all of you."

After briefly looking at each other, the women took their children and hurried away from the cowshed towards the riches that awaited them in the hall. The men followed, Gill last of all, and he glanced at Muriel with his single brown eye as he walked past.

"No slaves," she whispered. "Never slaves."

171

* * *

For another fortnight, Muriel spent every waking moment making each part of Dun Bochna as new and perfect as she possibly could. The work not only allowed her to show Brendan what she could do for him as his queen, and how much this place meant to her as her new home; it also kept her from worrying about him with every moment that passed without his return.

"He is a king now, Lady Muriel," Alvy would say. "From now on, he will often be called away to see to the safety of his people. And they do not all live within the confines of these walls."

Muriel would keep her voice light. "If even you believe he is a king, Alvy, it must be so."

"The kingmaking is in twenty-eight nights. What could happen in twenty-eight nights?"

For that, Muriel had no answer.

She would simply go on inspecting the houses for any holes in the thatched roofs, or for hinges that had rusted through. She would count the number of wooden buckets, discard those beyond repair, and order new ones to be made. And she would walk through the souterrains, the cool, dark, underground passageways where food was stored, looking at the shelves of apples, the heaps of dried seaweed, the baskets of hard cheeses, and the hanging sides of mutton and beef.

Muriel was especially pleased that the former slaves were now decently dressed in newly made clothes of dark brown wool, with boots and belts made of sturdy leather and long rectangular cloaks of the same dark brown wool. The cloaks would serve to keep the rain off and keep them warm while sleeping in the clean rushes of the King's Hall each night. She even found simple bronze circular brooches to pin the cloaks over each person's shoulder.

And as the days went by, it seemed to her that their faces looked less pale and gaunt... especially those of the children. Muriel saw to it that they all got their share of the plain but nourishing food that Dun Bochna always had in abundance.

Soon the former slaves blended in so well with the other servants that Muriel could hardly tell them apart– all except Gill, the white-haired man who was never seen without a strip of leather over his left eye and a dark woolen hood over his head.

All of her work made the time pass quickly. It made Muriel feel needed, as though she truly had a place here at Brendan's fortress. But at the end of each day, she still went to her bed alone.... and on each succeeding night she slept less and less.

Finally, as Muriel lay down on the ledge in the darkness of their home and pulled the furs over herself yet again, she reached out to touch the empty space where Brendan should have been. Her eyes begin to burn with tears. Tomorrow night, the moon would be full. If Brendan had not returned by moonrise, she would use the water mirror and seek him out herself.

* * *

The next morning, Muriel stood beside one of the houses and anxiously looked up at Gill. He was climbing on old wooden ladder with a tightly bound bundle of straw over his shoulder. "Do be careful," she called, as he stretched out facedown on the slick straw roof. "That ladder is old and worn. I should have someone bring another."

"Please don't worry, my lady," said Gill. " It is my task to do, and it will be done soon."

173

She shook her head. "I cannot help it. I do not like the look of this ladder. I've been inspecting many things these last days and have seen much that needs replacement. This is one of them. I will go and find someone to bring you another."

Muriel turned to go, intending to find another servant who could fetch a decent ladder; but just then she heard hoofbeats– and looked up to see Brendan riding through the gates.

His four men rode right behind him. Muriel hurried to stand where he could see her, and felt as though a great weight had been lifted.

Instantly he turned his big grey horse and cantered it towards her, vaulting down to the ground even before the animal could stop. He caught her in his arms and held her close.

Then, just as he leaned down to kiss her, Muriel heard the loud cracking of wood from behind them. Someone shouted and there was a thud as something heavy fell to earth.

Brendan gripped her by the shoulders as he drew back. Then he let go of her and dashed off towards the sound, towards the house where Gill had been working.

Muriel's instincts about the ladder had been right. Gill lay sprawled facedown on the earth with the broken ladder lying half across him.

Brendan rushed over to the man. "Lie still, lie still," he said, as Gill tried to sit up. "We'll send for one of the physicians. Lie still!"

But Gill pushed himself up to his hands and knees and began running his fingers through the grass as though searching for something. "Do not move!" Brendan said again, more urgently this time. "Whatever

174

it is, we'll find it. Alvy! Go and bring a physician. Hurry!"

Muriel wondered what Gill could be searching for. His cloak was still fastened, so it was not his bronze brooch that had fallen– and then she realized what it must be.

His ever-present hood had fallen back to reveal thick white hair, cut above his shoulders in the manner of a slave... but the leather strip that was always tied over his left eye was gone."

Brendan moved to Gill's head. "Let me see you," he said, crouching down to look closely at the man's face. "Ah, you must have slid against the straw roof. You are scraped and cut. Is there anything in your eyes? Let me see–"

There was a long pause. Brendan stared at Gill's face, and slowly stood up. Then, to Muriel's surprise, he backed away and stood a few paces away from the former slave, staring at the man and anxiously clenching and unclenching his fists.

Why would Brendan do such a thing? Muriel had already concluded that Gill had a scarred or missing eye, for he was never without the leather strip to cover it. But as a warrior and a prince, Brendan had surely seen scarred and wounded men before. Why would he recoil in horror from the sight of a disfigured servant?

Near the wall of the house lay Gill's strip of leather. Muriel walked over and picked it up, and then took it to Brendan. "This is what he was searching for," she said, holding out the leather piece. She looked at Gill, hoping to reassure him; but his head was turned away from her.

Brendan was almost as pale as he had been on the night she'd found him alone on the stormy sea.

"What is it?" Muriel, asked, more insistently. "It should come as no surprise if he is scarred. Think of what his life has been up to now. Why do you draw back from him?"

"Gill." Brendan's voice was very low. "Look up at Muriel. Look up at your queen."

Slowly Gill raised his head and peered up at Muriel with one brown eye. She crouched down to look closely at him, prepared for whatever Brendan might have seen.

His face was scraped and cut from sliding across the tightly bundled straw when the ladder snapped. He would have a few bruises, too, but he was able to move. He had nothing broken.

Gill's left eye, the one normally covered by his leather strip, was still tightly closed and watering. Perhaps Brendan had been right. Perhaps he had gotten a bit of straw into that eye, or what remained of it.

Gently she reached out and lifted the eyelid with her fingertip and looked closely at his eye... an eye that was whole and perfect and undamaged...

An eye that was brilliant blue.

V. THE SON OF A SLAVE

The full moon drifted high over the beach, bright white against the night sky and occasionally shadowed by faint grey clouds. The air was unusually cool and a mist was rising, creeping along the sand at the very base of the cliffs where a few wild grasses grew.

Muriel waded barefoot into the sea, dipped her bronze basin into the cold water, and carried it to a large seaweed-draped boulder. For the space of several heartbeats she closed her eyes and stood with her head lowered, bracing herself against the cold, rough surface of the rock.

She did not know if she could do this. She was afraid to think that perhaps the water mirror would fail her this time... and equally afraid to think that it would not.

Muriel became aware that two druids stood on either side of her. She looked up and saw a large crowd of men and women standing beneath the cliff wall, a few of them holding torches. Nearly all of the druids and the warriors and their wives, it seemed, had come out to witness this.

In front of them, on the sand between the crowd and the sea, stood Brendan and Gill.

Muriel breathed deep breath of the cool sea air. "Take them to stand at the place where the sea meets the land," she commanded. "It is not the sea, for a man can stand upon it; but neither is it the land, for the sea washes over it. It is a place that is both land and sea, and a place that is neither. It is a place of power."

She watched as the two men walked together and stood barefoot in the rushing surf. Both were dressed only in simple linen tunics and breeches with no gold or bronze or any other metals anywhere on their bodies.

177

Their heads and faces were bare and open to the night wind and rising mist. They were two men of equal height, one with short white hair ruffled by the breeze and the other with a golden brown mane flowing down over his shoulders.

"Stand back to back. Leave only a little space between you," Muriel told them. "The older man faces east while the younger man faces west, in the same path as the moon. At this moment, it will shine down equally upon you both."

The two men did as she commanded. Gill faced the cliff wall to the east and Brendan looked out to sea to the west. Muriel gazed down at the dark surface of the seawater in her bronze basin, willing herself to see nothing else, and lowered her fingertips down to the cold wetness.

"Gill," she whispered. "Show me who you are."

The moon shone down bright and clear. An image soon formed in the water mirror. Muriel saw a boy child with golden brown hair, a boy who wore the plain ragged clothes and iron bands of a slave. He had one eye of brown and the other of bright blue, and worked hard to carry feed and haul water into a fortress.

Odhran's fortress.

The image changed. Muriel saw Gill as he had been near the age of twenty. Except for the rough clothes and the perpetual exhaustion from his endless hard work, the man was the image of Brendan. He had the same golden brown hair, the same strong jawline, the same height and broad shoulders... and the same strange eyes.

The image changed again. She saw Gill with a young woman, who held an infant a few months old. As that child gazed upward, Muriel could clearly see its one blue and one brown eye.

The woman handed the child to Gill, turning away and hiding her face as she did so. Her shoulders trembled with grief. Gill took the infant and slipped away into the night-shrouded forest.

The images faded... yet their power remained. Muriel lifted her hands and held them still for a moment, waiting while drops of water fell back into the mirror; and then she touched her fingers to the water's surface again.

"Brendan... show me who you are."

Now she saw an infant left in the night at the gates of Dun Bochna. A man's strong arm, with an iron band at the wrist, pounded on the gates above the child. Then he ran away unseen just as the gates began to open.

Another image came. A queen in childbed, newly delivered of a stillborn son. Mercifully she did not know, for the midwives had given her a draught to let her sleep.

In the room with the queen was a king whom Muriel recognized. It was a young Galvin, dark-haired and vital, struggling with his grief and loss as he dreaded telling the truth to his wife.

A third vision now, this time of Galvin placing an infant boy into the arms of his wife... a boy now wrapped in new linen and a fine woolen blanket of purple and blue... a boy with one blue eye and one brown.

The queen took the beautiful child in her arms and held him close, even as Galvin placed his hand on the boy's golden brown hair.

179

The water stilled. The clouds hid the moon. The images faded as Muriel fell to the sand.

* * *

She awoke cradled in Brendan's arms, her head resting against his broad chest. With a gasp Muriel sat up and then pushed herself away, standing on the beach before him.

"Muriel! Let me help you," said Brendan, and tried to catch hold of her.

But she backed away with her hands held out in front of her. "I must tell you what I have seen," she said. "I must tell you!"

"Of course you will tell us," said Brendan. "But sit down first. Let me help you."

The rest of the people– the warriors and the druids and the women– had gathered close. Muriel continued to back away from them. "I must tell you now," she insisted, and found her way back to the rock where her water mirror rested.

She placed her hands on the boulder on either side of the mirror. Staring down at its dark surface, she tried to catch her breath… tried to think of what to do next.

"Muriel. Please. Tell me what you have seen."

She looked up to see Brendan gazing down at her from across the mirror. The dark sea glistened behind him and the high white moon shone bright above his head. His face was solemn and still, and the wind stirred his hair as he waited for her to speak.

As she looked at Brendan, Gill came to stand beside him. Their shadowed faces were reflections of each other.

"Gill." Muriel's voice was faint as she struggled for words. "This began many years ago, when you and your wife lived and served in King Odhran's fortress."

"I lived there all my life," Gill said quietly. "As did Brona, who was my wife."

Brendan glanced at him, but Muriel pressed on. "You lived in cruelty. In suffering. In pain."

"We knew no other way."

"And so, when a son was born to you, the decision was made that he would not live as you had. You yourself took him in the night to Dun Bochna, to King Galvin, in the hope that someone there would foster him even though he was the child of slaves."

"I did," whispered Gill. "The life of the lowest servant at Dun Bochna would be far better than that of any of Odhran's slaves."

"Did you know what became of the boy you left at the gates?"

Slowly Gill shook his head. "I knew that the gates opened and someone took him in… but no more. I never expected to know. All I had was the hope that his life would be better than mine."

"It was better than you dreamed," said Muriel. "That same night that you left your son at the gates, the queen of Dun Bochna was delivered of a stillborn infant… and to save her from her grief, the king gave her your child to love and raise as her own. A child who grew up not as a slave, but as a cherished prince…a tall, strong, happy child with one eye of blue and one eye of brown. A child whom the king and queen named Brendan."

The two of them stood motionless, side by side. "Look at your father. Look at your son," she said to them. "Gill, you have known who he was since the night

181

of the cattle raid on the mountain, when you first saw his face by the light of the moon. That is why you waited for us in the woods by the stream. That is why you were so willing to come and live here among us."

Gill tried to speak, though his voice began to fail. "If hope lay anywhere, it lay with him."

Muriel paused. "Brendan," she whispered. "Surely you know, now, who you must be."

His voice was so faint that she could scarcely hear it. "I know," he said. "I know it, now."

He raised his face to look up at the moon, and then looked down once more. "I laughed when you had your doubts, Muriel, about whether you were really marrying a king. I thought nothing of the signs at our marriage. I tried to forget seeing my brother drop the king's torque at Galvin's interment. I forced myself to ignore the message of the fidchell game. I never had any doubt at all about who or what I was… until this day, when I saw my true father's eyes."

The two men looked at each other, and then the son reached for the father. Muriel watched them embrace in the shadowed moonlight, until at last her own eyes filled with tears and she could no longer see them at all.

* * *

Somehow they all found their way back to the fortress gates in the darkness, following the torches that a few of the warriors carried. From a great distance, it seemed, Muriel heard one of the druids speaking as they walked. "We will hold a council among ourselves tomorrow," he said. "We will consult the laws and decide what must be done."

What must be done…

The words echoed in Muriel's mind as they all walked in silence through the gates of Dun Bochna. Once inside, the party quietly drifted apart in the darkness. The druids and warriors made for their houses, while Gill went to his place in the rushes of the King's Hall. He paused once, looking at Brendan as though he wanted to say something; but the subservient habits of a lifetime were strong in him and so he went on in silence.

Muriel and Brendan found themselves alone in front of their house. They stood face to face, the sky black and cloud-covered now, with the only light coming from the flickering torches scattered around the grounds. Muriel reached for the door and started to push it open– but he caught her hand and drew her back to stand in front of him once more.

"This is no longer my home," he said quietly.

"Brendan, of course it is your home. Our home."

He shook his head. "It is the home of a man of the warrior class. And we have learned that I am not a man of the warrior class."

"Please," she whispered. "Nothing has been decided yet. Please come inside."

"Muriel, we both know what will be decided. They have only one choice."

"Brendan–"

"They have no choice," he repeated. "A tanist must be of the king's own blood. He must be a son, a cousin, a brother. I am nothing of the king's blood. I am the son of slaves."

"Your father and mother did a great thing for you," Muriel said, tightening her grip on his hand. "They risked all to give you a good life. And they succeeded."

But he only shook his head. "It would have been better if they had kept me with them and let me live the

183

life I was meant to have... a simple life of labor, with none for companionship but other slaves and servants.

"There would be no heavy gold around my neck. No fine clothes on my back. No thoughts in my head of bold actions and cattle raids and men following me into battle. Most of all, there would be no beautiful queen at my side... no noble wife with the power of magic to come into my life and my heart."

He released her hand and turned away, his shoulders rising and falling as he struggled for breath. She started to go to him but then he spoke again.

"Tell me, Lady Muriel... is it better to have nothing and be content with it, or to have everything and watch it disappear? Who is happier– my father, or me?"

She caught her breath as the pain of his words filled her heart. "I do not believe any answer is a good one when it comes to such terrible questions."

"You are right," he agreed. "But I will have the rest of my life to think of them... all my life to dream of a woman such as you... a woman who would never have known me at all had I lived out my life as a slave."

She moved closer, though he was still turned away, and quietly placed her hand on his arm. "I would like to think that I would have found you somehow," she said "That in one way or another, our lives would have intersected and we still would have been together."

"We would have been nothing to each other." His voice was as still and final as death. "You would be a lady of nobility and magic. I would be a slave. We would be nothing to each other."

He turned to face her, but made no move to reach out. "You would marry none but a king, Lady Muriel, as you said many times. And you have good reason to do so. I saw it for myself, when I met your sisters. A man born into slavery is the last man you would have considered.

"A man like me."

He looked past her, across the torchlit grounds of the dun. She turned and saw three druids approaching, walking slowly as though reluctant to join them. But Brendan faced the druids with the same terrible stillness and resignation, and in a moment they stood before him.

Muriel saw that one of them held a stack of folded woolen garments with a plain bronze brooch resting on top of it. "I know why you are here," Brendan said. "Please wait." And he walked calmly into their house, leaving the door swinging open.

She hurried after him. In the darkness of the house she could hear him searching through the wooden chest that held his possessions, and heard the faint clink of metal on metal. She stepped aside when he walked outside again, but he behaved as though he did not know she was there.

"This is what you have come for," he said to the druids. In the torchlight she could see a shining heap of gold in his outstretched hands. The druids surrounded him and took all that he offered: wristbands, armbands, finger rings, and brooches… all of Brendan's finest gold pieces.

"And this." Tucked between his arm and his side was his tanist's torque. He held it out to them, and as the druids took it he let his arms fall back to his sides. All of the gold disappeared into a large leather bag, the torque last of all.

Brendan reached for the stack of folded garments on the ground near his feet. Over his simple linen clothes he pulled on the dark woolen trousers and tunic, wrapping the plain brown leather belt around his waist and tying it through the heavy iron ring. The leather of the boots was just as plain and coarse. Last of all he draped the rough wool cloak over his shoulders and pinned it with the small bronze brooch.

"The rest of it– the fine clothes, the good boots, the weapons– all of it remains here. I will not enter the house again."

The druids stood silent, as though they wanted to say something to him; but at last they turned and walked away into the night without having spoken a word.

Now Brendan stood alone in front of Muriel yet again, and he turned to her with something like a small smile... though his eyes still held that frightening stillness, that terrible emptiness.

He looked down at himself, smoothing the rough dark wool of his new garb. "My real father saw this as a great step up in the world only a short time ago. I must learn to feel the same."

"Brendan! Please do not say such things! Your father is– he was– he was King Galvin!"

He cocked his head and looked down at her. "Muriel, surely you cannot say such a thing after what you, yourself, have seen tonight."

"It is true that Gill gave you life," she went on, speaking rapidly. "And it was through no fault of his own that he could not care for you. He and his wife– your mother– made the unselfish choice to give you something far better than what they had."

Muriel took a deep breath. "But– did no one here ever question your parentage, Brendan? Even though you bore little resemblance to the king who raised you?"

He shrugged and looked down. "Sons may not always resemble their fathers in every way."

"True. They may not. But no matter what your appearance, no matter how strange your eyes, Galvin and his queen accepted you as their son. They, and all of their people, wanted nothing more than to have you as their tanist, one day to be their king. There is no doubt of that!"

At last he raised his head and looked into her eyes. "Someone must have known," he said, frowning as he thought about it. "The guards who opened the gates that night and found an abandoned infant dressed in iron and rags. The midwives present at the queen's childbed."

This time it was Muriel's turn to shrug. "A few probably did know. But they understood what had happened to their queen and respected their king's decision to ease her grief. And as the child grew and his strength and abilities and personality became evident, any lingering questions about his origins were set aside and forgotten."

"Until tonight."

Muriel closed her eyes. "Please. You must come inside. You are still my husband."

"I am not. Not any longer."

She raised her head and stared at him in shock, unable to believe what she was hearing. "Of course you are still my husband! If you will not stay here, then I will come with you. I will sleep beside you in the rushes of the hall if I must! Please, Brendan– I am so sorry for what has happened to you, but we must find a way. We must!"

He closed his eyes. "It is all too much right now. As you said, we should wait for the council of druids. They will help us decide what to do."

187

She tried to look at him, but his face was hidden in the darkness. Even his strange eyes were shadowed. His words made sense, but his tone was cold and dead.

Then, to her surprise, he stepped close and took her in his arms. "Stay in the house, Lady Muriel. Be safe and warm. Imagine my arms around you... arms that were once those of a king."

She reached up for him and pressed her body close to his, feeling his warmth and strength beneath the coarse wool and cold iron of the clothes he now wore.

"I must be alone for a time," he went on. "I am sure you understand. If I know that you are safe, I can go and be alone with my thoughts. The druids will hold their council tomorrow. They will have an answer in a few days' time... perhaps even by tomorrow night."

Brendan pulled her close one more time, gently stroking her hair. Then he drew back and bent to kiss her, his mouth as soft as the mist and as warm as the summer sunlight. Then he took her to the door of the house, helped her up the step so that she stood inside, and pulled the door closed in front of her.

All she could hear was his footsteps walking away in the darkness.

* * *

In the morning, Muriel awoke alone. There was nothing in the house with her save silence and stillness. The only thing beside her in the bed was a wide, empty space of smooth linen that was covered by a sealskin fur.

The terrible events of the previous night slowly surfaced in her mind... slowly, as if she could hardly bear to think of them. But think of them she must, for nothing in her life would be the same from this point forward.

188

Her worst fears had come true. The mirror had been right. Brendan was not and had never been a king. He would never be a king... not by birth and not by law.

But she had married him.

There could be no doubt of her love for this man. Last night her only thoughts had been for Brendan, whose entire life had come crashing down.

Yet his life was not the only one that had been shattered. What would she do now?

Muriel tried to think of how this was proof, if proof was needed, that she had not accepted him solely because of his station. She had never wanted to simply wait to find an available king and cold-heartedly marry him for her own purposes. She had been determined to marry a king whom she could love, and who would love her in return, or she would never marry at all.

She and Brendan had loved each other as much as any man and woman ever had. They had made the best of marriages. Even now, when she knew with certainty what he was, she wanted nothing more than to run to him and pull him close and do what she could to ease his pain.

She had told him she would sleep beside him on the floor of the hall, among the other servants, if that would allow them to be together. And she had meant it.

But another sort of cold dread sat at the back of her mind, the dread regarding the curse that hung over the women of her family. Her power of magic, her own spirit and vitality, were now at great risk, for the man she had married was born of the very lowest ranks.

It was almost too frightening to think about. But at this moment, all that mattered was that her husband had need of her. She would go to him and do what she could to help him.

189

Wearing only a white linen gown, she threw back her fur covers and got up out of bed. Through the high windows she could see that the sky was a faint grey. Peering around the tall leather screens, she saw that Alvy was not yet awake but still lay sleeping on the low ledge in the far wall, wrapped in a thick woolen cloak.

Muriel threw on the first woolen gown she could catch hold of. It was a blue-and-cream plaid, which struck her as fortuitous since she knew that Brendan liked to see her dressed in blue.

But why was she thinking of such trivial things right now? She pinned her long blue cloak over the gown, tied on her boots, pulled a wooden comb through her dark hair, and stepped out into the dawn to search for her husband.

* * *

The sun was high above the horizon by the time Muriel returned to her home, her anxiety rising higher by the moment. She had searched throughout the dun and spoken to everyone she saw, but no one had seen Brendan– not the servants, not the guards, not anyone she could find.

Even Gill was at a loss. "If Brendan is not with you, he is nowhere. I have not seen him."

She took the buttered oatbread and roasted codfish that Alvy offered her, knowing she must eat something if she was to have the strength to continue. "Keep looking," Alvy had counseled. "He's got to be somewhere. He would not leave you, no matter what has happened. Men sometimes have the need to go away to think. You'll find him when he's ready to be found."

Muriel could only nod, doing the best she could to swallow the hot buttered bread and drink a little fresh milk along with it.

At last, though fear gripped her tighter with every step, Muriel left the house. She turned away from the gates, faced in the direction of the sea, and walked past the houses and the hall.

She continued past the line of boulders placed on the ground that showed the safe limits of Dun Bochna. Beyond that line, no one ever stepped– and with good reason.

Her heart hammered as she ventured out onto the smooth and dusty ground. Its surface was littered with small rocks and untouched by anything save the wind and the rain. She approached the crumbling edge and stood as close to it as her trembling legs would allow her to go, standing on the edge of the world with nothing in front of her but the cold sea wind and a vast, sheer drop to the rocks and surf far, far below.

Yet she calmed her nerves and steadied herself, and slowly peered out over the edge to the beach. Far to one side, where the cliff receded and the narrow strip of sandy beach began, a small dark figure sat on a rock and gazed out to sea.

Muriel turned away from the cliff's edge, caught up the hems of her skirts in both hands, and raced through the crowded fortress straight for the gates of Dun Bochna.

* * *

Brendan sat on the same rock where Muriel had placed her water mirror the night before. His rough brown cloak was wrapped close around him with the top of it pulled up over his head, in much the same way that Gill always wore his own cloak.

191

Muriel hurried up to him. She was breathless from the long run down the steep back-and-forth path on the face of the cliff, and from the fear of what she might find. But even when she stood right in front of him, Brendan seemed not to notice. He simply went on staring out to sea.

All she could see was his face, so pale that it seemed almost grey... as grey as mist, as grey as the sky above them. His hair was damp and flat from the wet wind off the ocean. The same aura of stillness, of lifelessness, that she had found so unnerving the night before had now settled over him until it seemed unshakeable.

In his damp clothes, pale and wet and still, he resembled more and more the mysterious stranger she had rescued back at Dun Farraige. But that man, half-drowned as he was, had been full of life and determination and an unbreakable fighting spirit. The man before her now seemed drained and empty, as though he found it hardly worth the effort to breathe, as though his heart could barely trouble itself to beat.

A sudden apprehension struck her. Had he gone beyond the place where she could help him? Filled with a terrible fear, a kind of fear she had never known before, Muriel walked close to the rock where he sat and reached up to take hold of his arm.

"Brendan," she said, above the ceaseless noise of the waves. "Please talk to me. Tell me what you are thinking. Tell me what I can do to help."

For a long time he remained silent and still. He watched the waves as they rushed onto the beach and then receded over and over again, as they had done since the beginning of time. Then, just as Muriel was ready to shout at him or drag him down off the rock or even douse him with water to get his attention, she saw him take a sudden long, deep breath.

It was as though this were the first real breath he had taken in ages. And then, very slowly, he turned his head in her direction.

For a moment she felt nothing but relief. Perhaps she would be able to get through to him after all. But with a shock she realized that he was looking not at her, but through her, past her, far up the beach, to the place where the path from Dun Bochna met the sand, the place where nine druids and thirty warrior men now came walking towards him.

* * *

Muriel thought that Brendan would throw the cloak back from his head and shoulders in order to face the approaching druids and warriors with nothing hidden; but then she realized that was something the old Brendan would have done.

Gill had kept his hood up over his head to hide who he was, in order to keep Brendan– and anyone else– from ever suspecting that he could be Brendan's father. But now Brendan was the one who wanted to hide what he really was.

The nine druids stopped. They formed a line across the sand from the cliffs to the sea, as though blocking the way to Dun Bochna. The warriors gathered close behind them. At last, one of the druids– Lorcan, who had recited the contracts with some difficulty at the marriage ritual– stepped forward and began to speak.

"Brendan of Dun Bochna," Lorcan said. "The council of druids has reached its decision."

Brendan sat unmoving on the rock. Muriel stayed close to him and raised her chin to look at

193

Lorcan. "You have not wasted any time," she said, as cold fear crept through her.

"That is true. We have not," agreed the druid. He took another step forward. "Brendan," he said again. "You have been considered a member of King Galvin's family almost since your birth. You became one of our boldest warriors. You were chosen as tanist by the free men of our tribe. We had no reason to doubt that you should be our next king. But now such things have come to our knowledge that cannot be ignored.

"You were taken into the king's own family. He considered you his son, and as his son you were one of those who could rule over us as our sovereign. Such adoptive sons have been kings in times past. Yet it was always the case that they had first been born into some family of high rank, and so still carried the blood of free and noble men.

"The son of a slave, however– even if raised by a king– is not, under the law, one who could ever be considered to rule."

Muriel closed her eyes. Brendan said nothing.

"A new king has been chosen." Lorcan glanced over his shoulder, and two of Dun Bochna's warriors came forward through the row of druids.

Between the two warriors was a small man with a round face. His eyes were large and his glance was nervous, and he was dressed only in the long tunic and flowing cloak of a druid.

Then Muriel saw the sea-dragon torque that now rested large and heavy on his neck.

"Colum!" she cried, looking at Brendan and then back to Lorcan again. "Colum is a good man, but he is a poet! A musician! He is no warrior. I do not believe he ever wished to be a king!"

Brendan raised his head to look. "He is the image of Galvin, my lady. There will never be any doubt of his parentage."

"Colum is the choice of the free men of Dun Bochna to be their tanist," said Lorcan. "He will have his king-making ritual at Lughnasa next."

Lughnasa next... "What will happen to Brendan now?" Muriel asked. "I have made a contract of marriage with him. What of that?"

Lorcan turned to her. "We have discussed that matter, too, among ourselves. I am sorry to tell you, my lady, that under the law your marriage contract is invalid."

"Invalid," she whispered. "How can this be?"

"It was a union of deception. Yours was contracted as a marriage between a man and a woman of equal rank. Now we are aware that this was not true. A man born of slaves has no legal right to make such a contract. Therefore, we have determined that your marriage no longer exists."

She held tight to Brendan's arm. He sat quietly, listening to the druid's words.

"Lady Muriel," Lorcan went on. "You are, of course, free to return to your own family and take your bride gifts with you."

"And... that is to be the end of it? The end of my marriage?"

Lorcan looked closely at her. "If Brendan had family of any means, they would be required to pay your honor price for breaking the contract. But since they are only slaves, it would seem that you can gain no further compensation for this wrong that has been done to you."

Muriel pushed away from Brendan. She stood facing Lorcan, and all of the druids and warriors, across

195

the stretch of sand. "I want no compensation. Just tell me what you intend to do with Brendan and with Gill."

"Gill may remain among us as a servant," Lorcan said. "Or you could take him with you as your property, since he owes you your honor price but cannot pay it. As for Brendan…"

Lorcan looked back at the other druids, and then returned his gaze to Muriel. "We have no wish to destroy him. Yet a displaced king cannot remain among us. I am sure that you, my lady, being of high birth yourself, can well understand such things."

When she made no answer, Lorcan went on. "Your affection for Brendan is well known. If you wish, he may return with you to your home at Dun Farraige. The two of you could make a marriage contract there. But it will be a contract between unequals, and Brendan will be named a man supported on a woman's property."

Muriel turned away. Lorcan continued speaking as though he did not notice. "If such a contract is made, Brendan may rise to the rank of a craftsman, since would be married to a noblewoman. But he would have to master ironworking or wheelwrighting or somesuch, and he would never be your equal in rank."

Slowly she turned to look at the gathering once more, and echoed Lorcan's words. "You are saying that we could go to Dun Farraige… I could marry him again… and he could master a craft and live as a free man."

"Do you wish to do this Lady Muriel?" asked the druid.

She looked up at Brendan, intending to answer *of course I do!* But as she stared at him, the words would not come. She caught her breath and struggled to say

196

what must be said; but images of her dull and silent sisters filled her mind and she could not find the words.

Brendan actually smiled, if a bit sadly. 'You need not think of it now. There will be time for that later. Do not think of it now."

But Lorcan looked directly at Muriel. "You must decide soon, my lady. If you do not, Brendan will return to the servant's life to which he was born and be sent to the nearest kingdom that will have him. You must make your decision by morning."

The druids and the warriors turned away, taking Colum with them, and began making their way down the beach towards the path that led back up the side of the cliff. "Go with them, Muriel, please," Brendan said. "I will be back before long. Do not worry for me. I am at peace now. Go, so that I know you are safe and well."

"I do not want to leave you here," she said, allowing her pain to enter her voice. "Come home with me. Tomorrow we will go back to Dun Farraige and be married once more. We will make a life for ourselves there."

"They are leaving," he said, gazing out towards the men walking down the beach. "I will be there soon. Go now and wait for me. Please go."

She started to reach for him, but he was so deathly still, so quiet, that she let her hand fall. "I will see you soon," she whispered, and turned to follow the others down the windy strip of sand.

Muriel tried to tell herself that Brendan simply needed time alone to think, to absorb the terrible loss and wrenching change that had suddenly come into his life. Such an adjustment would be difficult for anyone to make. She would just have to give him time, give him understanding.

197

But again, the cold dread crept into her mind. How could she be so calm? She was in great danger, now, of losing all of her powers. Why wasn't she angry that she had been deceived? Why wasn't she furious that she had found herself married to a man who was the son of slaves, a man who may well cause her to lose everything?

Was she weakening? Was this the first sign that her spirit was beginning to fade?

Yet even as she struggled with those questions, a kind of peace settled over her. She had not been deceived. Brendan himself had known nothing of his origins. She was the one who had failed to heed the message of the water mirror... and now, knowing Brendan as she did, she did not believe she could ever have walked away from him no matter what the mirror said.

He was her husband. She was his wife. They had a true love for each other and he was nothing like the men her sisters had married. She would not, could not turn away from him now... not now when he needed her the most.

As she reached the path that led up to the cliffside to the dun, she could not keep from turning to look at Brendan one more time.

He jumped down from the rock. His rough cloak flew open and she could see that he still had his sword in its scabbard hanging from the old worn belt. As she stood paralyzed, unbelieving, he threw off the cloak, drew his sword, and walked into the sea– just as old King Galvin had done.

"Brendan! Do not do this! Come back!"

But of course, there was no response.

She turned and raced up the cliffside path. The party of druids and warriors had already started back down towards her, their attention caught by her cries.

"Look, there!" she shouted to them. "You know what he means to do. You must help him. You must stop him!"

The men strode down to the sand and got a clear view of Brendan. But to Muriel's shock, they simply stood quietly at the edge of the beach and watched.

"It is his choice," said Lorcan. "Perhaps the best one. We cannot have a king who is false, who has no right to rule. Brendan well knows this. He would rather give himself to the sea than become a pitiful outcast with no place anywhere in the world."

The druid looked at her with something like pity in his eyes. "He cannot have a king's life, but we can allow him a king's death. We will not interfere."

Muriel looked at them in horror. "You cannot let him die this way. You cannot! I cannot!" She kicked off her boots and ran down to the shore, splashing through the shallow water.

She was suddenly caught and held by strong hands on either side of her. "My lady, you must leave him," said one of the warriors who gripped her arms. "You must respect his choice, even as we respect it. As we did for the old king."

She struggled against the two of them. "This is no aged king making a merciful end to a long and happy life! This is Brendan! Help him! Stop him!"

But they only held her fast as her husband waded deeper into the sea, shouting at the waves and striking at them as they rose up to meet him.

Muriel could not break free. But neither could she let Brendan walk into the sea to his death as his foster father had done– the cold, relentless sea that surged around her bare feet.

She raised her chin and gazed steadily at Brendan, and at the waves. Then she raised both hands as much as she could against the grip of her captors. Holding her palms flat out towards the water, she then turned them sharply inward towards herself.

The waves swelled. The largest of them caught Brendan, lifted him up, and carried him back to shore, where he was dropped onto the wet sand in the shallows.

He got to his feet, angry and frustrated and covered with wet sand. Again he waded out into the sea, shouting and striking at the waves.

Muriel repeated the gesture, stronger this time, and another enormous wave rose up above the others. Brendan rode the face of that swell all the way to the beach's edge, struggling in vain to escape its grasp.

Two more times he tried to enter the sea, and two more times a great wave lifted him up and carried him smoothly back to the beach. At last, too exhausted to try again, Brendan lay panting in the rushing foam. With the last of his strength he threw his sword onto the dry sand of the beach.

Muriel let out her breath and closed her eyes.

The men holding her arms looked at each other, and let go. "I am sorry, my lady. He–"

"He is alive," she whispered. Then she picked up her skirts and ran down the beach to him.

Brendan lay where he had fallen at the edge of the rushing waves. "They threw me back," he said through salt water and grit, making no effort to get up. "Even the sea finds me unworthy. If you needed more proof, there it is. The water itself knows that I am no king."

"Brendan, let me help you." Muriel tried to get him to sit up, but he only lay gasping for breath on the wet sand as the water swirled around his trembling knees. "We'll take you to the dun. In the morning you and I will return to Dun Farraige. We will find a place there. We will–"

"You know very well what will happen to you if you try to stay with me," said Brendan. "Perhaps it is happening already. You must get away before it is too late for you… before your magic leaves you… before you lose your will, as your sisters did."

"I am willing to stay with you! It is my choice. Do you not think I am stronger than–"

He rolled over and tried to sit up. At first his head fell back and Muriel again felt a stab of fear as she saw how pale he was. But then he managed to sit slumped on the sand propped up on one arm, breathing deeply of the ocean air as though trying to gather strength from it.

After a moment, he looked up at her. "It was your mother's choice to stay with a man who was not a king, was it not?" he asked, catching his breath. "Your sisters' choice, too? And you know well what happened to them. You know that strength of will has nothing to do with it. It happened to the other women in your family. It will happen to you, too.

"You must go from me, Muriel. I will not see such a terrible thing happen to you. You must go away and make a new life for yourself."

She crouched down beside him in the chill of the creeping ocean. "I will not go from you. I will not leave you here."

Again he shook his head, and then struggled to his feet. "I saw you when they asked if you wanted to take me with you to Dun Farraige. You can do no such thing, and you well know it. And I would never allow it.

"Our marriage is no more. You heard what the druids said. It was a union of deception, for I deceived you into thinking I was a king. I, too, was deceived, but that does not matter here."

"Brendan–"

"It was the fault of neither of us, but it is over. Now you must go and never return."

Muriel, too, rose to her feet, staggering a little in the powerful pull of the tide. "Do you think a marriage is only the legal bond that the druids make? That it is a thing only of contracts and bride gifts and *tinnscra*? You are right when you say that those things can be unmade. But the marriage we have built between the two of can never be unmade."

She caught at his arm. "Have you forgotten our wedding night so soon? You know what I risked by giving myself to you, and yet I took that chance. That means we have made a true marriage, one that all the druids in Eire cannot touch!"

He refused to look at her. "I will set you free to live your life one way or another," he stated. "If I must, I will find another way to take my own life and leave you to yours."

A terrible chill rushed through her at his words, but she was determined to push back against such ideas. "You will do no such thing, Brendan of Dun Bochna," she said. "I will stop you from taking your life. Or if I cannot, then after you have done so I will do the same. Either way we will be together. Nothing can stop that now."

"Nothing," he murmured. Then he closed his eyes and let his head drop to rest in his hands. Muriel reached for him and at last he embraced her. For a long, long time they held each other as the water of the sea surged up around their feet.

"I do not know where I will be tomorrow," he said.

"For the moment, I do not care," she answered. Then she rested her head against his chest, listening to the beating of his heart and holding him as close as she possibly could.

As they stood together at the edge of the ocean, a pair of shadows fell across them.

Sudden fear struck Muriel as she realized someone was approaching them from behind. She whipped around, throwing her arms wide as if to protect Brendan from harm– and then saw Darragh and Killian standing before her.

Muriel could only stare at them as she tried to quiet her racing heart, but then found that her anger was only rising. "Why are you here? Do you mean to finish what he has started? You saw him walk into the sea, intending to let it take him. You did nothing more than stand and watch him do so!

"I will not let you touch him," she warned, trying to push Brendan back from them. "You will have to kill me first! Then you can answer for that to the new king and to my family! You will have to kill me first. You will have to–"

Muriel staggered and dropped back into the shallow water, reaching out for Brendan as she fell. He half caught and eased her down; and then, to her amazement, the two men got down on their knees before her.

Darragh reached for her hand. "My lady, you have nothing to fear from us. We are here to help him if we can. We are here to help you both."

"You would have let him die a moment ago." Muriel ignored Darragh's offer and let Brendan help her to her feet. "You would have stood and waited until his lifeless body washed up on shore, just as you did with–"

"But he did not wash up lifeless. He is alive. It was not yet his time."

She stood still, pressing close to Brendan, and regarded his former comrades. "You know he is no longer your king. He is no longer any part of Dun Bochna, unless it is as servant or slave. He is nothing to you now. And neither am I."

"You are wrong, Lady Muriel," said Killian. "He is still our friend. The two of you are still together."

She gripped Brendan's arm, not daring to let hope enter her heart. "He and I must be gone by morning. I will take him back to Dun Farraige. If you could get us horses and a bit of food, that would be more than I could hope for."

Darragh smiled. "We could do that. But is that the wish of both of you?"

Muriel looked up at her husband. "Brendan," she said, her voice firm and steady. "We must decide what we will do. We must decide now. We must be gone when the sun rises tomorrow."

She tried to catch his eyes, but he would not look at her. Muriel placed her hand on the side of his face. "You and I can ride together to Dun Farraige. We can again be married. It will be a different contract this time, but married we will be. We can still make a life there."

For a long time, Brendan was silent and still. He only stood gazing down at the surf crashing in and out around his feet. Then he slowly raised his head and began to speak, his voice so soft that she had to lean close to him to hear.

"I cannot go to Dun Farraige," he said. "Please do not ask me to do such a thing. If you do, I cannot refuse… and I would become as one who is dead inside, though he continues to walk and to breathe. I would become as your sisters are, though this curse would have a different cause.

"I know too well that I would never learn to live as a servant. I have been too long a prince, though I know now that it was undeserved.

"I am sorry I cannot do this for you. I never thought there would be anything you could ask of me that I could not do for you. But I know that if I should attempt to live as a servant, even for your sake, it would only bring disaster to us both.

"Please, Lady Muriel… do not ask this thing of me."

She could only look at him with fear rising inside her chest. "Then you must tell me, Brendan," she said, with rising panic. "What do you want to do? What can you do? We must find a way to allow your life to continue. If we cannot stay here, and we cannot go to Dun Farraige– where can we go?"

He allowed his head to drop forward again as exhaustion overwhelmed him. "I do not know," he whispered. "I cannot think. At this moment my mind is empty, walled off like a fortress. I am like a man struck down in battle, though I bear no wound that can be seen. I need time to heal. Time to think."

"Yet time is the one thing we do not have," Muriel pressed. "We must make a decision and we must make it now."

Darragh got to his feet. "Wait here," he said. "I will go and bring some help for Brendan, who is still our friend if nothing else." He turned and ran down the beach to the foot of the cliffs, disappearing as he started up the impossibly steep path to Dun Bochna.

* * *

Muriel and Killian each took one of Brendan's arms and led him to the base of the cliffs. He sat down against the rocks, and Muriel took off her blue cloak and spread it over him. Then she, too, sat down beside him to await Darragh's return. Killian kept watch a few steps away.

Brendan closed his eyes and looked pale as death. Muriel, too, began to feel exhaustion creep over her, sapping her strength and draining her will to go on.

This was not mere fatigue. This was despair, an enemy far worse. She must not give in to it. She must not!

Taking a deep breath, she moved closer beside Brendan, holding him in her arms and resting her head on his shoulder. She took some comfort from the faint warmth rising up through the cold wet linen of his tunic. Closing her eyes, she tried to think of nothing else but the slow and steady rise and fall of his chest and the gentle pressure of his fingers over her hands.

After a time, she became aware of footsteps on the sand... several sets of footsteps. She opened her eyes, blinking in the thin morning light, and saw Killian still standing a short distance away. Brendan straightened, pushing her upright as well, and together they looked down the beach.

Muriel blinked and shielded her eyes from the pale sun overhead, behind the grey clouds. She could hardly believe what she was seeing.

Walking over the sand with slow and measured steps was Darragh. On his arm, head high, carefully placing one foot in front of the other, was an old and noble man who was quite blind.

This could only be King Fallon, the former ruler of Dun Camas, defeated and blinded and exiled by Odhran. Brendan had said that the old king now lived in the shadows of Dun Bochna with his aged queen, Grania, who now walked behind him in the company of several warriors.

Following after the warriors were Gill and two other servant men.

By the time this strange party reached them, Brendan had managed to stand, though Muriel could see the trembling in his legs. She, too, got to her feet, and stood beside her husband as the old king approached.

"King Fallon," Brendan said, in a vice that was soft and steady. "I am glad that you are here. I am your servant. What may I do for you?"

The king turned his scarred and sightless eyes towards Brendan. "I, too, am your servant," Fallon said. "I am here to learn what I might do for you. if I can be of help to you, then my life might still have some purpose."

The faintest of smiles appeared on Brendan's face. "There is nothing that anyone can do for me, though I thank you for your kind words. My life is not what I thought it was. Now it is over. There is nothing more for me than that."

"As is mine," said Fallon. "I, too, am a man who was once a king… a man who, in the space of a single day, lost everything."

The entire group was silent for a time. Muriel could see the renewed grief in Brendan's eyes, even as he began to speak. "Your kingship was wrongfully taken from you by a cruel enemy. There is no doubt of who you are or who you were. You were born a free man of the warrior class and then became a king."

Brendan paced a few steps along the sand. "I have never been anything more than the son of slaves, no matter how fine my clothes, or how heavy my gold, or how loud my boasting of the marvelous deeds I had done."

"I am told that you are also a strong man with a beautiful young wife who offers you love," Fallon said. "It is too late for me to begin again. I will never have anything more than the memories of a life well lived, until it was taken from me by lies and needless cruelty.

"Those memories can offer me some comfort, as does my loyal wife who has vowed to stay with me until the end. You, though– you must listen to the message of the sea. You tried to give yourself to it, as King Galvin did, but it refused you. The waves threw you back."

"Perhaps the sea rejects a slave who is not worthy of a king's death."

"Perhaps the sea rejects a young man who should be seeking life."

Brendan closed his eyes. "I do not know what else to do. I cannot remain here. If I go and hide in the forest with my wife, how long until Odhran's men find me and finish what they started?"

He tightened his fists and paced a few more steps. "They patrol the forests relentlessly. They expect me to go straight to go with Muriel to Dun Farraige, but that is one thing I will not do. I will not live out my days on the bread of my wife's family, who will smile politely but never see me as anything more than a servant.

"As the slave that I was born."

Muriel looked away.

"You could go elsewhere. There is the whole of Eire to choose from," said Darragh.

Brendan shook his head. "And how shall we get there? Boats have no place to land, save at sheer cliffs, for a very long way on this coast. If we ride over land, we have to pass close to Odhran's borders. They will be watching and they will be waiting.

"If we camp in the forests, his patrols will find us. If we hide at the rath of some herdsman or farmer, it would cost them their lives if Odhran finds out they sheltered us. I will not put my own people– any people– in such jeopardy. I will not. I will not!"

"Does the sea tell you nothing else, Brendan?" Fallon asked.

Brendan glanced at the waves, which were dull beneath the grey sky, and looked at the old king again. "I know only that it does not want me. I seem to have no place on either land or sea."

Queen Grania came forward to stand beside her husband, and placed her hand on his arm. "Then you should seek a place that is neither land nor sea, Brendan, and make your home there."

Neither land nor sea…

Muriel studied this small, grey-haired woman with the peaceful blue eyes. What a queen she must have been!

"I was not always blind," Fallon said. "Look out across the ocean. Look beyond the waves. What do you see?"

After a moment, Brendan turned and stared far out to sea. He looked past the waves breaking all around and gazed out at the horizon. "I see an island," he whispered, staring at it. "I see the Island of the Rocks."

"An island," said Grania, "is not land, for it is separate and removed and isolated; but neither its it the sea, for it is solid and dry and unmoving. Perhaps this island holds your answer."

"It could provide us with a refuge for a time," Muriel agreed. "Odhran would never find us there. We could stay there in peace and think on what we should do next."

Slowly Brendan turned to look down at her and there was something like anger in his eyes. "What *we* should do?" he asked. "I have said that there will be no *we*. I would never allow you to be subjected to such a life. I once took a curragh with my men out to that island! The waves were so high, the cliff walls so steep, that it was impossible to land. There is nothing there but scrub grass, howling wind, and shrieking birds.

"Queen Grania is wise. I thank her for her counsel. The island may well be the place where I should go. But not you, Muriel. Never you."

Muriel shook her head, her voice equally firm. "I have already told you that my life is with you. You will never be separated from me again, no matter what you do."

She stared hard into his blue and brown eyes, and held his gaze until at last he looked down. "If you leave to sleep on the forest floor among the wolves, I will be there sleeping with you. If you walk over the edge of the cliff of Dun Bochna, you will find me falling through the air alongside you. If you go to the Island of the Rocks, I will sit beside you in the curragh as it glides over the waves.

"There will never be a time for you, Brendan, from this moment forward, when I am not there with you not matter what you choose to do."

Brendan started to answer with some retort... but it was clear that her words had reached him at last. He could only look back at her, his shattered heart and broken life clearly visible in his eyes... and yet Muriel was sure that she saw a trace of hope in those strange eyes, too.

One of Dun Bochna's warriors stepped forward. "A landing there is possible. Difficult and dangerous, but possible. There is a cove on the north side. I, too, took a curragh out there once with a few of my men. We tried it on a fine summer day and we managed it."

The old king reached out and found Brendan's shoulder. "It can be done," he said. "And I, too, will go with you when you do."

Brendan turned to King Fallon. "You would go with me?"

"I would. That is what I came here to tell you. I, of all men, have perhaps the closest understanding of what has happened to you. I no longer have any purpose in life unless it is to be of help to you. If I can do that, I may again have a reason to go on living... at least, for a time."

Brendan could only look at him, his head nodding ever so slightly.

"I will go, too," said Queen Grania. "Like you, Lady Muriel, it is my wish to remain with my husband. Like yours, mine well knows that there is nothing he could do to keep me from him."

Darragh and Killian took a few steps forward. "We will go with you as well," said Killian. "You have always been a trusted friend to us both. Now you are a man in need of friends. We will go there with you, and we will stay for as long as you have need of us."

Muriel slipped her hand into Brendan's.

Gill came forward last of all, with the two other servant men. "This is Duff. This is Cole. They, too, were slaves under Odhran until you set them free. We three will go with you, too, Brendan. If you will have us."

Brendan lifted his head and managed to draw himself up a little straighter. "I do not warrant any such love and respect and service as all of you have offered me this day. I should refuse it. But I will confess that there is nothing I would like more than to have your company, for a time, out on the Island of the Rocks."

With a sigh he lowered his head and pulled Muriel close, holding her tight with his strong arms as the wind from the sea– from the Island of the Rocks– blew over them.

* * *

The sun was just past its height when Darragh, Killian, Gill, Duff, and Cole came walking down the path from Dun Bochna to the beach. Above their heads they carried two long black curraghs. Muriel quickly noted that the boats were old and battered and greatly worn.

Behind the group walked Colum, with two druids and a few of the dun's warriors. The men all carried leather sacks that looked to be bulging with supplies.

Then a small figure hurried out from behind the last of the warriors. "Muriel!" Alvy cried. "Oh, Muriel! What is it that you mean to do?"

The two women embraced, one tall and dark-haired and the other small and frail with short locks of white. "I cannot leave him," Muriel whispered. "I

212

cannot. He is my husband. I love him. And he needs me."

Alvy peered up at her, looking hard into her eyes. "Are you sure? Are you sure that it is love and not– not the beginning of loss?"

Muriel smiled. "I know it is love. I can only hope it is not the start of a loss of spirit."

"I understand, dear one. But must you go to that island, so far away from everything?"

"There is no place else for us. This is our best chance. We will return. Perhaps not until the spring, but we will–"

"Take me with you!" cried Alvy. "I cannot let you go so far away alone. Please, take me with you!"

Muriel's eyes welled with tears. "Alvy, you cannot. I would never let you do such a thing."

"I am only an old servant woman. No one would miss me. Let me go and end my days caring for you!"

"Ah, but servants can be loved and cherished, too," Muriel whispered. "Please. Stay here for me and be safe. Promise me that you will be here waiting for us when we return. I will certainly have need of you then."

"I will always be here for you, dear Muriel," sobbed Alvy. "Right here."

Muriel stepped back a pace. "I will come back. I promise."

The two hugged each other again, and Alvy turned to walk away. "Oh, I cannot bear to watch you leave. Dear one, stay safe, and come home soon!"

As the retreating Alvy brushed past him, Brendan walked up to Colum. "You are very generous, Prince Colum. You are under no obligation to do anything for me."

"I... I find it hard to forget you were my brother." Colum clasped hands with Brendan and tried to smile. "Now, these curraghs are old, but seaworthy. In the sacks you will find food, water, extra cloaks and tunics, fishing hooks, and a few utensils. Darragh and Killian have their swords and daggers. You must take your sword as well."

Brendan released the other man's hand. "I thank you. I will not forget this."

I only hope it is enough." Colum glanced out to sea. "Are you certain you want to try this? Surely there is somewhere else you could go. Surely it would be better to just go with your wife to her people, and start your life over in that place."

Brendan shook his head and began gathering up the sacks of supplies. "I will be the one to care for my wife. I will never require her to take care of me."

"If you do make it out to the Rocks, and then decide to leave again, you will have to go before the autumn equinox," warned one of the druids. "After that, the waters surrounding the isle are so rough that it is impossible to get a boat on them. It will be difficult enough for you as it is. You are probably already too late."

"I am sure you will be there for only a short time, until you can decide on something else you wish to do," said Colum, as Gill and the other men loaded the rest of the supplies into the boats. "We wish you no ill. I, for one, regret that you cannot stay."

Brendan dropped a leather sack of grain into the first curragh. "There is no place for me here. Or at Dun Farraige."

He turned back to Colum and looked hard at him. "You are soon to be king. I am nothing but a slave and have no right to speak to you. Even so, I will tell you to beware of Odhran. He has been quiet for a time, but he will return when you least expect it. You must stay strong if you want to keep him away. You must be a warrior, not a bard, if you hope to defeat a man like him."

To Muriel's surprise, Colum laughed. "I know how you feel about him. It is no wonder Odhran found you an annoyance. You would have antagonized anyone with your constant raids."

Brendan frowned. "I am not sure you understand. If King Odhran is not at your doorstep right now, it is only because those constant raids earned his respect and taught him a lesson. He is hungry for power. You must deal with him as–"

"Yet you were never able to defeat him," Colum said. "You succeeded only in making him an enemy who hates you."

Brendan placed his hands on the side of one curragh and looked hard at his brother. "Do not underestimate him. Do not think of Odhran as anything but the most dangerous foe."

"I have been thinking on it. I may try a different method of keeping the peace. I want to offer him an alliance."

"An alliance! Colum, he would only take your offer as a sign of weakness on your part. I tell you, you must not think of doing such a thing!"

Colum must have heard the fear and desperation in Brendan's voice, for he smiled and then shrugged his shoulders. "It was only a thought," he said. "Odhran is just one of the many things I will have to contend with as king."

"Ask yourself what your father would have done. You cannot go wrong with that sort of guidance. Galvin was a good king." Again Brendan reached out, and this time he and Colum embraced each other. "I thank you for your generosity," he finished. "You will not see me again."

Brendan and his little party stepped into their two curraghs. Gill, Duff, and Cole got in with Brendan and Muriel, while Darragh and Killian went with King Fallon and Queen Grania.

The warriors on the beach pushed them off into the sea until the waves lifted up the boats. Then the men began paddling for the distant misty island that was simply called the Rocks.

* * *

Their two wood-framed leather boats, light as birds on the tumultuous sea, dipped and rose on the ever heightening waves. Muriel could only grip the sides of her curragh's wooden framework and try to focus on the floor instead of on the wildly heaving ocean.

She was aware of Brendan, Gill, Duff, and Cole paddling swiftly and patiently, driving their little craft up over each wave and then bracing back to ride it down the far side– up and down, up and up and over, up and down, again and again– and very soon Muriel found her head aching and her stomach rebelling.

One by one, all of them found themselves hanging over the sides of the boat and becoming more violently ill than they could ever remember. One glance back showed Muriel that the occupants of the other boat were faring no better. Yet by sheer force of will the men managed to keep their curraghs heading for their island destination, which loomed above them; a tall, sharply

216

pointed mountain with a wide base sitting all alone out in the sea.

Mercifully, the waters calmed somewhat as the boats crept closer. But as they did, Muriel realized that it was not just one island she was seeing. A second smaller one sat directly in front of the Island of the Rocks, with a long stretch of open water in between.

The smaller island also had a sharply pointed mount, but its peak was covered in a thick coat of dirty white– the legacy of the thousands of seabirds nesting there. As the two curraghs passed by, the birds began darting and wheeling overhead and swooping down over them.

Muriel bent low and threw her cloak over her head.

In what seemed to be nothing more than a final assault on Brendan's dignity, the swarms of birds flying over them soon covered the boat and all of its occupants with spots and blobs of droppings. Muriel felt that she would rather face those terrible sickening seas again than endure this rain of filth from the hordes of shrieking birds.

Perhaps the sea knew what it was doing by forcing them to pass beside this smaller island. There was no way to tell who was in these boats, for anyone inside– from the highest king to the lowest slave– would be forced to hide themselves as they passed or suffer the worst of insults. In these two little boats, there were no kings or queens or warriors or slaves. There were only nine desperate people using all their strength to reach what they hoped would be a place of safety.

Somehow the boats continued to advance and they got out from under the birds, but the seas grew worse again now that they were past the scant shelter of the small island. The bigger island called the Rocks, which looked much larger than it had from shore, lay directly ahead.

It towered above them. With a sinking heart, Muriel saw that this terrible place had no beach at all. There were only sheer rock cliffs dropping straight down to the sea. High, high up, there seemed to be a few level spaces where grass grew, but Muriel saw no place where they could land their boats. Brendan and the others had said it was possible, that they had done it before...

And then a dreadful thought leaped into her mind. Perhaps those warriors of Dun Bochna– and even Brendan himself– had told them a landing was possible while knowing only too well that it was not... while knowing that these fragile little boats would be smashed to pieces on the rocks and Brendan and his party would never be seen again.

It would certainly solve the problem of what to do with a man who should never have been called a king.

But surely those men would do no such thing. Brendan had been their friend and brother and tanist and king. And surely Brendan himself would not do this to the others with him now.

Muriel looked up and saw only the terrible mountain of rock towering over their boats and the enormous waves smashing its vertical sides. It might prove to be the last thing any of them would ever see.

Eventually the men forced the boats around to the far side of the island. As they moved from behind the towering mass, they were struck full force by the cold winds from the open ocean that ceaselessly tore at the Rocks.

Again the fragile curraghs rose and dropped wave by wave. Now Muriel could see that there was, indeed, a cove on this side, with a flat stretch of smooth wet rock within it where boats could be dragged for safekeeping– if the boatmen could get their crafts close enough without being hurled into the sharp, sheer rocks all around.

The little haven of flat rock was there and waiting for them, but the waves sweeping up to it were so powerful that there was a constant and enormous variation in the height of the water. The crest of one wave would put them high above the landing, but when it receded they would find themselves wallowing far below– and in prime position to be swamped by the next.

"It is impossible!" shouted Brendan, over the noise of the crashing waves. "We'll never get close enough. We'll have to turn back and go down the shoreline, and try for some other island."

"We cannot turn around!" Muriel shouted. Spray from the waves covered her face. "Everyone is exhausted. We would never make it back to shore. We must land now, or never!"

She sat up and turned around to where the second boat rose and dropped on the waves. "Stay close!" she cried, motioning them towards her. "Stay close!" Then she moved past the men to the prow of the boat, knelt down, and thrust both hands into the cold green sea.

"Calm," she whispered under her breath. "Smooth. Calm." She kept her gazed fixed on the spot where the wide, slanted flat rock awaited them. "Calm," she said again, to the sea. "Calm…"

219

In a moment, the wild motion of the waves began to ease. They became smaller and smoother, as on a beach, rolling with just enough force to carry the boats forward. She could sense the men behind her forcing the curraghs ahead with the last of their strength. They drew closer and closer to the hard, flat landing place that awaited them.

Muriel kept her hands in the water and kept speaking to the sea. Suddenly her fingertips brushed against rock. Then her hands were in the air as the last gentle wave lifted the boat up onto the rocky landing and the weight of its passengers kept it there beyond the reach of the sea.

There was a sudden violent crash of waves behind them as the sea roared to life once again. Muriel turned just in time to see the second boat ride up high on a wave beside them. She cried out to those within the boat, but it was no use.

One side of the wildly flung curragh tilted down to show her the floor of the craft with its four passengers bravely clinging to it. Then the wave collapsed upon itself and with a crash the boat came down on the rocks, spilling its people and supplies across the landing and cracking its wooden frame.

Muriel thought her heart was stop; but as the wave receded, she saw four people pick themselves up and move to stand against the sheer cliff wall nearby. Somehow they were here, and all alive, but only through sheer luck and their own determination. Her powers had failed the instant her hands had left the water.

The sea, which used to do her bidding, had almost killed them all.

Now they were stranded in this place, for nine people could not hope to ride home in a single curragh.

Their world consisted of no more than this shelf of stone with the sea crashing at their feet and the steep, forbidding rock towering far above their heads.

VI. NEITHER LAND NOR SEA

Darragh, Killian, and Gill quickly grabbed the broken curragh and dragged its heavy, sodden remnants up onto the rocks, and then did the same for the one still intact.

The rest of the men gathered the largest rocks they could find and placed them, with their paddles, inside what remained of each craft in hopes of securing them against the winds and tides.

"I hope they'll be here when we need them again," Killian said, stopping to catch his breath. "Though I don't know how we will get nine people into just one curragh."

"I'll see what I can do about repairing it," said Gill. "I've done some leatherwork."

"No time to worry about that now," Brendan told him. "We've got to find a place to make camp, or there will be no need for a curragh to take us anywhere. I thought I saw a few open spaces near the top of the mountain. There's nothing for us to do but try it."

He took a deep breath, looking at their leather sacks of supplies sitting on the flat, sea-washed landing. "Everyone take whatever you can carry. We'll climb up there and look for somewhere to live."

Everyone but Grania took at least one of the heavy sacks and threw it over his shoulder. Most of the men were loaded down with two. Muriel felt the muscles of her neck and shoulders straining with the unaccustomed weight of a large leather bag of oats and wondered if it was even worth hauling it. In a moment the cold dampness of the sea-drenched bag was seeping through her cloak and her gowns.

She shifted the sack and settled it as best she could, and then the entire party started up the treacherous steep climb.

Brendan went first, searching out footholds where they could step, clearing out small loose rocks so that the rest of them could find something like a path. Muriel went after him with Darragh behind her, followed by Grania, Fallon, Killian, Gill, Duff, and Cole.

It took an agonizingly long time to creep up the flank of the rocky crag that was this island. Honeycombing the cliff face were hundreds of burrows, many of them empty now, where puffins nested. Only a few still remained to finish rearing the last of their young.

The big slow birds merely hopped and flapped as the human invaders passed by; clearly they would not be difficult to catch. There would be meat at hand, at least until the last of the creatures flew away at the end of the season.

They paused to rest whenever they came to wide spots in the path, those places where slanted, soil-filled crevices allowed a few tough grasses to grow and thick lichens to cover the rocks. Muriel would allow the leather bag she carried to drop to the ground while she braced herself against the rock and tried to catch her breath. On their last stop she felt too exhausted to go another step, but told herself that the high, flat place they had seen could not be much farther.

Finally the little group struggled up the last piece of the path and found themselves on a grassy ledge jutting out from the rock face above them. The ledge was just wide enough for them to spread themselves out and begin to make a camp, just long enough to walk perhaps fifty paces.

Muriel set down her sack of oats, feeling a kind of physical and mental exhaustion that she had never known before. The combination of making the terrifying voyage, using her strength of magic to calm the waves, and then hauling the heavy sack up the dangerous path had left her feeling entirely drained.

Then she looked up and began to realize where they were.

She moved away from the rock face and crept cautiously towards the edge of their new little world, careful not to get too close. Not far from them was the Island of the Birds, and beyond it, across that terrible stretch of sea, the distant mainland was clearly visible.

Peering down at the crashing waves far below, she was amazed at how high up they were. This was nearly as high above the sea as the great cliff where Dun Bochna sat… but Muriel tried to put all thoughts of her comfortable home out of her mind. Life here would be very different.

"We'd better use the time we have before dark," said Brendan, setting down the bags he carried. "Gill. Take Duff and Cole and go back down. Get the wrecked curragh. Just break it apart and drag as much of it up here as you can. We can use the leather and wood to make some kind of shelter. The rest of us will try to make camp and see what there is to eat."

"Break it apart?" said Darragh. "Are you sure you want to do that? How will we get back?"

"There won't be much need for a boat if we all die of cold and damp up here," said Brendan. "We must think of surviving and do whatever is necessary. We'll start with the curragh. Go."

The three men turned and started back down the treacherous path. Gill turned to Brendan just before they disappeared and said to him, "We'll be back as soon as we can. Please. Be careful."

Brendan looked as though he were going to laugh. "It's a bit late for that, don't you think? But let me say the same to you. All of you be careful and get back just as soon as you can. You don't want to be on that path in the fading light."

Gill nodded, and then he and his men were gone.

Grania led Fallon to a place where he could sit against the rock face, well away from the ledge. The rest of them began searching through the leather sacks to see what they had.

"Drenched," Brendan said, tossing aside one of the sacks. "Everything is drenched with seawater. They gave us fresh water and oats and dried fish and apples, but all of it is wet."

Muriel came over to examine the rest of their goods. "Wet it is, but not soaked through. Whatever is in the center is still usable. If we are careful not to disturb what is nearest the outside, it will protect the rest. And as for the clothes…"

She held out the skirts of her own woolen gown. "All of us are soaked. Everyone should take off their cloaks and tunics and… and lay them over the rocks for the wind to dry. Place some smaller rocks on the corners to hold them down. We'll get them as dry as we can before sundown."

Rummaging through the sack that held clothing, she found two woolen cloaks and three tunics– mostly dry. "Here," she said, carrying the first of the cloaks to Grania. "I know that you and your husband are soaked.

Perhaps you could share this. I will do what I can to dry the ones you are wearing."

"Thank you," the queen said, accepting the cloak. "Just allow me to warm up a bit and I will help with whatever I can."

She could see that the older woman was shivering. "Do not worry yourself," Muriel told her. "Sit close to your husband beneath the cloak. There will be food ready soon. That will help."

Muriel took off her own cloak, untied her belt, lifted off her soaked blue-and-cream plaid gown, and stood only in her wet linen undergown. Quickly she pulled one of the plain brown tunics from the bag. Intended for a male servant, it was so long that it reached down past her knees.

Turning, she caught Brendan looking at her with renewed shock in his eyes. "I never thought to see you wearing the sort of thing that I must now wear," he whispered. "I am sorry."

"It is only a tunic," she said, walking over to him. "And it is mostly dry. I feel a little better wearing it. I got so wet from sitting in the prow of the curragh."

"But you should be wearing the best linen. The finest wool. You should have gold earrings and wristbands and brooches. You are a queen. You should not be dressed as a servant!"

His voice was beginning to shake. Muriel turned to him and placed gentle fingers on his arm. "The first time I saw you, you did not have clothes that were even as fine as this. You wore no gold. You had no weapons. Yet I knew, by your spirit and your strength and your courtesy, that you were no slave and no criminal."

She stared into his eyes. "You told me, then, that you needed none of the accoutrements of a king to know that you were one. And I will tell you now that if I am a queen, it is because I am loved by and bonded to a king. I do not need pretty gowns or gleaming gold to know what I am."

He tried to speak, but there were no words; and so they held each other close on the windswept rock, each one drawing comfort from the warmth and presence of the other.

After a time, Muriel raised her head. "We will make a life here, Brendan. It is risky, but it is better than the certainty of having Odhran hunt you down. There is no doubt that he would."

"I am not worth such a risk, perhaps." He raised his head and gazed out towards the mainland. "I should never have let this happen. I should never have allowed you to come here... not any of you. Most of all I should not have allowed it of you, Muriel."

"But we are here. And by choice." She caught his arm and shook it a little. "We need your help, Brendan. There is much to be done. Please. Help me. Help us all. We need only manage here for a short time, until we think of something better. Then we will go home."

He looked at her and slowly nodded. "I brought you all here. I suppose I'd better make it a home for you as best I can."

Muriel smiled a little, and turned away to see to the clothes.

Soon their campsite was decorated with cloaks and tunics spread out over the rocks to dry. The wind blew strong and cold in this place, though it was summer. Muriel fervently hoped that the broken curragh could be turned into some sort of shelter– if the three men could manage to drag it up all this way.

If they returned at all.

She closed her eyes and told herself not to entertain such thoughts. Their only chance of survival was to maintain hope. If they lost that, they might as well walk together over the edge of the cliff right now.

Muriel walked back to the rock face where the others sat. "We need a fire," she said to Brendan. "Is there anything to burn?"

"Fire," he repeated, and gazed around the site. "Fire…"

With a sinking heart, Muriel realized what he was seeing. The bare ledge held virtually nothing that would burn. The few tufts of grass they might gather would be consumed in moments.

"No trees on this island," Brendan said. "No peat. We would risk our lives just to get a few scraps of driftwood or a handful of seaweed, all in the hope that we can dry it out enough to get it to burn at all." He shook his head again. "At least we will not have to worry about a fire destroying our shelter. We have neither roof nor flame."

"All right, then," Muriel said, hoping to distract him. "We'll have to manage without fire for a time. People have done it before. The weather is warm enough and we have food to last for a while. So… our other thought is for water. Drinking water."

He made a small sound that was something like laughter. "You certainly do ask for a great deal, my lady. Food. Dry clothes. Fire. And now you also want water to drink?"

Brendan waved his arms and walked a couple of steps. "Look around. The place where your husband has brought you to live does not even have water. There is no stream, no spring. We will have to hope for rain– and when we get it, we will then have to hope that we do not

228

die from cold and sickness when we all stay soaking wet for days at a time."

He turned away and placed both hands against the mountainous rock face, looking away so that no one could see him. "What have I done?" he said, so softly that only Muriel could hear him. "What was I thinking, to come to this terrible place and bring eight other people with me? How can we possibly hope to survive? How can we possibly hope..."

Brendan let his forehead rest against the rock and fell silent, his fingers clutching at the cliff. Muriel went to him and stood close with her face against his broad back. She could think of no words that might help. All she could do was stand with him and offer him what strength she could, the way she had learned to draw strength and comfort from him.

After a time there was a touch at her shoulder. Muriel turned around the other way, and there stood Queen Grania.

"Prince Brendan," said the queen. "Please turn to look at me."

Muriel stepped back. Slowly Brendan raised his head. "I am happy to face you, my lady, though ashamed at the same time... for I am certainly no prince."

Grania pulled the rough brown cloak she wore a little more tightly around her. The sun was beginning to set behind the island and the shadows were lengthening.

"You must hear me," she began. Her voice was a little thin with age but strong nonetheless. "You must remember that if we are here, it is for the same reason: We are all here to help you."

He turned away again. "I am not worthy of help."

"None of us would be here if we believed that." Grania touched him on the shoulder and he faced her once again. "We are here on the most worthy of endeavors: to save a wounded king and help him to recover."

"King? I am not a king," he answered. " I carry no noble blood at all. Now I am paying the price for that deception, unwitting as it was... and so are all of you who came with me."

"But what of the many victories you have had?" Grania asked. "What of the many good things you have done for all the people of Dun Bochna?"

Brendan laughed, a short and bitter sound. "I have no answer for those things, Queen Grania. Perhaps the gods chose to amuse themselves one day by allowing a slave to grow up thinking he was a prince. Now they are laughing as he finds out what he really is: a man of no worth at all. A man who should have spent his life tending sheep and making buckets."

"You must never say that again, Brendan. If this place teaches you anything, it will teach you that you are indeed the king of those who depend on you for their very lives. We will help you, but you must also help yourself. When you are ready, we shall return."

He stared down at the frail and tiny queen, and then looked at Muriel standing beside her. "You are right," he said. "You are both right. It may have been a mistake to come here, but we are here now... and I cannot afford the luxury of weakness or complaint."

Grania smiled up at him. Muriel felt a great relief as she saw a spark of life come back into his blue and brown eyes.

She turned gratefully to Grania. "We are going to have great need of you in the days to come. It will take more than just strength and endurance to cope with this place. It will take wisdom, too, and generosity of spirit."

Grania laughed. "I hope it will be enough, my dear, for I can offer you little else. I cannot carry heavy loads, or drag wood to build a fire, or make my way down to the sea to catch fish... but I can tell you what I know about being a queen, though you need little in the way of instruction."

Muriel only smiled at that. "I know nothing of being a queen, even though for many years I hoped to marry a king. The only thing I know to do is love my husband and stay at his side, that we might face whatever happens together... no matter what it might be."

"And that is the best advice that I could give to any queen. You have learned that he cannot rule alone. That he needs you at his side. A king needs a queen to make him complete, for together they are far stronger than they could ever be apart."

Grania smiled. "It may sound simple, but often it is only the wisest of men and women who understand this."

"I will try my best. I promise," said Muriel. And then all three of them jumped as a scraping, clattering sound came up from the path which led down to the sea.

All of them froze for an instant. Then Gill and Cole and Duff appeared at the top of the path, each one dragging a heavy piece of the broken curragh up the impossible path.

The three men collapsed as soon as they reached the top. "We've got it," said Gill, raising himself up on one elbow as he gasped for breath. "Though it's a bit scratched and scraped, I fear."

"It is a treasure," Muriel said, crouching down beside him. "It means a little shelter. And maybe even some firewood." She smiled at him, at this man who was

Brendan's father, and gently touched his face. "Thank you. We all thank you."

He said nothing, but only smiled at her in return and reached up to lightly touch her hand.

* * *

By dusk, the little ledge had been transformed into something resembling a camp.

Cole and Gill had stripped the heavy oiled leather from the curragh and finished the job of breaking up its heavy wooden frame. They spread the wood out not far from the ledge, allowing the wind to dry it so that it might serve for torches or even firewood.

Duff and Killian then each took one of the daggers and worked diligently to cut nine narrow strips from the curragh leather. Each person could spread one beneath his cloak when they lay down to sleep, in an effort to keep out a little of the damp. The remaining torn and ragged pieces of leather were draped over their food supplies and weighted down with rocks to protect their food from rain as much as possible.

On the highest rocks of the campsite, anything and everything that could possibly hold rainwater had been set out: the small bronze cauldron, the two wooden cups, scraps of curragh leather pressed down into the crevices and depressions of the rocks, and, of course, the bronze basin that was Muriel's water mirror.

The group gathered together at the rock face. Brendan passed around a few pieces of dried fish for each person and Darragh handed out some of their dried apples. Muriel fetched the two wooden cups from the rocks and filled them with water from the leather waterskins. Water would be necessary as everyone struggled the tough, dry food.

"Wait. Where is Cole?" Brendan dropped the sack of dried fish. "Did he say he was going somewhere? When was he last seen?"

No one knew. All of them had been so engrossed in their own tasks that no one had noticed him. For a moment Muriel had a vision of the man taking a sudden fall over the sheer edge of that cliff. The roar of the sea was so loud, and so constant, that they would not even hear him scream.

There was a noise a short way down the path. It was the rattle of rocks, like something sliding or falling. All of them looked up to see Cole standing there, breathless, with a newly killed puffin in each hand. "I'm not sure how we'll cook them, but here they are," he said, and then frowned. "Is something wrong?"

"Not now," said Brendan, and to Muriel's relief he was smiling. "Come over here, Cole, and sit down with your riches. It's just that– next time, tell us when you're going off somewhere."

There was a sudden look of guilt on Cole's face. "Oh. I am sorry. No one ever wondered where I went before, as long as my work was done."

"Of course. But Cole, no one here is either servant or king. We are just companions trying to help each other survive. We will all need each other if we are to make it through."

* * *

Finally, as darkness descended over the island and a faint mist began to rise, the little clan wrapped up in their cloaks and lay down on their leather pieces, as close to the overhang of the rock face as they could comfortably get.

The overhang was the only shelter they had, for they had decided not to try to bring up the other curragh.

233

It was just too large and heavy to bring up in one piece, and even if they could manage the weight it would almost certainly be ripped and scraped against the sharp rocks. It remained where it was, weighted down by stones on the landing far below.

The wood pieces from the first boat's broken frame lay in the open so that the winds could dry them. There would be no fire tonight; the wood must be saved for emergency use. Cole's puffins had been thrown into the sea, for there was no way to cook them.

Muriel knew that she should go and lie down. She never remembered being so exhausted, so drained in every possible way. Yet she was still wide awake, her hands shaking as though she were actually too tired to make the effort to sleep.

She wrapped her still-damp, heavy blue cloak over her rough brown tunic and walked out towards the rocks at the far end of the ledge. Here, awaiting the rain along with the cups and the cauldron and the leather pieces, rested her water mirror.

The clouds were high this night, most of them light and fleet, and seemed to hold little promise of rain. Muriel looked out to the east. The mainland was there, though she could see nothing of it in the heavy darkness. When the clouds thinned and the stars broke through, she could just make out the white-coated peak of the Island of the Birds... but that was all.

Her empty bronze basin shone faintly by the starlight. Muriel started to reach out and touch it, but then drew her hand back and looked away.

She closed her eyes and told herself that she must go and lie down and try to sleep... there would be much to do tomorrow... but then she heard the sound of a footstep behind her.

Turning quickly, she saw that it was Brendan. Without a word she went to him, and the two of them held each other in the darkness at the edge of the world.

For a long time, neither of them spoke. The day had been so draining that they drew comfort and a measure of healing simply from standing and holding one another. Muriel wished she could remain so forever, feeling nothing but Brendan's strong arms around her and hearing nothing but his heartbeat... but eventually he drew back a little and looked down at her.

"It is so strange," he said, his voice sounding as though he were very far away. "I am angry with myself for allowing you to come to this place... yet I am so glad that you are here."

She smiled. "I told you that I will go wherever you go. I meant it. Now that we are here, we have to think of the future."

"Future?" He released her, and stepped back to lean against the mountain. "Look at them," he said, waving his hands towards the dark rock face, where all the others slept. "I know I promised you and Queen Grania that I would not allow myself to show any further regret. But how can I keep that promise when I look at the people in my care?

"A king is supposed to see that his people have food, and shelter, and protection from their enemies. My people have nothing but a handful of half-ruined food to eat. No shelter but a sheer cliff of rock. No fire at all.

"And as for protection?" Brendan just laughed. "At least they will be safe from enemies here, unless there is an enemy who is as mad as we are and tries to brave this impossible sea."

"We made this terrible journey to keep you safe and allow you to heal," said Muriel. "Did you think a king's life would be an easy one, with no testing and no hardship?"

"Perhaps I did," he whispered. "Always it was so easy for me... never a single doubt..."

He looked towards the rock face again. "If I were truly a leader, much less a king, I would not have allowed these fine men and women, whose only crime is misplaced loyalty, to be exiled here with me. Most of all, I would never have allowed you to suffer such a fate."

An edge of anger began to creep into Muriel's voice. It was the anger of frustration and exhaustion, and not a little fear. "Brendan! You still do not understand. If you have so little respect for me, and for these people who have come with you, as to think that we did so out of nothing but 'misplaced loyalty'– then perhaps you do deserve to be nothing but a servant."

He fell silent at that. She knew he was looking at her in the darkness. "I will tell you again, for the final time: None of us would have come here if we did not believe there was a future to be had with you– if we did not believe that you are, indeed, a king worth saving. So, Brendan, I suggest that you start behaving as a king should behave, for you now have eight people counting on you to do so. Our lives– our futures– depend on it."

He kept his silence for a time. For a moment she thought that he, too, was angry. But when he spoke again, his voice was as gentle as she had ever heard it.

"I do understand, my lady. I know what all of you believe. I will try with my last breath to live up to your belief. Yet there is one thing that a king must serve above all else, even above loyalty... and that is truth.

"Your doubts about my kingship were always the greatest. You were the one who turned out to be right.

Now we must all face the truth and see our situation for what it is: a dangerous, miserable exile, one which we will most likely never escape."

Muriel looked at him just as the clouds parted and a little starlight filtered through. He was very still, leaning back against the mountain, looking down at nothing. Beside him on the rocks sat the cups and the cauldron and the leather, all waiting for the rain... and sitting with them, like any other common household object, was her water mirror.

She turned away from the sight of the mirror and tried to look only at Brendan. "I am here because you are my husband. Because I love you. because I am bound to you. Where you go, I go. If I can help you, I will."

"Yet I can do nothing to help you." Bitterness rose up in his voice. "That is another truth for you, Lady Muriel.

"I thought to give you everything when I brought you to Dun Bochna. A fine big house, an endless supply of furs and fire, new linen and woolen clothes, the very best food, the most beautiful of all the gold ornaments to wear... and if there was anything else you desired, I had only to swing up on my horse and ride out to get it for you.

"But here I cannot even offer you a roof over your head. Here I can give you nothing."

"Here you can heal," Muriel insisted. "Here you will not be captured and held for ransom– or worse– by someone like Odhran. Here you will not be forced to live out your life as a servant."

"We are all servants here in this place," he muttered. "We are all slaves to the wind and to the sea and to starvation."

"We will find a way," she said quietly. "There is food here."

"Food? The raw flesh of birds?"

"The rain will bring us water."

"You will not have enough to bathe your feet. There are nine people here who must have enough to drink. And if you think to wash in the sea, it will be the last bath you ever take."

"We will find a way," she murmured again, and gazed at the dull shine of the bronze basin in the faint glow of the cloud-covered stars.

He took her by the shoulders and forced her to look at him. "Muriel! Listen to what you are saying! You should be angry that I have brought you here. You should be outraged that I have reduced you to eating bits of sea-soaked apple and sleeping on rocks beneath filth-covered cloaks! You should be fighting with all your strength, with all your power, to find a way out of here and be restored to the life you were born to– the life you deserve!"

She caught her breath and looked up at him, trying to resist the cold dread that she had held at bay for so long. "Perhaps what you say is true. I would have resisted... I would never have come to this place... would never have allowed *you* to come to this place... before..."

"Before what?"

"Before we were married."

They looked up at each other, their faces barely visible in the darkness. Muriel could feel only the pounding of her heart and hear only the roaring of the sea.

"You used your magic today to help us reach land," he said. "We would not have survived without you and your power over the sea."

She nodded slowly. "But what little I did manage took the last of my strength. It often leaves me weak, but every other time my power has quickly returned. This time it has not. I feel as empty as these wooden cups awaiting the rain... and I fear I will remain so."

He reached out and touched her bronze water mirror where it sat on the rock. "Look at this. It sits among the cups like any other thing you might find about your house... nothing special, nothing magical. Is this happening to you, as well? "You told me what would happen to you if you married a man who was not a king. You have done exactly that... and look at you now."

Brendan took a step forward. "Look there!" he said, pointing to the east. "The moon is rising. It is just past full. I will go and fetch some seawater to fill your water mirror. Will you use it? And if you do, what will you see?"

Slowly she raised both hands touched the sides of the basin. It felt cold and plain and ordinary, no different from any other plate or bowl or other common thing.

"Shall I fill it for you?" he pressed.

Muriel drew her hands away. "There is no need," she whispered.

"Why? Do you fear what you might see?"

"I do not."

"Then what are you afraid of?"

"I fear... that I will see nothing at all."

They both stood very still. Thick clouds obscured the last light of the rising moon so that deep

239

darkness fell over them. Then, slowly, with his head lowered, Brendan reached for her.

"Please," he whispered, and there was sorrow in his voice. "Come to me and let me hold you close while you hold on to me in return. The truth is a terrible thing sometimes, and this truth is the most terrible of all. I am a slave, not a king, and because of that you are now a woman married to a slave... and the wife of a slave has no magic. None at all."

He sighed deeply as she moved close and rested her head on his chest. "And yet, though we have lost everything else," Brendan whispered, "I find my love for you remains... though it rips my heart to know that I have nothing more in life to offer you than what I can give you here.

"I know it is not enough, dear Muriel. I know that you have lost far than I could ever make up for. Yet it is all I have, and I do not know what more any man can offer than all that he has."

Muriel could not find the strength to answer. She simply held her husband close and let her tears come through tightly closed eyes, while Brendan stroked her long dark hair and the sea tore at the foundations of the island far below.

* * *

Colum sat in the sunlit King's Hall, surrounded by his druids and a few of his warriors. He blinked several times, trying to keep his eyes open, for the afternoon was warm and the druids droned on about some small legal matter– something about who was owed what compensation for some minor annoyance– something about which Colum had not the slightest interest.

He shifted on his cushion in the rushes and tried to adjust the heavy tanist's torque around his neck, wondering how he would ever wear the king's torque when he found even this smaller one so heavy and uncomfortable.

The voice went on. "… one-third of the milk is to go to him for compensation, and one-third of the butter, and one-sixth of the–"

"Lorcan," Colum said, breaking into the recitation. "I have every confidence that you can determine the details of a fair compensation. Please send in the next case for me to hear."

The druid paused, a look of surprise and indignation crossing his face; but then he nodded to Colum, dismissed the complainant standing before him, and ordered the next one brought in.

Colum watched the man leave with two of the warriors, knowing they would bring in the next of many who waited outside for the king to heart their case. He thought longingly of his harp and of the poetry he had had to put aside until the long days of hearings were over.

He looked up as the two warriors walked back into the hall– alone. "Are there no more supplicants this day?" he asked, trying not to sound too hopeful.

"There are ten remaining, Prince Colum," said the first of the men. "But first I am to tell you that four riders from King Odhran's dun have arrived. They wish to speak to you. They–"

"Bring them inside," Colum immediately said. "Bring then in now."

The two warriors looked at each other and then glanced at the druids, clearly hesitating. "Now!" Colum insisted, and the two of them bowed to him and left the hall once again.

At least there would be a respite from these unspeakably boring recitations of the law. And he was curious as to why four of Odhran's men should wish to speak to him now.

Perhaps there truly was hope of making an alliance, something not even his father had attempted. Perhaps Odhran was willing to treat with Colum, where he would not with King Galvin!

Odhran's four men walked into the hall and stood before him. They were two warriors and two druids, and after nodding politely to Colum one of the druids stepped forward to speak.

"We greet you, Prince Colum, and send you a message from King Odhran. He wishes you and all of your men to know how very pleased he is that you are now the king of Dun Bochna."

Colum nodded to them in return. How was it that his father, and Brendan, had always thought these people to be so dangerous? They were certainly being most cordial to him now.

"We know that you and Odhran have never met face to face. We have come to see whether Odhran and a few of his most honored men might come to this hall to meet the new tanist– a tanist soon to be king– and provide you with a feast to celebrate Lughnasa."

Colum studied them, cocking his head and beginning to smile. "You would bring a feast?"

"We would. Lughnasa is the first harvest, the harvest of grain, and we will bring you bread and beer such as you have never seen."

One of the warriors took a step forward. "I am charged to tell you that it is Odhran's greatest wish to speak to you of an alliance between our two kingdoms."

"An alliance." Colum sat up tall, this time with a broad smile. "There is nothing I would like better than to make an alliance. The fighting has gone on long enough. If your king wishes to come to us at Lughnasa, tell him to come, for he is welcome."

The four men bowed to him and then left the King's Hall.

Colum sat back to relax, feeling very pleased and wanting to enjoy his triumph. But immediately his men and druids gathered around him and began speaking fast, one after the other.

"You intend to let Odhran and his men walk in here and sit down to a feast?"

"Odhran is not to be trusted. His word is no good!"

"He has proven that time and again!"

"Look at how your father dealt with him!"

"Look at how Brendan—"

Colum leaped to his feet. The tanist's torque bumped painfully against his collarbone. "My father and Brendan antagonized him with constant raids! It is no wonder Odhran is our enemy!"

He looked hard at all of them, knowing they would not dare argue with him. "Once I am king, things will be different. I will form an alliance with King Odhran. There will be peace between us. It will begin at the celebration of Lughnasa, on the very night of my kingmaking."

"But—"

"Enough!" He found it a pleasure to shout at the warriors and druids, and watch them do his bidding. "I

243

will spend some time with my harp now. The rest of this business can wait."

Colum went striding down the hall and headed out of the door to his home, not caring that his men all looked each other and shook their heads.

As king, he would be better than Brendan. Better than his father. He would show these warrior men that with a different way– Colum's way– Dun Bochna would know peace instead of constant petty war.

He could hardly wait for Lughnasa.

* * *

For nine lonely people, the entire world had been reduced to a wide, rough clearing on a mountaintop high above the ocean. They had fled to this place in an effort to keep one man alive– to protect him both from an evil king and from himself– but they had retreated to such a small and primitive corner that, at times, Muriel could only wonder if it would not have been better to take their chances on the mainland with Odhran.

But as the days went by, there was little time for such questions. There was far too much to do in the moment-by-moment effort to survive.

They soon found themselves divided up into three groups of three, the better to handle the many chores that must be done. Brendan, Killian, and Darragh became expert fishermen, using a net and hooks and crude lines to bring up endless supplies of cod and mackerel and pollack and wrasse, and even the occasional eel.

Muriel, Queen Grania, and the blind King Fallon stayed near the rock face and tended to food preparation and water collecting. Muriel because the tender of the newly caught fish, spending her days cleaning them and slicing them into thin strips and laying the strips out onto rocks doused with seawater. She would place stones on them so that the drying wind would not blow them away, and then constantly shift the stones to allow for thorough drying. And when she was not cleaning or slicing the fish she was chasing away the seabirds who thought they had found a ready feast.

Grania and Fallon would sit together to sew and repair the clothes and cloaks and fishing nets. Muriel was surprised to see how good Fallon was at sewing. His fine hands ran over the coarse stitches and instantly found any flaw.

Yet Muriel became increasingly concerned about Grania. The frail queen might have a spirit as tough as iron, but her body had less and less strength each day. Muriel saw how she struggled just to make her way from one side of the ledge to the other and how she shivered whenever she lay down to rest in the evenings.

"I will just stay here and listen to the sound of the waves," Grania would say. "The sea has been a part of my life ever since I went to live with my husband at Dun Camas. The sound reminds me of our life together there. It makes me feel happy to listen to it." Muriel could only smile at her and place the warmest of the cloaks snugly around her.

Gill, Duff, and Cole spent much of their time in the first days building a low wall at the edge of the cliff. It would give a little more protection from the east wind and– most important– help to keep anyone from accidentally getting too close to the fatal drop.

The three serving men were soon spending endless amounts of time in exploring as much of the steep and treacherous island as they could reach, often following the single path back down to the cove at the edge of the sea where the two curraghs had landed.

Each evening they would return with leather sacks bearing lengths of seaweed, precious bits of driftwood, small rocks to add to their protective wall, and even salt deposits carefully rubbed from depressions in the boulders where seawater had evaporated.

One of their most welcome finds was the occasion handful of a grass similar to watercress, whose thick heart-shaped leaves had a similar biting taste that went very well with the endless dried fish and water-soaked oats.

And when night fell, Brendan and Muriel would lie down close together on their leather pallet and cover up with all the cloaks they had, each one grateful for the warmth of the other in this cold, damp, and frighteningly barren place. Their greatest comfort here was the time spent alone in the mist-shrouded darkness, with the roar of the sea and the singing of the wind to grant them a measure of privacy.

Muriel would close her eyes and imagine she was back home with Brendan, safe and secure in their warm solid house with fur covers and straw-stuffed cushions to sleep on, and fresh hot bread and juicy roasted beef waiting for them on the hearth. She would pull him close in the darkness, their arms and legs entwined, and they would make love together for as long as they wished until the familiar sweet exhaustion set in… and then they would drift off to sleep in each other's arms, forgetting, for a little while, just where they really were.

A fortnight passed by… fourteen nights of a life far more difficult than any of them had ever imagined, except, perhaps, for Gill and Cole and Duff. They had suffered in ways that those of the nobility would never know. Yet even though the food was scant in this place and the work never ended, they were at least free men in a world that was entirely theirs.

Brendan, too, seemed to be growing stronger, with all the hard work to keep him occupied and moving forward. Muriel often heard him say that he would keep them all alive and get them home if it was the last thing he did in life.

But though Muriel, too, threw herself into the work so that they might all survive, she made no effort to use her magic. She never went down to the sea, never tried to call its creatures, never looked at her water mirror except to empty it of its rainwater as she did the cups and the cauldron.

Most of all, she tried not to think of how many nights must pass before the moon was full once more.

* * *

One evening, some thirty nights after their arrival, Brendan and his company gathered together around the welcome warmth of a small fire. The sun had just begun to set, leaving the group sitting in the shadow of the island peak above and gazing out at the sunlit mainland where the shadows lengthened across it.

As the days went, this one had gone fairly well. Though everyone had lost weight since the landing and grown thin and gaunt from the meager rations and hard work, they were not starving. Though their tunics and cloaks were ragged and worn, the efforts of Fallon and Grania kept them clothed. And though it was a lonely and isolated existence, they had grown to know each other well through the endless work that had to be done in cooperation each day.

On this night they had heaped up some of the driest of the driftwood and a few pieces of the broken currach frame, thrown on some dried seaweed and grasses, and managed to build a fire. All of the group sat as close to it as they dared, reveling in the heat and the glowing light.

Earlier in the day Cole had once again captured a couple of the slow puffins that made their nests among the rocks. He and Muriel had made short work of the newly killed birds and now, as the little fire crackled before them, they placed a cauldron full of water and sea salt and puffin pieces over the flames to boil.

It would be their first hot meal in many nights.

The late-summer evening was beautiful and warm and clear; the sea was as calm as it ever got; and once they finished eating, the little company sat together to talk for a time instead of just dropping into an exhausted sleep as they most often did. Muriel sat with her back to the east, knowing that soon the moon would rise.

She could not bring herself to look at it.

"So. I believe that tomorrow night the moon will be full," said Fallon, turning his head in Muriel's direction. "It will be the second full moon since the summer solstice. That means that this full moon marks Lughnasa. Am I correct, my lady Muriel?"

She smiled, knowing that he would sense her expression even if he could not see it. "You are, King Fallon. Tomorrow is Lughnasa. But I am afraid there will not be much of a grain harvest or a feast to celebrate it, nor a great bonfire to mark it, out here on this island."

"Then we shall have to find another way to honor this time of year." Fallon stood up, keeping one hand against the cliff wall, and faced the soft wind blowing in from the mainland. "I propose that we do so by making a decision."

248

"A decision?" she answered. "What decision is that?"

"I think it is time to ask: Has the time come for us to return to the mainland? Have we been gone long enough for Odhran to believe that Brendan is dead or escaped, and therefore no longer searches for him? Or should we wait as long as we can, to make certain our terrible ordeal will not have been in vain?"

The group glanced at one another. "The druids said we must return by the autumn equinox," said Killian. "Tomorrow night is Lughnasa. That means two fortnights more until the equinox."

"But the longer we stay, the rougher the seas become," said Darragh. "The equinox might well be far too late, especially with nine people in just one curragh."

"We might have to make more than one journey," Muriel said. "Though I dread to think of who would have to stay behind."

Gill raised his head. "If the danger from Odhran were truly past, would not someone have tried to come out here and tell you it was safe to return?"

"That seems likely," Darragh said. "They would not have to land. We could see them well out at sea, from this height. But we have seen no one."

"Yet they might not have come for fear of leading Odhran's men to us," said Killian.

Fallon nodded. "It is a dilemma. Do we dare return and risk finding Odhran waiting when we do? Or do we dare stay here longer, and risk starvation and cold and shipwreck?"

All of them were silent. "Brendan, you should take pride in what you have accomplished," Fallon continued. "We are your people. We have followed you by choice. You have kept us alive and safe in a place

249

that offers almost nothing. And I have not failed to notice that your spirit has grown stronger in the process, no matter how thin your body or how ragged your cloak."

"I thank you, King Fallon," Brendan answered, in a soft voice. "I, too, am happy that all of us are alive and here together. Yet it hurts me to see how thin you all have grown, how ragged your own garments have become."

Fallon nodded. "This island has been a retreat, but a harsh one. It was a refuge to preserve the life of a good and loyal man. But now, with the full moon of Lughnasa tomorrow, a decision must be made: Will we stay and risk the winter? Or will we leave and risk the journey home?"

They all turned to glance at each other. Muriel saw the pale, gaunt faces around her, and it seemed that the warm evening breeze suddenly held a chill as if in warning of what the winter in this place would be like. She drew her worn blue cloak a little closer ,and then looked at Brendan.

"We must go back," he said. "I know very well that we must go back and we must go soon. No matter the risk to me, we cannot stay here for the winter."

"I agree that it is difficult enough to survive here now, in the mildest weather," said Fallon. "The winter would likely prove to be our undoing. Yet I believe that you must make this decision."

The old king moved forward a few steps, keeping his hand on the rock face as he did. "What do your people think? It is important to know that. What will they do if we return?"

Glances flicked from one person to another. Eventually, Darragh was the one who spoke.

"My home has always been at Dun Bochna," he said. "I have served its king since I was old enough to lift a sword. And there is a woman there who waits for me."

He looked over at Brendan. "I will do all I can to help you, wherever you take us. Though I will not deny that I wish it were home."

Killian, sitting beside him, simply nodded. "Darragh speaks exactly as I would have."

Gill sat between Duff and Cole. He looked first at Muriel and then at his son. "Slaves never have a choice of where they go... but I am beginning to understand that my slavery is past. Of my own free will, I would go with you and help you in every way."

He raised his head and spoke to the rest of the group. "And I would do that for him even if he were not my son."

Duff and Cole glanced at each other. "Our lives, too, are with Brendan," said Cole, and Duff nodded in agreement.

King Fallon turned to Muriel. "There is no question of what I will do," she said. "I am with my husband. I will stay with him no matter where he goes."

All of them looked to Brendan. Silence descended, broken only by the ceaseless crashing of the sea and the warm crackling of the group's little fire.

Brendan stood up and walked a few steps towards the rock face, placing one hand upon the stone and then leaning his forehead against it. "You have all pledged your loyalty to me," he said, into the deep shadow cast by the island's towering peak. "So now I must choose what we will do."

"What are your choices?" asked the old king.

Brendan took another few slow steps across the little campsite. "I can stay here and truly be a king– the king of nothing at all," he said, with a small and bitter laugh. "I can be the king of this terrible place, with trapped and suffering subjects. We can stay here until we all perish from the boredom, or from starvation… or until a raiding party from Odhran's kingdom finally learns where we are and comes to finish me off. And what would happen to all of you then?

There was silence. "Or, we could risk putting nine people in a small curragh and take our chances on the sea, just as we did when we first set out for this place."

Fallon stared at him with unseeing eyes. "So, Brendan. What will you choose?"

Muriel could hear him breathe deeply of the night air. "I have only one choice. I will do the only thing I can even think of doing."

He turned to face the seven people who listened to him now. "I am no true-born king… but no true-born king ever had better friends than these, or a father so steadfast, or a wife of such beauty… beauty matched only by her loyalty."

Brendan raised his head. "I will return to the mainland. There I will leave you to your lives at Dun Bochna. I will go with my wife to Dun Farraige, there to serve as a craftsman or a herdsman for the rest of my days."

He tried to smile. "Perhaps Odhran would not bother with me if he knew I truly was no king any longer, but merely another servant… a man who spends his life hammering out weapons instead of using them, or following the cows with a herding switch instead of taking them in bold and praiseworthy raids."

Brendan managed a small laugh. "I am sure he would find great amusement in leaving me alive so he could watch the arrogant, troublemaking prince reduced to such a station in life."

"Yet a life it would be," Fallon answered. "And you could take satisfaction in knowing you had improved the lives of many, including your own father. You would know that your wife is loved and cherished and protected and that she never doubts that you will be with her always."

Brendan nodded. After a moment he slowly walked over to where Muriel sat on the damp and mossy ground, and knelt down in front of her. "I must live the rest of my life without kingship," he said. "If you remain with me, you will live the rest of your life without magic. Are you sure that that is your wish?"

Muriel reached for his hands. "There are things other than power," she said. "My decision was made before we ever came to this place."

"But was it really your decision? Or are you simply going the way of your sisters, with little of your strength of will left to you?"

She shook her head. "If anything can take the place of kingship and magic, it is love. And none can say that we do not have that."

He pulled her close and they embraced. The wind picked up and whirled around them.

"In the morning, then," King Fallon said. "In the morning, all of you will return to the mainland and begin your lives anew."

* * *

In the morning Queen Grania was dead.

When Muriel sat up on her makeshift pallet, the first thing she saw was King Galvin sitting against the high rock face. Beside him, her head resting on his shoulder, was Grania.

Muriel got up and walked over to them. It seemed strange that they would be sitting so; usually they were the first ones awake, with Grania sorting through the food supplies and Fallon moving step by step along the mountainside and feeling for any grasses or plants that could be harvested for food or dried for tinder.

But this time both were still.

As Muriel reached them, Fallon turned his head in her direction. "Good morning, Lady Muriel," he whispered. Though his words were polite, as they always were, she could hear a tremor in them. "I am sorry to tell you that Queen Grania has died in the night." Gently he stroked his wife's silvery hair and rested his cheek against her head.

Muriel crouched down in front of them. She could see that Fallon was right. The woman's face was pale and still. Her eyes were closed and her hands had fallen limp to the mossy ground.

"I am sorry, King Fallon. She was so brave here in this terrible place, with so few of the comforts to which she must always have been accustomed. She thought only to help and comfort me, and all of us."

Slowly Muriel stood up, though deep sadness had settled over her. "I knew her for such a short time. Yet I mourn her passing as though she had been with me far longer. I can only imagine how empty your own heart must be right now."

Fallon lifted one hand and Muriel reached out to take it. "Thank you for your kindness," he said. "If you will tell the others– tell Brendan– so that we might prepare her–"

"Of course I will." Briefly she covered his hand with her own, and then she stood up. Just as she turned to go, she saw Fallon kiss his wife one last time and bury his face in her neck. His shoulders trembled as he wept, but that was all; Muriel realized that with his ruined eyes he could not shed a tear, not even for his beloved queen.

* * *

As best they could, the little group prepared Grania for her final journey. It was decided not to bury her in the shallow soil of the island, with its many scavenging birds. Once she had been laid out on her cloak, with her long silver hair combed out smooth and gathered over one shoulder, they pinned the heavy wool fabric tightly around the body. Then Brendan and Darragh lifted her up onto their shoulders and started down the path to the sea with Killian, Duff, Gill, and Cole following close after them.

Muriel remained above with Fallon. Both stood quietly not from the low wall at the cliff's edge. "You will tell me when they have completed their task, won't you, Lady Muriel?" the king asked, standing close beside her and holding her arm.

"I will tell you," she answered. The winds picked up and whipped their cloaks around them. "And... I am so sorry we could not give her a proper interment."

Gently he touched her arm. "Do not be sorry. She has always loved the sea. Now it will be her home forever."

As she and Fallon stood waiting for the others to return, Muriel glanced up to look at the sky. Above the peak of the island she could see the edges of clouds gathering. There would be another rainstorm soon.

If it came before they departed, it would provide them with a little more drinking water... and they should certainly fill their waterskins to the limit if they could. The men would have hard work ahead of them to paddle the curragh back to the mainland, and would need fresh water. And if they should have trouble finding a safe place to land and have to stay out on the sea, the group would need all the water they could carry.

They would be wise to take food, too, though it was just as well that there was not much to take. The single remaining curragh would already be overloaded with eight people inside.

Muriel could only hope that departing the island would be easier than their arrival had been. At least this time they would be going away from the rocks, and not towards them. If they could just get the boat away from the treacherous waves breaking against the steep sides of the island, they could ride the currents and an incoming tide all the way back to the mainland.

A howling gust of wind grabbed at her, forcing Muriel to take a step forward to catch her balance. Fallon turned his face towards the cliff behind him. "A good storm is coming."

Muriel saw that the clouds were thicker and darker now, gathering behind the island. "It is. I hope it does not linger and delay our leaving. I would not like to be on those waves past sunset."

"Nor would I." The old king turned his head to stare sightlessly at the sea. Then he raised his head and Muriel felt him tense. "Brendan and his men have finished their task," he whispered.

She looked out to the ocean, where the waves grew higher and higher, and saw the brief shine of something on the water.

Looking closer, she saw that it was the gleam of a golden brooch that fastened a cloak around the body of a queen... a body now sweeping past them in the grip of the stormy sea.

Muriel nodded slightly. "They have finished," she confirmed, and Fallon bowed his head.

As he did, the wind struck again harder than ever. It went whipping around the ledge and sent the entire group's cloaks and leather sleeping pallets flying and whirling around the campsite.

"Oh! Wait here," Muriel cried, and left Fallon's side to chase down the blowing things before they went flying off into the sea.

In a moment she had everything secured beneath heavy rocks, but the wind continued to grow more violent. Just as she returned to Fallon, a torrent of rain lashed down on them both.

She caught the old king's arm and tried to lead him away from the edge, but he stood immovable. "Please tell me. Is she gone? Is it finished? Has the sea taken her?"

Muriel pushed her wind-whipped hair out of her face and wiped the rain out of her eyes with her sleeve. Looking out over the cliff through the grey curtain of rainfall, she saw nothing but the heavy white-capped waves rising to enormous heights before crashing back down to the sea.

"It is over," she said. "Please, now. Come with me. The men will be back soon. Come with me to wait for them. We'll find a little shelter against the rock face."

For many moments King Fallon remained unmoving; but at last he gave in and allowed Muriel to lead him through the pouring rain and back to the rock face. There he sat down in silence, ignoring the storm that tore at his long iron-grey hair and ragged woolen cloak, and turned away from the roaring sea below.

After what seemed like a very long time, Muriel heard a clamor coming up the long and treacherous path from the landing. Pulling her cloak tightly around her, bending low against the howling wind and cold rain, she struggled to her feet and went to meet Brendan and the five others.

The men appeared at the top of the path, all of them drenched to the bone and cold and pale and exhausted... none more than Brendan.

"It is done," he said, moving close. "We gave Queen Grania to the sea. The sea took her."

"I saw," Muriel told him, and then looked up at King Fallon. "We both saw."

Brendan glanced at Fallon, and nodded. "I know you did."

The rain and wind lashed down even harder. "It's the worst I've seen out here!" Muriel cried, as the three of them hurried back to the scant shelter of their campsite.

"It is," Brendan agreed, as the three of them sat down against the rock face. "We could see the western horizon from the landing. It is a wall of black cloud. There will be no leaving today."

Muriel could only lean her head against Brendan's shoulder and close her eyes tight against the rain. "I am glad," she whispered.

"Glad?" he asked. "I would think you would be dismayed at the thought of being forced to stay here for yet another day. How can you be glad?"

"Because... now there will be one more day when we can stay alive and stay together."

His arms tightened around her. Yet in her mind was another reason why she felt relief. This was one more day in which she would not have to face the sea, in which she would not have to learn whether it would respond to her ever again.

Another day where she would not have to learn whether she still any power of magic at all.

After a time, Muriel opened her eyes... but the first thing she saw was her water mirror, sitting high on a rock and overflowing with rain. She closed her eyes once more.

* * *

All day, the storm raged. Brendan and Muriel and their six companions stayed huddled against the rock face, eating the last of their dried fish and watching the storm as it raged against the sea. It swallowed up the mainland and soon even the Island of the Birds vanished into the heavy cloud cover.

Finally, not long before the sun was due to set, the wind began to lessen. The rain slowed until it became a mere sprinkling. The sky lightened to a softer grey and they could once again see the Island of the Birds, though the mainland was still obscured.

Somewhere out there, the body of a queen had been taken by the sea. Muriel was powerfully reminded of her own ancestor, of that nameless woman who had also given herself to the waves. But while that sacrifice had been futile, Muriel felt only awe that Grania had chosen to live her last days helping two kings.

Both of those kings had lost their kingdoms through no fault of their own. One had been Grania's own husband, who would never have left her behind at Dun Bochna to come out here with Brendan. By being willing to go with him, Grania had allowed Fallon to

259

have a purpose in life again: helping another displaced king find his way back to life.

A sacrifice it had been… but Muriel would do all she could to see that it was not wasted.

The company stirred, getting slowly to their feet, and did what they could to begin to dry their clothes and shake the water from their belongings. But they quickly found that the clearing sky was accompanied by air as cold as winter.

As Muriel moved about the campsite, with the light fading into dusk, she noticed that a mist was rising from the wet ground at her feet. Slowly and steadily it rose from the crevices among the rocks, from every place where there was earth enough to grow a bit of grass or moss.

It began to flow down the rocks and weave its way about the ledge. Soon the island was entirely covered in the cold white fog, which continue to rise and weave and move slowly all about them as twilight fell and covered everything in silent darkness.

* * *

On the ledge high above the sea, voices floated through the mist-heavy night.

"Lady Muriel," said King Fallon. "Soon we will leave this place and try for the mainland."

"Soon," she repeated, her voice low.

"I know very well that your bond with the sea allowed us to land here those many nights ago," Fallon went on.

"It was hardly enough, but I was glad I could offer even that much."

"I also know that you have made no effort to use any of your powers since then."

Brendan turned towards him. "Did my wife not tell you of the curse that rests on the women of her family? That those who marry any man but a king are doomed to lose their power of magic, and walk through life as a grey and fragile shell?"

"She spoke of it to Grania. Grania whispered it to me."

"The power I had was over the sea," Muriel said. "there has been no reason for me to try it while we are up here."

"Your water mirror holds nothing but rain," the old king answered.

"The moon has been hidden behind the clouds."

"Tonight it will be full."

"The mist–"

"Blinds you?" Fallon stepped closer. "Do you believe that because I am blind, I can no longer see? Listen to me, Lady Muriel. When Odhran took my sight, I thought I had become weak and helpless. I thought I was a man with no further reason to live, for he had lost all of his power.

"But Grania soon taught me that far worse than losing the power of sight was the fear I had of doing without it." Fallon motioned emphatically. "I had not become powerless because I was blind. I was powerless because I was afraid.

"Two things take away power: force and fear."

Muriel stared at him, her breath coming quickly. "King Fallon… I thank you for your wisdom. But I believe our situations are far different. Your blindness came from an enemy's treachery. Mine is… mine is from…"

"Lady Muriel," the old king said. "These women of your family whose lives became so empty: Did any of

261

them try to use their powers once they married? Or did they simply *fear* that they could not, and so they never tried at all?"

She started to speak, and then paused. "In truth, I do not know," she admitted. "I know only that my sisters became like two who hardly knew they were alive at all, much less that they could wield any power of magic. I do not believe they ever again tried to do so."

"Then you are wrong about why their magic left them," said Fallon. "My wife and I spoke of this at length. It was not because of the men they married. She and I both reached the same conclusion. Their magic was gone because they *feared* it was gone. The presence of that fear and doubt was, in itself, enough to drive their powers away.

"The women of your family were not cursed with being powerless. It is clear to me that they were cursed with fear. Nothing leads to being powerless like fear. They, too, were blind, as blind as Odhran left me, as blind as you believe you are when the rising mist shuts out the moon."

One step at a time, Fallon walked across the mossy, rocky ledge until he stood directly in front of Muriel. "Sometimes, you must be willing to walk headlong into the mist and test yourself. You must be willing to trust your inner sight even while outwardly blind. You may be surprised to find that your spirit will rise up even stronger each time you do so.

"There are other battles than those that come on horseback to steal your cattle. A spirit of the sword is one sort of power. A spirit of the mist is quite another."

All of them sat in silence for a time. The fog continued to move and weave around them, as if the cold breath of the sea had risen up from far below to envelop them and hold them prisoner. It only grew thicker and colder as they waited.

"It is a mist that holds us captive now, King Fallon," Brendan said at last. "I have never seen any so heavy, so thick, so white."

"Each of us will walk out of the mist when it is time to do so," said Fallon. "When it is your time, you will know." He took one more step towards Muriel, and reached out to touch her sleeve.

"I thank you all for honoring Queen Grania this day. I will go now and rest for a time, and remember her in my own way." He bent down and placed gentle hands on either side of Muriel's face, and then kissed her forehead. "Do not fear the mist, Lady Muriel."

Next he moved to Brendan and touched his shoulder. "Let no man tell you what you are." Brendan returned the gesture, placing his own hand briefly atop the old king's arm.

Then Fallon turned and walked away towards the center of the little campsite, soon disappearing into the thick white fog.

* * *

The weariness of the day hung heavy on Muriel. She leaned her head on Brendan's shoulder and closed her eyes, trying to think of nothing else but the strength of his arms around her and the warmth of his skin against her cheek... and trying to shut out the sight of the unnerving, all-encompassing white mist.

Yet sleep stayed with her for only a short white. She awoke with a start to find that it was still night.

Brendan was deep in slumber, his breathing slow and regular. Though she wanted nothing more than his company right now, she knew the exhaustion that must weight upon him. He would need all of his strength, as would the rest of the men, if they were to row the curragh away from the treacherous waves of this island and get it safely back to the mainland.

She eased herself upright, taking care not to disturb him. He shifted a bit but remained asleep, his golden brown hair shining in the moonlight.

Moonlight.

Muriel turned and saw the entire wide ledge of the campsite, the sea glistening beyond it, and the blackness of the mainland all lit by the moon... the enormous white moon shining high in the dark night sky.

The mist was gone. There was only the clearest sky, and the brightest moon, that she had ever seen.

Its light showed her the outlines of six men lying asleep at the base of the rock wall.

Six men. One was missing.

Fallon.

The old king had kissed her on the forehead, spoken to Brendan, and then stepped off into the mist. He knew the layout of their camp very well and had never strayed beyond the ankle-high wall of loose stones that Cole and Duff had piled just inside the precipitous drop.

Muriel had assumed that Fallon had gone for a little water after talking for so long, and then would make his way back to his pallet to lie down and sleep. Indeed, she had dropped off to sleep herself almost as soon as she had watched him go.

But now there was no sign of him.

I will go now and rest for a time, and remember her in my own way.

Slowly Muriel walked to the low stone wall, and then carefully stepped over it so that she stood on the very edge of the island. Remaining very still, looking down only with her eyes, she watched the waves lashing and breaking in moonlit whitecaps as the tide rolled out far below... and realized that there was a small, dark figure washing back and forth against the rocks.

Then the outgoing tide lifted the figure up off of the rocks and bore it away on a high white wave, with a faint gleam of gold in the moonlight before it was gone.

"Farewell to you, King Fallon," Muriel whispered. "Your work is finished here. Join your beloved queen in the Otherworld, and take our love for her with you."

Muriel stood for a long while at the edge of that terrifying drop. Then she took one step backward, and then another, until her cold, wet boots touched the low stone wall. Quickly she stepped over the wall and hurried back to the safety of the campsite.

Her water mirror sat on the boulders where it had been since the time of their arrival. Its shining surface, brimming with rainwater, gleamed in the light of the high white moon.

She closed her eyes and turned her face away from the sight of the bronze basin. So many times she had touched her fingers to the cool surface of the water within. So many times she had seen strange and beautiful and impossible things as easily as she saw the sun rise over the land and set again over the sea. Never had that power failed her, and she had come to take it for granted.

But no more.

It did seem to her that she had expended the very last of her magic in her efforts to bring the two curraghs to a safe landing on this island. Those terrible waves had calmed in response to her touch and her words, and all nine people had survived. But the moment she lifted her hands from the sea, she had felt empty and drained. It was as though her powers had drained away with the water that ran from her fingertips.

It was true that in the past, the magic had its limits. Using it had often left her feeling drained, but always that feeling had only been temporary… the way a runner might tire briefly but then come back stronger for the effort.

This was different. This was the cold and empty feeling of power lost, never to return.

Yet she could not help opening her eyes and looking towards the rocks again. Her water mirror still sat shining in the moonlight, as beautiful as it had ever been.

As the wind from the sea passed over it, she seemed to hear it singing as it sometimes did… drawing her closer… causing her to walk slowly, slowly, one step at a time, until she was standing before the mirror and gazing down at the shining surface of the water within.

Behind it lay the magnificent view of the darkly glowing mainland and the glistening moonlit sea.

The faint singing continued. She could hear it as she raised her hands, spread her fingers, and slowly lowered them to touch the cool water.

The singing stopped.

Muriel felt that her heart would stop as well. She peered down at the dark surface, but saw only the white disk of the reflected moon… and nothing more.

She took a deep breath, raised her fingers, and placed them in the water again. As before she saw only the moon, but now the image wavered as her hands began to tremble.

Snatching her hands from the mirror, Muriel turned away from it… turned away from both the mirror and from the magnificent view of the world where she had once lived… a world from which she was now exiled. Neither could she look at the water mirror and the magic it represented, for that, too, was a world from which she was surely shut out forever.

There seemed to be nothing left but this small and terrible island. Muriel knew that if she no longer had the power to calm the waves or call the creatures of the sea to help her, this might well be their home for the rest of their days.

* * *

There were footsteps approaching. Muriel looked up to see Brendan standing there, his face somber in the moonlight but his eyes full of concern for her.

"Muriel," he said, throwing his rough, dark cloak back over his shoulder. "What is it? What has happened?"

She looked up and started to answer, but could not. Instead, she stepped aside to let him see the water mirror sitting on the rock.

"Oh…" Brendan walked over and placed his hands on the rock on either side of the bronze basin. "It is a thing of beauty," he murmured. "And I have not forgotten what King Fallon said. Do you fear to try the mirror? You must not. You will–"

Placing a shaking hand on his arm, she stopped his words. "Brendan… first I must tell you something. I must tell you that King Fallon has spared us all witnessing his death."

He frowned. "Spared us? What do you mean?"

She took a deep breath. "When he spoke to us this evening, his final words were of Grania… of how he

267

wished to go and remember her in his own way. Then we saw him walk into the mist. I thought he was only going to get a little water before sleep. But the truth is, he continued to walk across the campsite and across the stone border and out to the ledge... and now he has joined his queen."

Brendan closed his eyes. "I should have known. I should have stopped him."

Gently she held his arm, and then withdrew her hand. "None of us could have stopped him. Not for long. Not forever. It was his wish."

"He was a great help to me, and to us all, in this place. He did not deserve such an end."

"His life was more important than his death. And it was a very good life, wasn't it?"

Brendan smiled, his face clearly visible in the bright moonlight. "It was. And even now, I remember what he said to you. To both of us. You must try the mirror, Muriel. I will leave you alone with it if you wish, but try it you must."

She stepped away from him. "I did try the mirror."

"You did? What happened? What did you see?"

"I saw... I saw the thing I feared most to see. I saw nothing."

"Nothing..." Brendan turned back to the mirror, reached out with one finger, and lightly touched its edge. The clear water wavered at the brim.

Brendan studied the water closely and then tasted the clear drop on his finger. "This is rainwater, sweet and pure. Did you not tell me that your mirror required water from the sea?"

"It was made so," she said faintly. "But I still should have seen something. I should have felt something. The moon has never been so powerful as it is tonight."

Brendan touched the beautifully etched waves and leaping dolphins that covered the sides of the bronze mirror. "This is an instrument of the sea," he said. "Wait here."

He caught up one of the small leather waterskins and raced across the campsite, allowing the precious contents to pour out as he ran, and then disappeared down the path that led to the sea.

* * *

Muriel waited in the moonlight for him to return. She tried not to think about Brendan going down that slippery, treacherous path in the darkness, hurrying over the broken rocks and creeping past the sheer drops along the edges of this island.

This same sea had claimed Galvin and Grania and Fallon, and had tried to claim Brendan on the night she had found him– a night that now seemed very long ago. She had saved him then, but could not hope to do so now. All she could do was wait for him to return.

* * *

The moon had moved only a little through the sky when Brendan reappeared, with the leather skin filled with seawater over his shoulder. The instant she saw him, Muriel was relieved that he had returned safely; yet she also felt a renewed stab of cold apprehension, for now she had no choice but to try her magic yet again. This time, she would have no excuse if it failed.

"Here," her husband said, a little breathless. Muriel knew he must have fairly run all the way. "Here is what you need."

269

She took the leather sack from him and held it close to her heart, stepping back a pace as Brendan lifted the bronze basin and flung the rainwater to the winds. With great care he placed the basin back on the boulders and turned to look at her. "Now. Fill it with the water from the sea."

There was no turning away from it now. Slowly Muriel walked to the rock, lifted the sack, and emptied the cloudy salt water into the bronze dish. Setting down the leather bag, she stood watching the mirror and waiting for the water to quiet and be still– and then, in one swift move, she closed her eyes and plunged her hands into the seawater.

At first it was just cold, as the rainwater had been before. But where the rainwater had been smooth and clear and empty, the water from the sea roiled and swirled with the dissolved metals and salts and very life forces of the creatures that lived within it.

As she stood with her fingers in the mirror, Muriel began to feel its life and power through her hands and her arms and all the way to her heart.

She opened her eyes.

Now she looked down at the shining surface of the water and saw the place that was uppermost in her thoughts: Dun Bochna. This was the fortress across the water, the place where she had thought to make a home with Brendan and rule beside him as his queen.

In the mirror she saw a great fire blaze into life on the cliff, beside the stone walls of the fortress. It was a bonfire consuming a huge stack of wood, with people leaping and dancing and celebrating beside it.

"The Lughnasa fire," said Brendan.

Muriel glanced up. He stood a few steps away with his back to her, gazing out across the sea. There was a fire visible on the mainland, though it was just a spot of orange light from here.

It was the same sight that the mirror showed her. Muriel felt something like relief, something like returning confidence. This vision was not her imagination. The mirror was indeed showing her what was happening right now at Dun Bochna.

"Your magic has returned?"

"It never left me."

Muriel felt the truth of the statement. Fallon had been right. It had been her own fear holding her back all this time. She looked down at the mirror again, tensing her fingers, willing all the power she possessed to reach into the water and show her all there was to see.

"King Colum," she whispered. "Show me the king." Then she caught her breath as the images began to change.

Now she saw the inside of the King's Hall, filled with happy revelers at the great harvest festival of Lughnasa. The place was brightly lit with torches and lamps, and it was filled with music from harps and drums and with the laughter and shouting of brightly dressed men and women. All of them sat together at the feasting boards, enjoying the fresh hot breads and cakes made from the newly harvested grains.

There was King Colum, young and smooth-faced, sitting beside an older, sharp-jawed man with long hair of iron grey and piercing, narrow eyes.

"What is Colum thinking?" she heard Brendan whisper. He stood beside her now, gazing into the mirror just as she did. "How could he invite Odhran into our fortress walls? Would he invite a vicious dog into a pen with sheep?"

Muriel caught her breath at realizing that Brendan could see the images, too. She had never heard of any such thing happening before. Only a mistress of the water mirror could see its messages… until now.

It was no small bond that she and Brendan shared.

Odhran reached out to clasp Colum's wrist. They saw Colum accept a flat gold cup from the other king, who then picked up his own cup. Both men drank deeply. "Now we are allies," Odhran said with a smile. Colum nodded and looked somewhat relieved, but there was still apprehension in his eyes. He took another drink from his goblet.

"Allies?" said Brendan, through clenched teeth. "There is no such thing as being the ally of a beast. How could Colum do this?"

"Colum has not one attribute of a king," Muriel said, "except his father's face." Together they stared at the images in the mirror, held by the ominous story unfolding before them..

The feasting and reveling continued but Colum remained subdued. He set down his cup and stared at the plates before him, seeming oblivious to the noise and color around him. Slowly his head lowered and his shoulders rocked forward, until he pitched face down onto the table. Odhran slapped him on the back and then went on talking and laughing with his men.

"He brings an enemy like Odhran into his house and then spends the whole night drunk on wine," said Brendan, with clear contempt. "Perhaps it was the only way he could find courage."

"That is not wine you are seeing," Muriel said. "Look closer."

Colum lay still as death on the furs. A thin line of saliva ran from one corner of his mouth. His eyes were half open, but saw nothing.

One of his own men, the druid Lorcan, sat beside him. After a time the druid thought to have a second look at his king, who lay unmoving among the laughing revelers. He leaned over and peered closely at the younger man, and at first seemed to think that Colum had merely fallen asleep at the feasting boards. Most of the men in the hall would end up thus; but it was early yet, and the king was not normally the first to fall.

"Poison," whispered Brendan. "Odhran has poisoned him."

The druid, getting no response from Colum, rolled him onto his back. One look at the king's face told him all he needed to know.

He cried out. The men of Dun Bochna leaped to their feet and crowded around their king. There was a short, tension-filled silence– and then the King's Hall erupted with shouting and rage and the ringing sound of weapons being drawn.

The feast was forgotten as the warriors of Colum and the warriors of Odhran brought the battle to each other within the bright confines of Dun Bochna's hall.

The images wavered and disappeared. Muriel lifted her fingers from the water and rested her hands on the stone on either side of the basin, hanging her head and breathing deeply of the cool night air.

"The have killed him!" raged Brendan. "He invited them in, a little lamb thinking to make friends with the vicious dog. And the dog killed him! Not even in battle. Not even with a chance to defend himself or send a champion. The cowards fed him poison and he

273

was dead before anyone even knew what had happened!"

He paced across the moon-bright ledge. "How could his men have allowed this? How could they allow Odhran and his men to gather inside the hall like friendly cousins at the feast?"

"Colum was the king," Muriel said. "If he so ordered, they would support it– whether they liked it or not."

"I would not have let Odhran step within a day's ride of Dun Bochna," Brendan said. "You were right when you said Colum was no king. He was a solemn, gentle man who should have been left to his harp and his poetry."

He looked down, his mouth tight and his fists clenched. "This is my fault. If I had been there, this would never have happened."

Muriel straightened and turned to watch him as he continued to pace. "You must not blame yourself. You would never have left Dun Bochna had you any choice."

"I did have a choice. I did leave it. And now Colum is dead and Odhran battles the men who once served Galvin, who once served me. And I can do nothing to stop him."

He turned away from the sight of the mainland and shut his eyes, his fists clenched in anger and frustration. "Once I had a title, but no right to perform a king's duties," he whispered. "Now I have no title… but I cannot turn away from the duty, whether the people there ask it of me or not."

Muriel went to him, reaching out and trying to take him in her arms; but he did not respond. He stood rigid, trembling with rage, his breathing ragged and his face turned away from her.

"Brendan, look at me, please," she said, taking hold of his arm and trying to turn him. "In the morning, we will return. We will offer what help we can."

"In the morning it will be far too late. We can only hope that the king's men can defend their fortress and not fall to the treachery of a man like Odhran."

Taking hold of his hands, Muriel leaned her head against his shoulder. At last he raised his arms to hold her. With a sigh of relief she took comfort simply from standing in his strong embrace once more… and then, as she looked up at him, she caught sight of the mainland.

Her eyes went wide with horror.

* * *

"Darragh! Killian! Wake up! We are leaving. We are leaving now!"

Brendan moved across the moonlit campsite with determined strides, shouting into the night in a determined effort to rouse his companions. Muriel hurried after him, trying to catch his arm and make him listen to her.

"You cannot hope to return tonight! The journey is all but impossible in the light of day. it is certain death to try it in darkness!"

"A brighter night I have never seen. The sea is calm and the sky is clear. There could be no better time. *Darragh! Killian!*

The men were finally sitting up now, and rising slowly to their feet at the base of the rock face. "What is it?" Killian finally asked.

"We're leaving. Now!"

"Leaving? Why would we–"

Brendan grabbed Killian by the shoulder and turned him to face the mainland. "Look!"

The entire group stopped talking and looked. For a moment there was only a stunned silence among them… and then everyone began talking at once.

"What's happened?"

"What is burning on the mainland?"

"That's too big to be just the Lughnasa fire."

"It looks like the whole of Dun Bochna is ablaze!"

"It is," said Brendan. "We've got to go now. there will be no reason to go later. Colum is dead of poison and Odhran now battles for the dun. We can only imagine what other evils Odhran and his men have done. There is no one to help them but us."

"I am not sure what we can do," Darragh said. He stared out at the spreading spots of bright orange flames that were easily seen even from so far away. "We are seven men. We have two swords and two daggers."

"Seven men?" asked Gill, and then looked around. "Where is King Fallon?"

Muriel turned to him. "King Fallon has joined his queen," she said. "They are together now in the Otherworld, and at peace."

The men looked at each other. "Then I am glad for them," said Gill.

Brendan moved to the water supply and carried two of the leather waterskins to a flat spot at the start of the path. "If you are with me, then get your cloaks and come to the boat. Gill, stay here with the Lady Muriel. I will return for you as soon as it is safe."

"You will not return." Muriel dropped her empty bronze water mirror into a leather sack and closed it tight. "At least, not for me. I cannot speak for the others,

276

but I have no intention of staying here and watching you travel away without me."

"We will have seven people in one tiny curragh," Brendan answered, "trying to make a crossing in the dark and not knowing what might be waiting even if we do reach the shore. I do not know which is worse– to have you go or to have you stay– but at this moment, the thought of you making the crossing and then facing the battle to come leaves me cold with fear for you."

"The time is long past when you could afford to fear for me, Brendan." She raised her chin and looked at him and the others. "You see what is happening right now at Dun Bochna. Do any of you wish to remain on this island while Brendan gores off to battle King Odhran?"

After a short silence, she carried her leather sack to the start of the path and placed it by the waterskins. "That is what I thought you would say. I will not stay here, either. Our time here is done! Get your water, your cloaks, your weapons! Get them now!"

They all hurried to do as she commanded. But even as they worked, Darragh and Killian moved close to speak with Brendan.

"I must ask you," Darragh said, lifting another waterskin to his shoulder. "How can we hope to help Dun Bochna? As I said, we have two swords and two daggers between us. We have no other weapons, unless you count four oars and a cauldron. We're certainly no army. What do you mean to do, Brendan?"

"He is right," said Killian. "If you approach those gates with an army of six hungry, weary men– two of them unarmed, three of them entirely untrained in the art of battle– all of us will be taken prisoner or killed where we stand. And as for you? They know you by sight. I do

277

not dare think of what Odhran will do to you, and laugh while he does it."

"You did not desert the people of Dun Bochna," added Darragh. "They deserted you. If you lost the kingship, it was through no fault of your own. Do you truly feel you should die for those who cast you out?"

Brendan dragged out the last tunic and threw it down on top of the waterskins. "The laws are clear on who may be chosen king."

"Laws!" Darragh walked after him. "It takes more than blood to make a king. Colum lies dead in his hall, fallen to treachery. It is you, the outcast, who plans to save Colum's people!"

Brendan sighed. "I thank you for your loyalty, Darragh. But this is not something we can argue about. We must save Dun Bochna. And you were right when you said we cannot march to the gates as if we were an army, for we are not. We will have to find another way."

He turned back to Muriel. "You heard what Killian said," he told her. Perhaps we can scale the walls without being seen. I must decide what to do before we are at the gates. Odhran has certainly posted watchmen."

Brendan looked out at the mainland again, at the growing orange spots of fire. "There is so much chaos there now. Nothing but fighting and flames…"

Muriel stood in front of him and gripped his shoulder to get his attention. "I know you, Brendan. You want to ride in through the wide-open gates of Dun Bochna and save your people from an invader. But you know very well that you cannot do that this time."

"So–" He waited in tense silence.

"If you cannot go as a king, go as what you are."

He frowned, staring hard at her with those strange moonlit eyes. "I am the son of slaves," he said. "You would have me go to Dun Bochna as a slave? "

"Not as a slave, Brendan. A servant."

"A servant."

"Think of it! A man marching boldly and openly through the gates of the dun, swinging a sword and having the manner of a king, would be cut down on sight. But who would notice one more poor servant running about in the confusion, trying to get his servant wife to safety?"

"His wife!" Brendan stared at her. "Muriel, you cannot think to come inside the fortress with me. You are right, perhaps, that the way for me to get inside is to go as what I truly am: the lowest of servants. But do you think I would let you to come with me into such danger?"

"The crossing will be no less dangerous."

"The crossing is necessary. Otherwise, we stay here and starve. No one will be attacking as we take our curragh back to the mainland. We will not be surrounded by enemies and fire!"

Gently she touched the side of his face. "I am the one who can help you in the crossing, where swords can do no good. And I may be able to help you in the battle to come with Odhran." Muriel stared deep into his blue and brown eyes. "You know this, Brendan, as I know it. I am not afraid, for our fates are now joined, and we will face our future together… whatever it may be."

He took her hand and folded his fingers with hers.

"Your kingship has returned," Muriel said.

"It never left me," Brendan answered. They embraced, unafraid of what might lay ahead.

279

Muriel took a step back as Darragh approached. "Everything is ready," he said. "There wasn't that much to pack, as you can imagine. We can leave as soon as you wish."

"We are ready," said Muriel. "I only need to get my extra cloak."

"Of course, you would not want to leave your lovely cloak," said Brendan, with a small laugh. "You will not want to be without it– in whatever sort of home we may come to live in."

He grinned, and she grinned back, both of them feeling reborn by their newly reclaimed powers and by the task that lay ahead of them.

Muriel walked the few steps to her bedroll, where she picked up her ragged brown servant's cloak and the wide strip of leather from beneath. Then, from the cloak, a tiny bunch of flowers fell down and rolled out across the damp mossy ground.

Puzzled, Muriel reached down and picked up the little bouquet. It was three stems of spring gentian, the dark purple-blue flower with petals like a five-pointed star.

There had been no flowers growing here when they first arrived. But somehow this fragile little plant had managed to find its way out here to this empty, windswept island and take root. Sometime earlier this day, Brendan must have gathered enough to make her a little gift.

She looked up to see him standing over her and smiling. "I once promised you, my lady, that there would always be flowers. For some time, I forgot that promise in the fear and hardship that we faced here. But I have learned that even in a place such as this, wherever you are I are together, Muriel, there will always be flowers."

* * *

Carrying the last of their belongings in the worn leather sacks, the little company made its way down the shadowed, twisting path to the sea far below. And Muriel saw, as they crept through the darkness, that a mist was again beginning to form in the low mossy crevices of the rocks.

At first she did not know whether to feel relief or fear– fear because a rising mist could make their crossing more hazardous, or relief because a mist could be the forerunner of rain. Rain would help to put out the fires now consuming Dun Bochna.

But the mist faded and vanished as they reached the base of the island, leaving their journey– and the danger to come– clearly visible in the brilliant night.

The curragh was a dark form in the moonlight. It rested high on the slanted rock, out of reach of the treacherous waves. Brendan jumped into it, as did Gill and Duff, and they began throwing out the big rocks that kept the leather boat from being swept away in the wind and water.

Then Muriel took Brendan's hand and stepped into the curragh. She held tight to one side as the other men shoved the boat halfway into the water and then quickly stepped inside.

In a moment the sea took them. It lifted the crowded little boat and sent it into a sudden backward dive into the deep trough of a wave before the men could get paddles over the side.

"Get it turned round!" shouted Brendan. "Turn it round!"

With all the strength they possessed, the group worked to force the small curragh to turn for the mainland. But then there was another sudden backward drop into a huge trough.

Muriel looked up to see the crest of a monstrous wave towering over them.

"Muriel!" cried Brendan. He was right. The men could do no more. Now it was up to her.

Wedging herself into the prow of the boat, Muriel reached over the sides and plunged her hands into the sea. *Calm,* she thought to it. *Calm. Smooth.*

Though her heart pounded and fear threatened to overwhelm her, she forced herself to keep still and concentrate.

Calm.

The back end of the curragh rode high, and then higher still, up the side of the enormous swell. After what seemed like forever, it lowered back down to the surface of the sea. Muriel knew that the monstrous wave had subsided enough that they would not be swallowed.

The night was calm but the sea was not– not in this place, where the water's journey towards the mainland was greatly disturbed by the island in its path. The water objected to this and leaped and jumped and smashed hard against the huge rock, as though trying to push it out of the way.

The boat continued to ride the huge waves as it backed away from the cove. Muriel stayed in the prow with her hands stretched into the water. Up and down, up and down, dry night air and cold seawater alternating against her skin. She kept her eyes shut and thought only of calming the waters and gentling the powerful waves.

Calm… smooth…

The men worked hard with the paddles. Slowly the boat lumbered around. Raising her eyes, Muriel could see the dark mainland ahead, set off by the glowing moonlit sky– land that was entirely black except for the ominous orange-yellow spots that burned straight ahead.

The waves eased somewhat as they made progress away from the Island of the Rocks. Muriel's hands remained in the water now, so smoothly did the boat travel forward.

Yet she began to realize that the smooth sea created yet another problem: The calm waters offered very little tide to carry them forward.

The men were already weakened by many days of poor food and exposure to wind and rain and cold. She could hear their labored breathing as they struggled to get the heavily loaded curragh to the shore.

It would take them far too long at this rate. They were barely halfway to the Island of the Birds and the mainland lay much, much farther away. It would be up to her to help them again.

Muriel leaned as far out over the front of the boat as she could get and then reached into the water as far as possible, stretching her fingers wide. She kept thoughts of a calm, smooth sea in the back of her mind, but added to it the picture of a group of smooth grey swimmers… the friendly, smiling ones with seemingly limitless strength.

Let us borrow your strength, friends. Help us reach the land. Many of us will die if we do not reach it now. Let us borrow your strength!

There was a sudden sharp thump against the bottom of the boat– and then another, and another. Then the curragh seemed to rise up and shoot forward, heading straight for the distant orange glow far away on the land.

Behind her, the men slowed their paddling. All of them sat back and took the opportunity to catch a breath. On either side of the curragh, out on the moonlit sea, dolphins leaped and splashed as they took turns pushing and keeping pace with the rapidly moving boat.

Now the Island of the Birds loomed before them, a shadow covered with a blanket of dirty white. It was silent now since its thousands of inhabitants had settled in to roost for the night, and the curragh's escort of dolphins sent the boat hurtling past it and into the sea towards the mainland.

As they traveled the long dark stretch of water, the sudden sharp thumps on the curragh's hull were reminders of the dolphins who carried them. The little boat continued to fly over the moonlit sea as Muriel kept her hands in the cold rushing water and thought of calmness… smoothness… and the great strength of these laughing children of the sea who drove them forward.

She closed her eyes and felt the power flow through her.

There was a sudden drop and the curragh wallowed and slowed, pitching all of its occupants forward for a moment Muriel found herself nearly shoulder-deep in water as a swell washed up over the front of the boat. She opened her eyes to see the dolphins flee, leaping into the air as they returned to the open sea.

And then Muriel realized that her fingers brushed rough sand and shells, just as Brendan and Gill jumped out into the waves and shoved the heavy curragh up onto the beach.

VII. THE CHOSEN KING

Slowly Muriel sat up. Her dark hair fell into her face. The long journey spent controlling the ocean and calling the dolphins had left her arms cold and aching, but most of all she felt severely drained and exhausted from the entire effort.

Yet she was exultant. They were here. They were safe. She raised her tired arms and allowed Brendan to help her out onto the narrow strip of sand upon which they had landed.

All of them looked up to see a mass of flames rising into the blackness of the sky, there at the edge of the cliff where Dun Bochna lay. The great fire raised a terrible glow against the clear night sky and swallowed the stars in its glare.

Brendan was the first to turn away. "Quickly, now. Darragh, Killian, take off any sign that you are not a servant. Pull off the gold brooches, the bright cloaks– though they are not so bright now. Your boots are so worn that any other servant would refuse to wear them, so no need to take them off. Here are our last two undyed cloaks. Put them on."

Brendan and his two warriors threw the rectangular cloaks over their heads, pushing the plain bronze brooches through the coarse brown wool. "Hide your swords and daggers beneath the cloaks. Muriel…"

He took her by the shoulders. "Do this for me. Stay here on the beach, where I can hope that you are safe. I will come back for you as soon as… as soon as I have made sure that Odhran will never threaten anyone again."

Muriel could only look up at him. She had been the one to tell him, out on the island, that he must go to Dun Bochna as a servant and not a warrior. But now she felt paralyzed at the thought of seeing him walk up that path that led only to fire and battle and death.

She looked into those blue and brown eyes of his, one light and one dark in the glow of the moon. "How can I stand here and watch you walk alone into the flames?"

"But I am not alone. I have Darragh and Killian. I have my father and his friends." From the shadows, Gill and Cole and Duff raised their heads.

"We need not fight their whole army," Brendan went on. "I need only slip inside and get to Odhran. Once the invaders have no king, they will flee back to their own land. It is always so."

Muriel took hold of his arms. "I know I told you to do this thing– to dress as a servant and slip inside– but look at Dun Bochna now! How can you possibly hope to save any of it, much less get to Odhran, when the whole place is going up in flames?"

Brendan glanced up at the glowing orange sky. "We must believe. And we shall save what we can. That is why I have come. And Muriel…"

He pressed her hand to his heart. "You were right before about my needing you. You can help me save our home. Look, there: The flames consume it. What does Dun Bochna need right now, more than swords, more than anything to save it from fire?"

She stared at him. "Rain," she whispered. "Torrential rain. But the sky is clear! There will be no rain tonight."

"Think of it," he said urgently, bending forward to touch his forehead to her own. "You have power over the water like no one I have ever known. Call upon the rain and bring it here."

"The rain…" She took a step back. "What power I have lies with the waters of the sea, not with rivers or rain. I cannot make it rain. I have never been able to make it rain!"

"My lady, you have done many things that you thought you could not do. You are more powerful than any of your forebears. Surely you must see that now! Help me. Do this for the love we share between us. Bring the rain that will put out those fires."

He pulled her close and kissed her, and then stepped back. "I must go now or there will be no people left to help. When we return, we will meet you here. Stay safe and keep my love with you… and use it to help you bring the rain."

* * *

Muriel stood at the base of the cliff, watching as the shadows of Brendan, Gill, Duff, Cole, Darragh, and Killian moved quickly and silently up the switchback path towards the fiercely burning dun. When they disappeared above the top of the cliff, Muriel stood and stared at the spot. She could only hope that would not be the last time…

After a moment she took a deep breath, picked up the hem of her long, ragged skirts, and began to run towards the sea. She had a duty to Brendan and to his people.

Our people.

She turned as she reached the edge of the water, splashing through the white foam and following the beach towards the place where the fires burned high above. As she ran, she reached up and pulled the golden dolphin brooch from her worn blue cloak and let both fall to the sand. They were quickly followed by her brown leather belt with its gold ring.

Soon she looked up at the point where the stone half-rings of Dun Bochna met the edge of the precipice. Those stone walls now enclosed a raging inferno. With her breath coming quickly, she reached down and untied the worn leather strings of her battered boots and kicked them off. Last of all she pulled her blue-and-cream plaid gown over her head and threw it aside.

Now she wore only her cream-colored linen undergown, loose and flowing to her ankles and also dirty and ragged from the many days spent on the Island of the Rocks. Her wrists and throat were bare. Her hair hung loose and unadorned. There was nothing about her to say she was a highborn woman, much less a queen. There was nothing to set her apart from any other servant.

Just as Brendan had willingly become a servant when he could not be a king, she would do the same. She would surrender her station to become as one with the humblest creatures of the earth and the sky and the sea... for if she became as one of them, their powers might become open to her in ways that would never be possible if she remained closed off by thick clothes and heavy gold and protective stone walls.

Now she was a servant of the elements, a handmaiden of the natural world, for it was the only hope she had of saving her husband's life.

* * *

Moving in silence and as quickly as they dared, Brendan and his five men reached the top of the cliff. Immediately they shielded their eyes from the glare of the billowing red-orange flames that suddenly came into view.

It seemed as if the whole front end of Dun Bochna was on fire. The heavy smoke barely moved at

288

all in the warm, still air, leaving it hanging over the burning rooftops in a thick grey-black pall lit from below by the orange flames.

Then the sound reached them: the roaring and snapping of the fire, the shouting and crying of the people as they ran back and forth in the blaze. And the smell reached them, too: the smell of burning wood and straw, along with the scorched odor of metal and earth.

They hurried around the great length of the outer stone wall until they were at the gates. "I feared these would be shut," Brendan said. But the two massive wooden gates stood half open, one beginning to smolder from the flying sparks. Men and women hurried frantically through them with buckets in a futile attempt to put out the inferno inside.

"Come with me!" Brendan called to his men. "Draw your weapons. Hide them under your cloaks. And stay close. It's Odhran we want."

They crowded together and ran inside, pulling up their cloaks against the onslaught of heat and smoke. The flames roared in their ears and they could hear the crashing of roofs caving in.

There was also the sound of cattle bawling and horses snorting in fear as the fire reached their pens. Brendan could see the panicked horses plunging back and forth in the heat and smoke, and the terrified cattle milling about and pushing up against the smoldering rails of the pens.

But there was no one to help them. All of the dun's inhabitants were working to get the people out of their houses and out of the dun, and then trying to fight the huge blaze with nothing but little buckets of water.

Someone clutched Brendan's arm. He turned to see Gill nodding towards the trapped animals. "Go,"

Brendan said. His father was not trained for battle but if anyone could rescue the horses and cattle, it would be him. "Take Duff and Cole with you. I expect to see all three of you safe and whole when this is over."

"We expect to the same of you," said Gill. The two slapped each other's shoulders and then Gill and the other men ran towards the pens.

Brendan, Darragh, and Killian moved on towards the King's Hall, which was as yet untouched by the flames. Odhran and his men might have run by now, but Brendan did not think so. Much of the dun's wealth in weapons and armor and gold was kept in the hall. They would surely stay until the very last moment in order to steal it all.

* * *

Muriel dashed ankle-deep into the cold, rushing sea, into the foam sliding gently back and forth across the sand. Raising her arms, she gazed far out to the moonlit horizon and thought with the utmost concentration of mist and cloud, of water and storm. She willed a thunderhead to form out there, far out to sea, where the rain and storms always came flying in.

Mist and cloud, water and storm!
Come together over the sea!
Come to Dun Bochna, come to me!
Mist and cloud, water and storm…

She repeated the words over and over in her mind, staring at the sky where it met the sea… hoping to see clouds rise up and surge towards her… hoping to bring the rain that would save the people of Dun Bochna.

She saw nothing but clear black sky, glittering with stars and lit by the shining white moon. Behind her,

290

the glare of flames high overhead grew larger and brighter with each passing moment.

* * *

Throwing their cloaks around their faces in an effort to block out the smoke, Brendan, Darragh, and Killian hurried through the grounds of the dun. They dodged flying cinders, burning houses, and panicked people who raced about trying to save their families and belongings. As they passed the last of the flaming dwellings, its roof fell in with a terrible crash and sent up a huge shower of flying sparks and burning chunks of straw.

The three men stood for a moment in the heated air, trying to breathe; but instantly they jumped back into the shadows as some twenty of Odhran's warriors, all wearing swords and daggers and all carrying ropes, nets, and empty leather sacks, walked towards the King's Hall as calmly as though they had just arrived for the feast.

With smoke trailing past their faces, Brendan and his men peered out at the invaders from behind their cloaks. Brendan's grip tightened on the concealed hilt of his sword and he forced himself to stay still.

There had been a time when he would have charged boldly after the whole lot of them, with a few trusted men at his back and boundless courage in his heart, to take back all that rightfully belonged to Dun Bochna. And though he found that his courage had not left him, he knew it was required of him now to do anything but face his enemy directly.

Muriel had told him that he could best help his people now by being their servant and not their king. And now he saw that she had been right.

He stood up, as did Darragh and Killian, and then moved towards the King's Hall. Reaching its doorway, he and his men peered in with lowered heads like frightened servants with their swords carefully hidden beneath their ragged cloaks.

"You, there!" someone shouted.

A man wearing thick leather armor with a wide plaid cloak pinned over it stood inside the hall, beckoning to them. Brendan tried to keep the anger from his eyes as he recognized Aed– one of Odhran's men, the king's champion, the one who fought if the king were challenged.

"Help us with this. Move!" the warrior shouted. "Your home is burning. Or haven't you noticed?" He laughed and spit on the floor before rejoining the rest of Odhran's men at the far wall.

Aed stepped over the body of Colum as he left.

Brendan's eyes scanned the hall. There, at the very back, watching as his horde of men took all they could grab of Dun Bochna's wealth and crammed it into leather bags and wooden boxes, was a tall, thin, aged man with grey hair and sharp eyes and a grim, humorless face.

Odhran.

The invaders were alone in the King's Hall, Brendan saw. There was no one left to defend it. With their king dead and their fortress in flames, the people of Dun Bochna had retained no thought for gold plates or fidchell boards. Even the warriors were trying to save their families, their houses, their food. There was no one to confront Odhran except Brendan and his men.

He and Darragh and Killian stepped inside just as the plundering mob of Odhran's warriors crowded past with their sacks of stolen treasure. They were

292

fleeing the hall like field mice escaping a burning home. "Get over here!" shouted Aed, waving his arm at Brendan again. "Burn if you want, but not before you finish carrying out our property!"

Aed stayed close to Odhran's side. Brendan knew nothing would move him from that place, for Aed was the king's champion, Odhran's guardian and personal defender, the one who would fight to the death for him. He was the one Brendan would have to overcome if he hoped to get face to face with Odhran and defeat him once and for all.

"Hurry!" shouted Aed, and Brendan saw that he was looking up at the opening directly above the firepit. "The roof is catching!" And Brendan, too, saw the smoldering straw and ominous glowing spots at the edges of the enormous thatched roof.

"You two hold Odhran," Brendan murmured to his companions. "Leave the champion to me." Darragh gave him a small nod and the three of them crept across the rushes, stepping carefully around the motionless body of King Colum. Darragh and Killian went with lowered heads toward Odhran. Brendan walked silently towards Aed.

He took no pride in what he was about to do. He had never drawn a weapon on any man except in fair combat, had never struck anyone down without the battle being a lawful one. But Aed, and his king, had done nothing according to any rule of fair play or honorable combat.

For the second time, they had attacked a fortress unannounced and burned it in the night– and destroyed its king. And they would keep right on doing these terrible things until someone did what was necessary to stop them.

Two kings had been unable to stop Odhran, but those kings had been expecting lawful combat. Odhran and his men did not yet realize that they were no longer facing a king. They were facing a man they had dismissed as the lowest of slaves, a man willing to face them as a servant.

Two king's tactics had not withstood Odhran's deceptions. Perhaps a slave's tactics would succeed where noble ones had failed.

Brendan moved slowly, shuffling through the rushes even as bits of burning straw began to drop near his feet. He waited until he saw Darragh and Killian lift up two of Odhran's sacks, until he saw Darragh glance over at him...

"Now!" Brendan threw back his cloak, swung his sword high, and ran straight for Aed. At the same instant, Darragh and Killian threw their heavy sacks at Odhran and knocked him hard to the floor.

"What is this?" For an instant Aed stood motionless, stunned by the sight of his king felled by two he had taken for ordinary servants– and that slight hesitation was all Brendan needed.

"It is justice!" he shouted, and with a single stroke half severed the head of the king's champion from his body. With a look of shock in his glittering eyes, Aed slowly toppled to the floor with one hand clawing at his gaping neck.

"It is justice," Brendan said again. "Justice for murderers and thieves. If you had not poisoned Colum and burned the dun, you would have earned a fair fight. But there has been nothing fair about you or your king."

He turned his attention to Odhran. The man lay flat on his back, gasping, trapped beneath a heavy wineskin and a sack filled with grain– with Darragh and

Killian each standing on the sacks, swords in hand and pointed at Odhran's throat.

"Let him up," Brendan said, aiming his own sword at the captured enemy. "Take the supplies. Get outside. Save what you can. Most of all, save yourselves. And get back to Muriel as soon as you can. Go. *Go!"*

The two warriors grabbed up the sacks, pausing only long enough o grip Brendan's arm for an instant. Together they raced for the door.

"Now, Odhran," Brendan said. "Get to your feet."

* * *

In the heat and glare of the half-burning hall, Odhran rolled and jumped up and then stood with his back against the wall. Glaring, he drew his sword. "I thought you were dead, Brendan. But no matter. Now I will have the pleasure of killing you myself."

"I think not," Brendan said.

Odhran smirked. "Your new attire suits you well," he said, his cold eyes flicking over the rough and ragged brown wool that Brendan wore. "I always knew you were no king. You are a thief, a criminal, a lowborn slave… one who is not fit to rule over dogs."

"Then we are truly alike, for I have always heard the very same about you."

Smoldering bits of debris continued to rain down on them from the roof. Out of the corner of his eye Brendan caught sight of actual flames bursting to life and eating into the tightly bundled straw there, filling the dim and smoky hall with more garish light.

Odhran glanced up. "As Aed tried to tell you, your home is burning. Will you do nothing to save it?"

When Brendan did not answer, but only stepped closer and leveled his sword, Odhran laughed. "I suppose you do not care if the King's Hall's burns. You would have no reason to be in it except to carry out the filth." He shrugged. "Stay here if you like. Burn along with it. I will rebuild the place and make it fine enough for its new owner, King Odhran!"

With that, he crouched low and made a fast dash for the open rear door. Brendan stopped him, slamming him viciously up against the wall.

"If you want this hall, you will have to fight me for it," he snarled, pressing his sword against Odhran's throat. "I will burn it down around me than see it belong to you."

"Burn with it, then!" The vile king shoved him back and ran for the door again. With a determined leap, Brendan grabbed him and knocked him back to the floor just as half of the burning roof crashed down in a huge shower of flame.

Twisting free, Odhran crawled for the open door and tried to shield his face from the heavy smoke and blowing sparks. Brendan caught hold of him and threw him outside, thinking to pin the man on the ground and disarm him– but then his own stinging eyes and smoke-filled lungs forced him to pause for breath.

Again Odhran broke away. Brendan lunged for him, but his opponent had regained his feet and run into the dark towards the cliff's edge. Brendan struggled to get up and then ran after him.

For a moment Brendan feared that his enemy had escaped him. Odhran had not been living on the edge of starvation for two fortnights, had not just struggled to survive a desperate sea voyage, had not gotten the full force of the smoke when the roof of the hall collapsed.

But neither was he a man fighting for that which he truly loved. Brendan understood that a man like Odhran loved nothing except, perhaps, himself.

The greatest king with the strongest army could not be more determined than Brendan was now, for he had broken through the mists of doubt and saw clearly what he was battling so hard to save: his people, and his home, and his beloved wife.

Brendan tightened his grip on his sword and ran harder than he ever had in his life.

Suddenly he was out of the smoke and away from the burning buildings. Leaping over a row of rocks, he came to a stop as he realized where he was: the wide empty space at the edge of the cliff... the final gap between Dun Bochna's buildings and the sea.

Pacing back and forth not far from the edge, with sword in hand and alone without champion or guard for perhaps the first time in his life, was Odhran.

Brendan glanced back over his shoulder. Torrents of fire leaped and billowed from the houses and the King's Hall and the outbuildings along the inner stone wall, leaving a barrier of flame and heat and suffocating smoke between him and the front gates.

There was no way out.

And there would be no escape by climbing the two surrounding walls of the dun. What had once worked with the cliff to keep invaders out now effectively trapped Brendan inside. In the still, heavy air, thick smoke had settled into the wide space between the double walls. Anyone who tried to vault over them would suffocate before he could climb back out again.

The orange-lit smoke continued to swell out and over the precipice above the sea. It flowed past Brendan

297

and filled the air much like the white mist had done out on the Island of the Rocks.

But this was far different. Brendan was forced to drop to the ground and try to breathe as the smoke enveloped him. The space of clear air between him and the edge of the cliff, between him and Odhran, grew ever smaller. This was no mist. This was death for him and for his enemy.

The only escape was the sheer drop before them.

* * *

It was not working. She would have to do something else... something that might bring the rain.

Muriel let her thoughts go to the cliff far above, where Brendan risked his life to save a kingdom no longer his. If he had the power to save the dun and its people, he had it only because he had offered up everything he had.

Including his own life.

It was the hallmark of a king, this willingness to sacrifice himself if it meant he could save his people. Brendan had clearly shown it when he had climbed that path and gone to the burning fortress, there to confront the invading Odhran and his well-armed, well-fed men.

Brendan was still acting as a king even though the title had been stripped from him. And if she believed that he was a king after all, by his deeds if not his birth, then his queen could behave no less nobly.

Brendan had walked into the fire. She would walk into the water.

Long ago, her nameless ancestor had also walked into the water. But Muriel knew that if a sacrifice was needed this night, it would not be in vain. As Grania had done, Muriel had come here to help her beloved and trusted husband. She would help him save the home of many, many people if she could... and if the sea required her life in return, it now seemed a small thing to ask.

Muriel fixed her gaze on the horizon and raised her arms once more. This time she walked farther into the water, until the gentle waves washed up over her knees.

Mist and cloud, water and storm...

Far out to sea, lit by the brilliant white moon, clouds began to gather. She waded farther out, waist deep now, hands trailing in the water.

Mist and cloud...

* * *

The wind struck them first.

It brought a draught of fresh sea air and pushed back a little of the intolerable heat and smoke. Brendan gasped and raised his head from the ground, his eyes stinging, and breathed deep of the cool wet wind.

It smelled like rain.

He sat up and looked out to sea. No longer could he see the moon, for it was hidden behind solid blackness. As he watched, the stars above his head vanished one after another as a huge stormcloud moved slowly towards the land.

"She has done it," he whispered, getting to his feet. "She has done it!"

* * *

The wind sent her hair whipping into her eyes and drove the waves so hard that their spray burned her face. Still Muriel walked forward, shaking her head to throw back her hair, and walked until the sea rose up to her shoulders.

Water and storm...

A rippling flash of lightning danced purple-white in the sky and raced through the heavy rolling clouds that now obscured the moon. Again and again the jagged streaks flashed and tore at the heavens. Thunder rumbled and wind howled. And as the storm-lashed waves lifted Muriel off her feet and dragged her down beneath them, the last thing she was conscious of was the water all around her.

It had begun to rain.

* * *

Brendan stood tall in the downpour, his sword raised. A hissing, spitting sound arose all around him, as the driving rain crashed down upon the fires. He looked back at the fortress and saw the flames began to diminish though they continued to rage, angry and flaring and determined to consume as much of the fortress as possible before they could be destroyed.

Then a motion behind him caught his attention. Lightning flashed and he saw Odhran waiting at the edge of the cliff, sword still in hand.

"Come to me, Brendan!" the king shouted against the thunder. "I will send you to the fish far below. One last step over this cliff and you will be gone from us forever!"

Brendan shook his head. His enemy had a mad glint in his eye. "Come away from there. If you want a battle, bring it to me! I am not fool enough to fight at the edge of a cliff!"

Odhran laughed. "I am not surprised to see that you are frightened. I do not fear the height any more than I fear your sword! I know exactly how far I can go. You are nothing but a cowardly slave and this proves it! I am a king! I am afraid of nothing!"

"That does not make you a king. It makes you a fool. And a coward. You think to wait there until the rain kills the fires and your men come and rescue you. Nothing more."

Odhran paced back and forth just a few steps from the drop. "If you want me, slave, you will have to come out here and get me– out here where only a king dares to walk, where a slave fears to step! Here–"

His boot slipped on the wet rocks. He caught his balance and then took another step, safe and secure once more. But Brendan saw the muddy edge behind him start to crumble even as the king stepped away from it. A few pebbles rolled past his feet and disappeared over the side.

In the drenching rain and pounding thunder, Odhran did not notice. He was far more concerned with glaring at Brendan from the relative safety of the cliff's edge, knowing there would be no attack so long as he stayed in such a dangerous spot.

Odhran's wet boots slipped again. He almost fell to the ground, but managed to keep his balance by bracing one foot against a rock. "There, you see? I am safe, even here. I am a king! I walk in places where no slave would ever dare to step!"

Dark lines appeared in the rain-soaked earth beneath Odhran's feet. Instinctively Brendan moved towards him. "Come away from the ledge! Come away from there! Come away–"

But Brendan flinched at Brendan's sudden move. He took only a single step back, but it was enough. The fragile, storm-damaged edge of the cliff crumbled beneath him. He scrambled for purchase but the rain-slicked rocks gave him nothing. He dropped out of sight, screaming in terror and rage all the way down to the rocks far below.

"You were right, Odhran," Brendan said, from where he stood. "There was no need for you to fear my sword. But you should have feared Muriel's rain."

* * *

Brendan turned away from the crumbling cliff, facing away from the howling wind. Wiping the water away from his eyes, he watched as the rain drove down on the burning buildings of the dun. It was not long before the flames began to die out.

He began to make his way across the grounds towards the gates. The flames still leaped and snapped but grew smaller and lower all the time, and at last they died out almost completely.

He found the King's Hall largely intact. Half the roof had fallen in, but now it lay steaming and smoldering in the wet, charred rushes of the floor. There were no more glowing spots of fire to be seen anywhere in the dun.

The damage had been halted. The fortress was now swathed in darkness as the fires were doused and the storm clouds blocked the moon.

Moving carefully, avoiding the smoldering chunks of debris and trying not to slip on the muddy ground, Brendan used flashes of lightning to see what remained of Dun Bochna.

The houses nearest the rear of the fort, nearest the hall, had for the most part only lost their thatched roofs. But the closer he got to the front, the worse the damage became. Some houses were burned halfway to the ground while others were little more than heaps of blackened, smoldering clay. Half-burned wickerwork stuck out of the fallen walls like bones.

Most chilling of all, Brendan saw no people and no animals anywhere– not dead, not injured, not alive. He was at once both greatly relieved and filled with dread. Either everyone had gotten out, or they had been trapped inside the burning, collapsing buildings... or between the two outer stone walls of the dun, there to die in the suffocating heat and smoke.

Another flash showed him the charred remains of the once-massive front gates. They were now nothing but smoldering timber hanging at strange angles from the iron hinges. Brendan walked out between the ruined gates, splashing through the rivulets of water pouring down from the walls over head.

The wind eased. Still the rain came down. Behind him, wisps of steam drifted up from the burned-out buildings, rising up into the rain like mist and disappearing into the darkness.

He could only hope that this was not all that remained of his former kingdom. Surely the people must be hiding somewhere. Surely the fires could not have consumed them all, leaving no trace! Brendan moved on, following a wet and muddy track that led to the edge of the forest.

Suddenly he stopped. Lightning showed what he had nearly stumbled over: the body of a man. He crouched down to look at it, turning it over, his heart hammering as he looked at the face. Again the lightning came, and he saw that this was not one of his men but one of Odhran's.

Brendan stood up. The lingering ripples of lighting showed that he was surrounded by bodies. The invading army, driven out of the fortress by blinding, choking smoke and weighed down with stolen treasure, had run straight into an ambush.

He looked up as a tall dark figure stepped out from beneath the trees. It moved straight towards him, first walking, then running, slipping and sliding on the muddy ground, until it was right in front of him; and then his father reached out and held him in a tight embrace.

"They're all here," Gill said, stepping back. "All the people. All the horses. Most of the sheep and cattle. Even all the gold that Odhran's men tried to steal!"

Lightning flashed again, more distant now. Beneath the dripping trees Brendan saw the familiar faces of the men and women and children who had once called him king. Behind them were milling cattle and nervous horses and heaps of bags filled with supplies and with treasure.

All the people were soaked by the storm. Shock and loss were evident in their eyes. But they were alive, and Brendan knew that they would begin rebuilding their homes almost as soon as the storm was past.

But there was one person whose face he did not see… one person who would have run to him if she had been there beneath those trees.

"Muriel," Brendan whispered. "She is not here."

Gill shook his head. "She is surely waiting for you down on the beach."

"Of course she is," Brendan said, but his voice caught. "She is down on the beach, waiting for us, exhausted from bringing in this magnificent storm."

He turned around. "Darragh! Killian! Come with us to the beach! Muriel is there, waiting for us to find her!"

* * *

Down the path that led to the sea, a path now more like a running river as torrents of rainwater poured

304

away from the dun, the four men slipped and slid in hopes of finding one more life. Half running, half jumping, all of them covered with mud, they raced all the way until finally leaping down to the sand.

"Muriel!"

Brendan ran out onto the narrow beach, past the curragh still sitting where they had left it. The tide was high and the waves crashed into the sand at their highest point. But there was no sign of Muriel.

The rain began to lessen. As Brendan ran down the darkened beach the lightning became more and more distant, and the flashes farther apart, as the storm began to die.

"Muriel!" he called again.

Surely she would answer. Surely she knew he was here, and would stand up from among the rocks wet and cold from her conjured rain. She would run to him and take comfort in his arms.

But there was nothing here but the crashing wavs and the faraway rumble of thunder.

He stopped. For the first time in his life, Brendan knew fear far greater than any he had faced in battle. He had been willing to sacrifice himself, if need be, to end Odhran's tyranny and drive him out of Dun Bochna. He should have known that Muriel would be willing to do no less to save the place that had become her home, to save the people who had become her own, all because she loved him.

He would have given his life in a heartbeat if it would have saved her own.

Then came one last rippling flash of lightning. In its glare, Brendan saw a small white-clad figure lying motionless in the foam at the edge of the sea. The waters rushed back and forth over long, dark hair.

"Muriel," he whispered, and dashed to her side.

He knelt down beside her and half lifted her up, pulling her close to him, trying to warm her cold still body with whatever life he had left to give. Her head fell back. Her eyes were closed, her wet hair was still in the grip of the rushing sea, and her skin was cold and pale as death.

He bent down and pressed his ear to her chest, listening for any sign of life– the slightest breath, the faintest heartbeat– and as he hugged her close, rocking her back and forth, unable to speak, he felt the slow beat of life within her. It was faint but steady, and then a gentle arm came up to fall across his shoulder.

Brendan lifted her up, away from the cold dark sea. He carried her back to the path, back to the burned-out fortress that had been their home, holding her close every step of the way.

* * *

"We were so desperate to put a fire out just a short time ago," said Killian. "Now all we can think of is to start one again."

Brendan smiled. He sat beside Muriel in the dark remains of the King's Hall, propped up against one wall on a pile of the driest rushes they had been able to find. She lay with her head resting against his side, tucked in beneath a stack of half-damp, half-scorched woolen cloaks scavenged from the least damaged of the houses. Alvy sat close on the other side of her, constantly smoothing Muriel's cloak and hair.

Her eyes remained closed, but a faint touch of color had returned to her cheeks and her breathing was soft and regular. The awful chill was beginning to leave her body, replaced by the warmth of his own.

"Is the fire started yet?" Alvy asked again. "She must have a fire!"

Killian continued working at the firepit with his flints. The sparks flew each time he struck the stones together, but at last he shook his head. "Far too wet," he said. "Nothing here to burn. It's all drenched."

"You are welcome," Muriel whispered. She turned over on her side to move closer to her husband, sliding deeper beneath the heavy cloaks atop her.

Brendan grinned. "She's right. We asked for rain, and we got it. We have nothing to complain about."

Cole got up from where he was sorting through the rushes, pulling out any that weren't too wet. "I'll see what I can do," he said, and walked out into the night.

Brendan looked down at Muriel again and kissed her forehead– and then became aware that someone else had walked into the hall.

It was Lorcan, who had been the most highly placed of King Galvin's druids– and who had been the same for Brendan and then for Colum. Right behind him came all the rest of the druids and then the dun's warriors. Brendan eased out from beside Muriel and stood up as everyone else who lived at Dun Bochna, it seemed, crowded together in the burned-out hall.

"Brendan," Lorcan said, stepping forward. The black sky above his head, visible through the half-fallen roof, glittered with stars and shone with moonlight now that he storm had gone. "Before anything else is done, we must know for certain what your future holds."

Brendan glanced down at Muriel. "I understand," he said. "I will leave you just as soon as she is well. We will return to her family at Dun Farraige, or perhaps build our own rath out in the forest. I will ask what she wishes just as soon as she–"

Lorcan held up his hand. "You do not understand. We have come to ask you to take your place here, as our king."

"King," repeated Brendan.

He looked around the room at the familiar, anxious faces staring at him in breathless expectation. Brendan started to walk towards Lorcan, but then stopped and raised his head.

"We know all too well that I have not the blood to be king," he said. "I am the son of slaves. That is no shame to me, for my father is a fine man no matter what his station... and though I never knew my mother, I have no doubt that she was equally worthy of honor and respect. Yet there is no escaping the fact that, by the law, I am not one who can ever be considered to rule you."

He studied the gathering again, looking at the druids and the warriors and the women, and even at the waiting servants in the shadows and in the darkness.

"Why would you say such a thing to me, Lorcan? Has the smoke affected you? Or are you joking, to lift the spirits of your people after such tragedy as we have witnessed tonight?"

"Brendan, I beg you," said Lorcan. "Listen to me. We have known you since you were an infant. We know what sort of man you have become. You were the one closest to the heart of King Galvin, the one he himself wanted to be king after him... as did all of the free men of Dun Bochna."

Brendan paced a few steps across the soaked and blackened rushes. "All this was true before," he said. "Before you knew what I truly was. Then you gave me no choice but to leave this place forever. Now you say you want me to be king! Why have you changed your decision?"

There was a low sound of conversation as the people turned to each other and began to whisper. Then, from within the ranks of the warriors, a solemn grey-haired main appeared– a man with wide shoulders and the air of a warrior.

His long plaid cloak was scorched and blackened, his fine tunic torn and filthy with soot and smoke. But there was no mistaking that he was one of the nobility... one of the warrior class. He was a man who could have been a king himself.

"I am Fergal," the man said, "brother of Galvin. In this one year, Dun Bochna has known three rulers. The first was Galvin, who served for so long and so well. Then Brendan, young and strong and laughing and fearless. Last was Colum, a gentle, peaceful man.

"We lost our first king through age and sacrifice; the second through an accident of birth; and the third through treachery. It seemed to us that we were cursed, meant to have no king at all.

"Yet we know that you, Brendan, though born a slave, nonetheless came to us here as the son of King Galvin. You came to us here that first time, when it would have seemed impossible."

Another grey-haired man, also wearing a soot-blackened tunic and cloak, moved to stand beside Fergal. "I am Dermot, a physician in this place. Though captured by an enemy and set adrift to die, Brendan, you returned home in triumph. You came to us here a second time, when it would have seemed impossible.

Another man, quiet and dignified, came forward. "I am Lorcan, a man of law in this place. Though banished and disgraced through no fault of your own,

Brendan, you braved shipwreck and fire and a rogue king's army to wrest our home from the grip of an outlaw and save us all. You came to us here a third time, when it would have seemed impossible."

Dermot spoke again. "You, once our beloved prince, have returned to us once more– though we had no reason to believe you ever could."

Lorcan spoke again. "It is true that our laws would seem to preclude you from being a king. Yet we have learned to listen to the messages of the natural world, as well as to our own laws. We have never seen a message so clear as this."

Fergal spoke again. "Three times you were apart from us. Three times you came to Dun Bochna, against every chance. It appears, Brendan, that if any man was meant to be our king, that man is you."

Silence feel over the hall. Brendan looked at all of the gathered people staring at him from the shadows, and he could feel the tension as they awaited his reply.

He turned and gazed down at Muriel, sitting up now and listening intently, and reached out his hand to her.

Slowly she got up, wrapping her old blue cloak around her ragged linen gown, and walked barefoot over the rushes to stand close beside Brendan. He reached out and put his arm around her waist, pulling her close.

"I have my mother and my father to thank for bringing me to you for the first time," he said. "But it was this lady, Muriel, who saved me from the sea when Odhran set me out there to die. She used her powers over that sea, and the creatures who live within it, to bring me home once more… and to bring the storm tonight that kept our home from burning to ashes altogether."

He looked down at her again and gently kissed her forehead. "If I am a king– if I am alive at all– it is only because I found my queen. I already know the love you must have for her, and with her at my side I will serve you as your king for all the days left of my life."

"King Brendan!" cried a voice from the darkness of the hall.

"Queen Muriel!" said another.

Brendan held her close once more, and then looked up at Fergal. "There is something I would ask of you."

The older man glanced up at him. "You honor me by asking. What is it that I can do?"

After helping Muriel back to the warmth of the cloaks and the rushes, Brendan stood tall. "You, Fergal, are the brother of Galvin, who was the best of kings for the people of Dun Bochna. And I know well that you, too, would have made a king of equal worth."

Fergal gave him a slow nod.

"Everyone here knew King Fallon and Queen Grania. They knew that Dun Camas was overrun through treachery and cowardice. I would ask something of you now, Fergal. I would ask you to go to Dun Camas and give them what help you can– including, if need be, serving the people there as their king."

A slow smile spread across Fergal's face. "I will leave for Dun Camas in five days' time," he said, and the hall was filled with the sounds of approval as the people all spoke to each other and then crowded around Fergal.

Then they all turned and fells silent as a figure appeared in the doorway– a figure holding a flaring, snapping stick of wood serving as a torch.

Brendan reached for his sword– but then relaxed again when he recognized Cole, standing just inside the door and staring in bewilderment at the great crowd gathered inside.

He raised up his makeshift torch. "I told you I would find a fire," he said. "The roof of your house fell in, Brendan. But when it did, it sheltered part of the hearth from the storm. There were still a few embers glowing there."

Brendan and Muriel looked at each other and smiled. The hall erupted into shouting and laughter, and soon it was bright with a newly kindled fire blazing in the great central hearth.

* * *

Nine and thirty days passed– long, busy, sunlit days spent in the rebuilding of a kingdom.

All of the people of Dun Bochna came in from its every corner to help: the farmers from their raths in the forests and fields; the herdsmen down from the mountaintop pastures; the warriors who kept watch at the borders.

They joined the men and women who lived in the fortress itself to reconstruct the burned-out houses and animal pens and armory and King's Hall. Everyone from servant to druid to warrior to noble all pitched in to help.

They carried bundles of hazelwood sticks and buckets of clay to build new walls. They hauled wagonloads of oat and wheat straw from the freshly harvested fields to make new roofs. And as the buildings took shape, the craftsmen and spinners and weavers went to work creating new tools and cushions and boots and cauldrons and cloaks and tunics and gowns to replace those damaged and destroyed by the fires.

The pens went back up along the inner stone wall, and soon the cattle and sheep and horses were safely inside once more. New gates for the front of the fortress were built from strong oak timbers and hauled up into place by twenty strong men.

And then one morning, the gates stood open.

The leaves on the oak, willow, and rowan trees had begun to turn to the reds, golds, and deep purples of early autumn. The blackberry bushes were heavy with clusters of berries and the apple trees dropped fresh green fruit to the windblown grass. The newly rebuilt dun, its buildings gleaming white with new clay, their straw roofs shining like gold in the morning sunlight, sat waiting for its people to return.

But on this particular morning they all stood gathered together on the top of the hill beside the great fortress, beside the open space of sand and ash that once again held a great stack of wood awaiting sunset and torches.

The bonfire would be even larger this time, for among the wood was much of the debris from the night the fortress had burned. If ever there was a night when a great fire should burn, it was this one– this autumn equinox.

At the highest point of the hill, Brendan stood surrounded by his warriors and his druids. He stood tall among them, his golden brown hair ruffled by the cool sea breeze. Over his black leather trousers and soft grey tunic he wore a newly made cloak woven of blue and purple and white, a cloak so wide that it was gathered in five folds across his chest– yet it was fastened with plain bronze brooches no finer than a servant might wear.

As Brendan watched, the crowd parted and allowed a group of six people to walk through. At the head of the little group was Muriel, and in both hands she carried the king's gold sea-dragon torque.

Her gown was of the softest and finest wool; yet, like Brendan's tunic, it had been dyed only in a plain shade of grey. Her cloak was like his, too, blue and purple and white, but fastened only with a servant's bronze brooch.

The two fortnights spent out on the island had left her weakened and thin; but under Alvy's care, her beauty and health had once again been restored. Her black hair fell in waves to her shoulders, her fair skin glowed, and her blue eyes shone bright as she looked up at Brendan.

Just behind her walked Darragh and Killian. Following them, dressed in the bright wool plaids and fine golden brooches of free men, were Duff, Cole, and Gill.

Muriel stopped in front of Brendan. He smiled at her for a long moment, as if the two of them stood alone together, and then he looked out at the crowd and began to speak.

"It is well, I think, that my own kingmaking should be held at the time of the autumn equinox, for that is a time of balance– a time when the day is equal to the night and neither is greater than the other.

"Today is also a day when three servants become free men." He nodded at Gill and Duff and Cole. "And it is also a day when a king becomes a servant."

The men and women of the gathering turned to glance at each other, but kept their silence as he continued. "You see the brooches that my queen and I choose to wear. They are of bronze, as a servant might wear, and not the gold of the nobility. There will be other gold for us to wear. Always we will keep this small mark of the servant to remind us of the true place

314

of a king and queen– as servants of their people, not just their rulers."

Brendan paused and looked at his gathered people, trying to meet the eyes of each one. "It is customary for the chief druid to place the king's torque around the neck of the new king. Yet I would ask that another place the torque for me this day.

"I was not born to be a king. And though you have asked me to serve you in this way, and I am happier than I can say to do so, I must make certain that none can ever again say I have no right to it."

He looked at Muriel again. "I would ask that my chosen queen place the torque for me. As it was in the oldest of days, it is a queen, more than anything else, who makes a man a king."

Brendan got down on both knees before her. He kept his eyes on hers as she slid the heavy gold torque around his neck. Then, as everyone watched, she kissed him gently on the lips and held both of his hands as he got to his feet once more.

Next Brendan turned to Lorcan and took the small, delicate queen's torque from the druid. Pulling the ends of the gold torque slightly apart, he slid it around Muriel's neck, gently placing the heavy gold so that the beautifully made sea-dragon heads rested on her collarbone just above the neckline of her soft grey gown.

The pair stood together for a moment, and then Brendan spoke to his people again.

"I was born a slave, and raised a prince, and made a king. But I would never have been a king had I not first been a servant, both to my lady and to my people. I accept the charge you give me as your king, but I will never forget that first I am your servant."

315

"Brendan and Muriel!" cried a voice from the crowd, and soon all of them joined in. Then the new king and queen led their people back down the grassy hillside path, back to the feast that awaited them in their fortress home by the sea.

The End
SPIRIT OF THE MIST
The *Celtic Journeys* Series
Janeen O'Kerry

Thank you for reading. If you enjoyed SPIRIT OF THE MIST, please consider leaving a review on its Amazon.com webpage.

For more information about the author and her other books, please visit Janeen O'Kerry's page on Amazon.com.

Made in the USA
Coppell, TX
06 March 2022

74578195R00174